SURGICAL STRIKE II

ASSAULT ON THE EMPRESS

Books by Jerry Ahern

Surgical Strike Series

The Survivalist Series

The Defender Series

They Call Me the Mercenary Series

SURGICAL STRIKE II

ASSAULT
ON THE
EMPRESS

JERRY AHERN

SPEAKING VOLUMES, LLC

NAPLES, FLORIDA

2012

SURGICAL STRIKE II

ASSAULT ON THE EMPRESS

ISBN 978-1-61232-201-8

Chapter One

The ragged-edged black rubber blades of the windshield wipers could barely keep up with it, the dingy white crust of ice spicules completely covering the glass just inches ahead of his nose except for the two wet streaked wedges they had carved and worked unceasingly now to maintain. Their fragile-seeming grey armatures whipped to and fro at a pace that was beyond frenetic and, when watched too intently, almost hypnotic. His left thigh and left arm were soaked through to the skin; throughout the drive, he had periodically cranked down the window and used his bare left hand to scrape away the ice which would build up on the sideview mirror with annoying and rapid regularity. He hated vehicles that were designed for anything but right-hand drive. The gearshift was in the wrong place and, a right-handed chain-smoker, it was constantly necessary to keep the cigarette between his lips with the smoke streaming up into his eyes or reach blindly into darkness and half the time stab the cigarette in his hand against the shift knob.

Seamus O'Fallon jiggled the stick into neutral and cut the Volkswagen's engine, then jerked up the parking brake. He pushed off the light switch then took the stick match from his teeth, flicked it against his thumbnail and lit his cigarette. After knocking off the fiery tip of the last one and smelling the rubber floor mat smoldering for several minutes, he had abandoned any further attempts. He inhaled almost gratefully now. Before he shook out the match, he shot the cuff of his left sleeve and looked at the face of the old Gruen watch in its light. It was nearly nine o'clock; and, by ten, he had to be across town to meet with the others. But there was time enough. He shook out the match finally, the smell of sulphur still on the air with the windows rolled up against the sleet, the sulphur mingling nause-atingly with the heavy stench of the burned rubber from before.

He slipped his right hand into his Macintosh pocket and closed it over the rough checkered wood and the cold steel of his revolver.

"Idle hands are the Devil's Workshop," it was always told to him as a child. And it was the one piece of advice he had always taken to heart. Just because there was Fein business tonight didn't mean that the other matter couldn't be gotten out of the way as well. He pulled an unlined black leather glove onto his left hand.

"Martin, you'd best be waitin' in the car, boyo. I been thinkin' it all over, I have, and me mind's made up. This was a one-man job from the start and McGill'll be less on the itch if there's only one of us to knock on his door," he told the carrot-haired boy in the passenger seat beside him.

"But Seamus, I—"

"I know, boyo. You're after gettin' experience; but, mark my words, you'll have ya a belly full of that tonight. So, there's a lad and stay in the car, now. O'Fallon'll return, he will." And O'Fallon wrenched the door handle and stepped out into the street, tugging the brim of his slouch hat low and hunching his shoulders high against the wind-driven liquified ice.

As he moved his loafer-shod feet, the stuff crackled beneath them and the shoes were thin-soled enough that he could feel the little chunks of ice gouging into him.

He started round the front of the car and onto the sidewalk, hands in his pockets, the right hand warming up the .357 a bit. There was a light on in the second-floor window at the end of the row and he walked quickly because of the cold and damp. McGill would have his tonight for sure.

When O'Fallon reached the white-splotched red-brick build-ing, he stopped and looked back once. Young Martin was a regular card, he was, so eager and all, reminding O'Fallon of his own youth. There'd be killing enough for the boy, if he lived that long, and that was certain. As he smiled, ice touched his lips and he spat it away.

O'Fallon stepped into the foyer, the wood-framed glass door blowing shut when the wind sucked at it, the fingerprint-smudged glass rattling almost angrily. O'Fallon smiled at the thought and started up the green and pink stripe runnered steps, the carpet threadbare at the center of each tread, as good as new except for the dirtiness of it at the edges.

O'Fallon stopped at the landing for the first floor and looked down the stairwell into the foyer. Nothing and nobody. He had the gun nice and warm to the touch now as he took the stairs two at a time. McGill would know somebody had entered the building. Only a man who was deaf or dead could have missed the slam of the door. The railing was knicked and bruised and in spots the stain was worn so thin that the bare wood showed.

He stopped on the landing, looked down again. It was all clear. O'Fallon walked straight for McGill's door and rapped on it with the knuckles of his left hand, his right hand out, the gun behind the skirts of the Macintosh tight in his fist.

" 'Tis me, McGill," he said not too loudly for the neighbors but loudly enough for McGill.

The door opened on a security chain. "I been expectin' you or somebody."

O'Fallon smiled. "It wanted the personal touch, it did."

"Let me get the woman out."

"There's a back entrance you have, then?"

"No."

"Ahh, but she'd see my face."

"You don't have to, Seamus."

"But faith I do, McGill. Easy or hard?"

The door closed and for a split second, O'Fallon thought it would be easy. But the chain didn't rattle and the door was closed almost all the way.

O'Fallon threw his weight against it, the old frame door cracking, the security chain ripping away and taking a chunk of the jamb with it.

McGill, his swarthy-looking face sweat dripping, was barefoot and wore nothing but an athletic shirt and boxer shorts with blue stripes on them. A woman with indifferently dyed red hair lay on the bed, the greyed white sheets drawn up under her chin, her eyes so full of color and so wide they reminded him of blue willow pattern china plates.

He stabbed the gun forward.

McGill made the sign of the cross.

"Ahh! A man of God! Say your Hail Mary then or whatever it is double quick."

The woman started to scream, so O'Fallon shot her first, one between the eyes. At the distance of ten feet or so, it wasn't that much of a shot. The scream stopped. His ears rang from the gunshot and the web of his hand hurt from the recoil. "Is it finished ya are now, McGill? With your prayer of intercession and all?"

"Yes."

"That's wonderful now." O'Fallon fired again, another shot into the head at the distance of three feet, hitting exact center right where the nose began, McGill's body rocking back, then falling sideways right and thudding on the floor. "Death to traitors, McGill; but, ya knew that when you talked to the RUC."

O'Fallon put the revolver behind his coat again and walked from the room, into the hall, down the stairs. From the floor above, he heard a shout. Sounded like an East Indian, he thought. "What is happening?" the high-pitched voice implored in a strange singsong.

O'Fallon kept walking, to the first landing, not looking up, down the next flight and to the foyer, his gloved left hand to the door, wrenching it open, holding it against the wind and then onto the street. His right hand slipped into his Macintosh pocket still holding the gun.

The sleet was blowing, if anything more intensely than before. O'Fallon walked quickly to the Volkswagen, Martin throwing open the door as he neared it, the dome light without a bulb and the interior of the car not illuminating.

O'Fallon slipped behind the wheel.

"I heard the shots, Seamus."

"My ears still ring with 'em, Martin. But there's a goodly drive ahead of us still, there is. And we can drive with the gladness in our hearts of knowin' that McGill'll never whisper over us to the coppers again, boyo."

"You shot him . . . er . . . twice?"

O'Fallon gunned the Volkswagen to life. "No. Ya shouldn't be after askin' such questions, boyo. But I'll tell ya rightly enough tonight and never again. There was a harlot in his bed and she saw me face, boyo. No two ways about it." He looked at Martin, just barely able to see enough of the face in the darkness to get a little of the boy's expression. There was a touch of sickness and melancholy there. But if young Martin survived, that'd pass. And if it didn't pass, young Martin wouldn't survive.

O'Fallon released the parking brake, balanced the clutch and the accelerator as he pulled off the leather glove he'd worn, then worked down the window to scrape clean his mirror. He couldn't see much but started into the street anyway. There was little traffic but there was less time. . . .

The old Gruen on his wrist showed five after ten when he glanced at it fleetingly by the yellowed light of a street lamp as he turned the Volkswagen into the alley behind the baked goods plant and slowed, the corrugated metal garage door looming ahead through the swirl of sleet. O'Fallon had geared down into second as he made the turn and, despite the protestations of the engine, kept in second for added traction, the alley—unimaginably almost—slipperier than the streets had been getting here. He double clutched and geared into first, the Volks lurching slightly, a sudden chill hitting the right side of his face as young Martin rolled down the window and began the thing with the red-filter-lensed flashlight. Automatically, O'Fallon leaned closer to the windshield and peered upward to the lace-curtained window just above and to the right of the garage door. There was a green-filtered light flashing back through the window. As O'Fallon began braking, the corrugated door began to rise. Had it been a film, he thought, the door would have risen in perfect synchronization with the approach of the Volks and there would have been no need to stop. It was not a film and he had to stop a little hurriedly in order to avoid clipping the lower lip of the door with the roof of the car. The Volkswagen skidded a little but stopped nicely. He started ahead, losing traction, catching it, half slalomming through onto the slush-rutted grey-brown concrete beyond the doorway.

He stopped the car again, twisting the door handle and stepping out into the slush. The door was already slipping downward. Larry O'Toole was coming toward him from the scaffolding-like wooden steps which led to the garage office, O'Toole wiping his palms along the thighs of his ill-fitting brown trousers and building a smile. "Seamus, we were worried about ya."

"Ahh, 'tis good to be missed, O'Toole; but, the O'Fallon wouldn't have missed this for all the tea in China." And he clapped Larry O'Toole on the back and felt for the shoulder holster harness he knew should be there. It was a trick he had learned from an old hooker, never quite sure which was, in fact, older, the trick for spotting a gun or the woman who turned tricks for her humble living. "Martin! Help however you can." He didn't wait for an answer, starting for the rear of the garage, his arm still around O'Toole. There was a group of men coming through the wooden doorway at the rear of the garage, the doorway leading from the bakery. His right hand went into his Macintosh as he made a smile appear and he nodded to the men, some of them doffing their hats or caps to him, others smiling deferentially or mumbling respectful greetings.

O'Fallon crossed through the doorway, pulling the door after him, keeping Larry O'Toole just ahead of him now. He could smell the bakery yeast, and the sourness of it on his empty stomach was an uncomfortable sensation. The second doorway was open as well, the doors less than six feet apart, once a way between the bakery and the garage but—from the workmanship—thirty years or so ago enclosed. He passed through the second doorway, the yeast smell stronger, closing the door after him.

Pipes, gleaming, stainless steel, ran along the ceiling and at intervals along the wall on his left, the shining metal in sharp contrast to the overall dinginess of the damp sweating brick. O'Toole started talking. "The lorry's loaded and ready to go, Seamus. The lads all know their part."

"I'd be after havin' a look inside myself, Larry."

"Of course, Seamus." O'Toole nodded, digging his hands into his pockets. O'Fallon's right fist tightened on his gun. He had replaced the two spent cartridges when he'd stopped the Volkswagen for a red traffic light.

The baked goods factory was L-shaped and they walked side by side now out of the leg of the L into the upright, the delivery van parked by this building's garage entrance. It was black, the bright red lettering making the jet of the black all that much more pronounced. But a few minutes in the slush would make the vehicle look as though it had been seeing harsh service.

"Did the traffic and the sleet make it rough driving, Seamus?"

"For fact they did, the reason Martin and I were almost late." The yeast smell was mingled with the smell of exhaust fumes now as they neared the van. O'Toole walked ahead more briskly and began opening the sliding side panel door. O'Fallon's left hand found the brim of his hat and he took it off his head and shook it, the wetness already penetrated through.

O'Fallon approached the van, leaning forward to look inside. "Aww, shit."

"What is it, Seamus?"

"Larry. Do an old man a favor, would ya, boyo? I'm out of

the weed, but there's a carton half-filled on the desk in the office back in the garage. Could I be askin' ya . . ."

"Of course, Seamus. Be with you in a mo'." And Larry O'Toole shot him a big, toothy grin and started away in a fast, long-strided walk.

O'Fallon listened for the click of heels and for the sounds of the door opening. He heard both and quickly steped up into the van, grabbing up an AK-47 at random and checking that the firing pin was present and it seemed in working order. He set it back, grabbing up one of the Uzi submachine guns and doing the same. He weighed the full magazines stacked neatly inside two wooden slat crates, the weight feeling right, that the cartridges themselves hadn't been tampered with. He replaced the magazines and flipped down out of the van, lighting a cigarette. He heard the slam of the door and could just hear the click of heels. "Larry, you'll be after thinkin' the O'Fallon's gone daft, boyo, but I found my cigarettes after all!"

Larry came around the angle of the L and flipped the packet in his right hand, then started to laugh. . . .

O'Fallon sat in the passenger seat, looking to his right at O'Toole who drove. The jaw was a little slack, the eyelids blinking a little more than they might have; but, otherwise, Larry O'Toole seemed cool enough.

"Slow up, Larry," O'Fallon ordered, the outer gates of the fence surrounding the barracks looming just ahead. The sleet had turned to snow, and the snow covered the frozen stuff already on the street and on the roads and the going had been so slow they were running forty-five minutes behind. It was nearly midnight. O'Fallon lit another cigarette with the butt of the last one, inhaling deep. There were lights in both guardhouses and only two men were out, the weather an unexpected but welcome ally.

The guards were Royal Ulster Constabulary, so swathed in winter gear they looked like overweight black bears. O'Fallon pulled on the uniform cap and inhaled again on his cigarette. "Be ready, lads," he ordered. O'Toole's face looked positively ashen now. The steady thumping of the windshield wipers was the only sound except for the purring of the engine.

The guards had seen them and moved toward the pie-wedge shaped grey-white deflection barriers. "Slow her down some more, Larry."

"Right."

O'Fallon inhaled again on his cigarette, the revolver in his right fist under his thigh.

Larry O'Toole stopped the van.

As one of the guards approached the driver's side, O'Toole lowered the window, a rush of cold air and flurry of icy snowflakes filling the front seat compartment like a tiny whirlwind. "State your business," O'Fallon hissed, his and O'Toole's eyes meeting. Did O'Toole know he knew?

The guard stopped by the open window.

O'Toole spoke quickly enough. "Special Air Service. Here to run a night exercise, Sergeant."

"Right, sir! May I please see the Captain's orders."

O'Toole looked at O'Fallon almost pleedingly. O'Fallon smiled and leaned across to be nearer to the open window. "I can take care of that, you vile motherfucking peeler!" His left hand snapped the cigarette neatly into the right eye of the RUC sergeant and his right hand stabbed the revolver forward, double actioning a shot into the same eye, the RUC sergeant already screaming from the cigarette burn to his eye.

The RUC-er's head snapped back. O'Toole started wrenching at his door handle. O'Fallon leaned back quickly and raised the muzzle of the little revolver to the level of O'Toole's left temple and hissed, "Shootin's too good for ya, ya bleedin' bastard squealer. But it'll have to be doin' now, won't it?" He pulled the trigger and O'Toole's head, because of the angle at which O'Fallon had shot, rocked forward, slamming into the steering wheel, blood spraying onto the inside of the windshield. Already, O'Fallon heard the first submachine gun, the van charged with icy air now with the sliding side door open as it was. O'Fallon's right hand rammed the revolver into the pocket of his jacket and he threw his body weight against O'Toole's, the body rolling out as the driver's-side door opened, into the snow. O'Fallon slipped behind the wheel. Two of his men were already over the deflection barrier, another two right behind them, young Martin one of them. More submachine-gun fire, the yellow-lighted windows of the twin guardhouses seeming to implode as his men riddled the structures with bullets.

The deflection barrier lowered, O'Fallon taking up the radio set from between the seats, depressing the push-to-talk button. "Move, lads!" He threw the set down and stomped the accelerator as the barrier dropped flush to the roadbed, the exterior gate swinging open—young Martin. The interior gates swung open inward and he pulled the van through, hearing the breathless exclamations of the men as they clambored back aboard, the clicking and scratching of magazines being withdrawn, replaced with fresh ones. "Pass me up an AK, Martin."

"Yes, Seamus."

He extended his left hand, felt the front handguard and the chill of metal, drew the weapon toward him. "Thank ya, Martin." Already, he was starting the van forward, the snow heavier here, making the driving actually easier. Inside his head, Seamus O'Fallon was ticking off the seconds. Thirty-four had gone by so far. Fifty-eight remained as he'd figured it.

He caught a glimpse of the second lorry in the sideview mirror, speeding through the open gates. But this was no van, but what the Americans so picturesquely called an eighteen wheeler, the lorry picking up speed now.

There were lights coming on in the barracks hall and in the smaller windows where the trainees slept.

O'Fallon skidded the van to a halt, cutting the wheel sharp so the van would form a wall between them and the barracks building.

He jumped from the driver's seat, almost losing his footing, working the AK's bolt, his men closing ranks around him as he opened fire toward every light he saw, the roar of gunfire around him deafening. He had spent his magazine and he threw the assault rifle into the opening in the side of the van as he walked away from where the others still stood to fire, the huge lorry still coming, faster and faster, the driver's-side door opening, Keogh swinging out from the opening, his body wrapped in heavy padding and almost unrecognizable as being human at all.

Keogh jumped, the lorry aimed right for the center of the barracks.

O'Fallon had his whistle out and blew it sharply three times, then swung up behind the wheel, already getting the van into motion, his lads jumping in through the open side door, Martin among them as O'Fallon cut the wheel hard left and accelerated. His rear wheels were spinning, but then caught. The van's rear end fishtailed as he fought the steering wheel, still counting seconds. Twenty-one remained.

Keogh was running, looking positively ridiculous with his padding.

O'Fallon slowed the van only minutely, Martin shouting, "We've got him safe, Seamus!"

O'Fallon didn't care, but evidently Martin did. O'Fallon stomped the accelerator to the floorboard, still counting seconds.

He began mumbling them aloud when he reached only ten left. "Nine . . . eight . . . seven . . ." The guardhouses were just ahead, the gates still wide open and the deflection barriers still down. "Six . . . five . . . four . . . three . . ." Through the interior fence, then the outer fence and the van bumping and jostling as it crossed over the seams between the deflection barriers.

"Two . . . one . . ."

The explosion made the already bloodied glass of the windshield vibrate, all other sounds—the near-over-revving of the engine, the rattling of equipment, the siren that had begun wailing an instant before—masked beneath it. O'Fallon turned into the road and snapped a look right. A gratifyingly huge tongue of orange and yellow and white flame flicked skyward into the night, the road surface vibrating with the shockwaves.

One hundred and twenty dead at least. All RUC.

He screamed to his fellows,,"Ahh, a thing of beauty lads, a thing of beauty! Ha!"

Chapter Two

Nothing about it made sense. Meeting aboard the train which traversed the distance between Tirana and Durazzo was madness. And even if by some miracle all went well, once he was at Durazzo and had it, there were dangerous miles to be traveled down the Albanian coastline before reaching Valona and the quick transfer by night across the Strait of Otranto to the comparative safety of Italy. And once there, what?

When the previous president had begun his one-man crusade to replace dangerously but usefully planted agents with long-distance electronic intelligence gatherers, a number of the old-timers had predicted just this sort of thing: When a man was needed on the spot, he wouldn't be there; no one would be there and someone would have to be sent in.

It was nice to know, Thomas Alyard thought as he gazed at his reflection against the night-black window of the train, that he was "someone." He ran the fingers of both hands back through his dark brown hair.

The phone had rung. The girl he'd been keeping company with for the last six months had leaned across him, her bare breasts brushing against his face, answered, roused him to full wakefulness, told him, "Somebody who says his name is Mario, Thomas. He wants to speak with you."

Thomas Alyard didn't know a man named Mario, but he did know a code sequence that started that way. "This is Thomas Alyard."

"This is Mario. You need to come at once. Signore Brownlee is very sick."

"What seems to be wrong with him?"

"His fever is one hundred and two how you count it."

"Has the doctor been called?"

"It took one hour to reach him."

"I'll be right there." Alyard hung up, reached for the Bible in the nightstand drawer beside the bed and glanced quickly at Appalonia. She was very beautiful and, more important at the moment, already asleep. He squinted in the yellow light from the bedside lamp as he flipped pages. At last, he turned to page 102 and read the first full verse on the page, the temperature of the nonexistent Mr. Brownlee giving him the page, the number one for how long it had taken to contact the doctor telling him the verse. Verse one of Leviticus, where the Lord called Moses and spoke to him from the Tent of Meeting. The basement intelligence suite at the Embassy. That had seemed to make poor sense as well, going to so obvious a location for his assignment. And after he had been told what his assignment was to be, it had seemed even more nonsensical than ever.

It was a logical given that bacteriological work was never done near large concentrations of people. Just in case. Or, at least, never done near large concentrations of your own people.

Yet, a secure location was required. And the more remote the better.

Hence, Albania, a ragged bite taken out of the west face of the Balkan Peninsula between Yugoslavia to the north and Greece to the south. Communist, of course, but separated from the chaotic democracy of Italy by only forty miles of the Adriatic at its nearest point.

The compartment in which Thomas Alyard sat was empty except for him, the route between the capital of Tirana and the coastal city of Durazzo not the most heavily trafficked even during more conventional hours. Albania—a country comprised largely of farmers denied all but the most rudimentary contacts with the West, and hence stifled in the iron fists of a party leadership that was among the most reactionary of Communist governments.

Central Intelligence Agency Case Officer Thomas Alyard had flown from Italy to Greece, leaving the Athens airport that was uneasily shared with Helenikon United States Air Force Base by private plane which, after too many stops, had gotten Swiss businessman Thomas Rheinhold to Tirana just three hours before the train was to depart. There had, as yet, been no sign of David Stakowski.

And meetings delayed were frequently meetings compromised.

Alyard sometimes wished he was living in a book or a movie. As an American "agent," he was certainly the good guy, and in books and movies, the good guy was easily able to enter enemy-occupied territory with all sorts of weapons. There was occasionally some daring-do required, but there was always the slavishly loving heroine to fall into bed with afterward. But this was reality and he had no weapon but his wits, and the edge of this solitary weapon was dulled by the lack of sleep and the sudden, prolonged travel since "Mario's" wake-up call. He had left word that Appalonia be told some convenient lie so she wouldn't be angry with him when he returned, but there was no way to know if anyone had bothered to tell her anything. He didn't want to lose her. He was not in the market for a love-struck gypsy girl or a defecting Russian cipher clerk. Appalonia satisfied him more than any woman ever had.

More cheerful thoughts were needed, but there were none to be had. So Alyard focused his attention on the details of the assignment, running them over again in his head. David Stakowski, age twenty-nine, was a CIA Case Officer as well, but assigned to the United States Embassy in Moscow as a cultural attache, the universal euphemism for "spy." Stakowski had been running an Eastern European newsman named Wilton Voroncek. Voroncek had requested money through Stakowski, a quite large sum with which Voroncek would pay his agent-in-place who held a position of some responsibility at The Peoples' Institute For Biological Progress, a biowarfare laboratory on the Drina, the river which knifed through the northernmost portion of Albania out of Yugoslavia, the laboratory all but inaccessible because of the rugged mountains which surrounded it. What Voroncek had paid his man for was the solitary existing sample (supposedly) of an as-yet-unnamed virus, as well as the destruction of the laboratory notes and tapes and any other data vital to its efficient duplication by the Soviet scientists who had created it from the work of a now dead (natural causes, it was presumed) German scientist of considerably advanced age.

It was estimated that it would take Soviet scientists at least three months to duplicate their work without the inspirational leadership of the dead German, about as long as it would take the teams of scientists already being assembled in the United States scheduled round-the-clock to analyze the sample of the viral agent and duplicate it. Each nation would quietly let the other know that it had the virus and the doctrine of mutually assured destruction would once again spare mankind enduring a weapon of unimaginable destructive capabilities. What the virus caused was something Alyard had not been told, if anyone knew.

The trick was to get the sample from Stakowski, who was as hot as a two-dollar pistol, and then spirit it to America. Stakowski would never be able to get out of Albania with it, might well have to sit it out in Albania for months until he could quietly slip over into Greece or get across the Adriatic to Italy.

The problem arose out of Stakowski's inexperience. The logical procedure, once Stakowski was approached by Voroncek, would have been to get the agent-in-place out from under Voroncek's control and put him under control of someone experienced in clandestine operations of such delicacy, cutting out Voroncek and Stakowski completely. If the agent-in-place would work for no one but Voroncek (some private liaison, for example; or, something as basic as a sense of comfortable security), then Voroncek would be put under direct control of the more experienced field officer. But any way the problem was viewed, logic would have to dictate Stakowski's quick and total exclusion. Logic had not only been unable to prevail, but as Alyard understood, logic had never once been considered.

Alyard lit his pipe, watching the grey smoke as it curled round his reflection on the window.

Voroncek would have pocketed the bulk of the money for his own profit, of course. What would some laboratory supervisor who had spent the last decade or so living in the mountains of Albania do with that kind of money anyway? Why add to the fellow's troubles? A hundred thousand dollars was allocated, likely meaning the agent-in-place who did all the dangerous dirty work had gotten a quarter of that or less. But, as Alyard understood it, the issue of money was academic now. The theft of the specimen and the destruction of the notes and lab tapes were discovered more quickly than any of the wizards planning the thing had supposed, the agent-in-place getting as far as Split on the Yugoslav coast where Voroncek was to have met him to receive the specimen and where Stakowski was to have met Voroncek. A boat was to have taken Stakowski across the Adriatic to San Marino. But nothing ever really got that far.

Once the theft at the laboratory was discovered—the security at the laboratory was KGB—the agent-in-place was immediately pegged as the culprit.

The agent-in-place (no name had been supplied Alyard at his

briefing and he suddenly wondered if anyone knew it or thought it even important enough to bother knowing) had been cornered in Split. But whoever the nameless fellow had been, he had to have been tough. When Voroncek had rendezvoused—late—his agent-in-place had already been shot to death, twice in the throat and once in the chest, but managed to stab to death his assassin. Voroncek had taken the specimen and then compounded all the foregoing stupidity with a stroke of unbelievable idiocy: Voroncek had gone directly to the pre-arranged meeting with Stakowski. The KGB or the Albanian secret police—no one was sure yet— had been at Voroncek's heels and an actual gunfight had broken out. The results included Voroncek's death, Stakowski's getting control of the virus and barely getting away, and some assorted deaths and gunshot wounds, Stakowski almost miraculously not among them.

Stakowski had then done something moderately intelligent. Instead of heading for freedom, he had gone into Albania, like a purposeful salmon going against the flow of the security stream. It had worked, up to a point. If Stakowski didn't show up soon, apparently it hadn't worked that well.

Alyard's pipe had gone out and he started to refill it when he heard the knock at the compartment door, sharper sounding over the rattle of the train car as it sped over the tracks.

Thomas Alyard asked in German, the agreed upon language since Stakowski spoke it, and as a Swiss Thomas Rheinhold would speak it too, "One moment, please?"

He approached the door, his pipe stem turned outward in his hand. He wasn't entirely weaponless, the stem a tough phenolic resin material and, when used properly, capable of inflicting considerable injury when thrust to a vital area.

Alyard opened the door a crack and peered into the corridor. It was Stakowski, looking a bit shopworn and rather tired but otherwise just as bland as his photograph. Hair that if a woman had worn it would have been called ash blonde, a little on the longish side for anything but a musician, an actor or a college boy; a chubby face with cheeks that in the photograph had seemed almost rosy but now seemed merely flushed with exertion, the lips grey and parched looking, gold-wire-rimmed glasses adding to the look of confused innocence the face seemed almost to exude; narrow shoulders under a rumpled, once-expensive look- ing Harris Tweed sportcoat, a khaki trench coat folded neatly over the left forearm; a double chin all but obscured the Windsor knot of the tie, some phantom regimental or old school stripes.

But the code phrase was still required, if only Stakowski knew it. "I, er, was needing to exchange a large note for smaller denominations so I could purchase cigarettes. Could I trouble you?"

"I have little on me in Albanian leks, I'm afraid. Only Swiss francs. Wait!" And Alyard started to dig in his pockets. "I may have a bit extra."

"You would save my life."

Thomas Alyard took his left hand from his jacket pocket and switched the pipe to it. He opened the door the rest of the way, Stakowski almost collapsing inside. "Thank God," Stakowski whispered hoarsely. "I had no picture."

"Here—sit down," Alyard told the fellow, guiding him to the opposite seat from his own, then sitting down on the edge, staring intently at Stakowski for a moment. It almost seemed as though Stakowski was beginning to hyperventilate. "Wait . . ." And Alyard stood, pulled over his overnighter and dug into it for a moment, the pipe going back into his teeth. He found the beaten metal hip flask and opened it. "Here. Have some of this." Stakowski seemed to hesitate. "It's all right. I don't have diseases or anything. And let's hope you don't." Stakowski nodded then, taking the flask. "Looks like you've had a rough time." Stakowski drank from the flask, coughed, wiped the mouthpiece on his sleeve and handed it back. Alyard wiped it again and took a swallow from it himself. "Do you have it?"

"Yes."

"Were you followed? Or do you know?"

"I was followed to the train, but not to your compartment."

"Do you have any kind of a weapon?"

"Yes, this." Stakowski reached under his jacket, Alyard tensing just in case, Stakowski's right hand reemerging with a pistol, but in no position to shoot it, the gun—a Walther PPK—held as though it were radioactive. "Here." Stakowski offered it to him, Alyard nodding, pocketing it as he went to the compartment door and locked it. He took the gun back out and began to examine it. "I'm scared to death."

Alyard removed the little pistol's magazine, worked the slide back. No round had been chambered. "It takes a brave man to admit fear," he told Stakowski to be more or less comforting. The PPK was in .380, 9mm Short in European parlance, the magazine containing only six rounds, solids. "Any more for this?" Alyard raised his eyebrows as he slapped the spine of the magazine against the palm of his hand and then shoved it up the butt.

"No."

Alyard worked the slide, chambering a round, setting the safety to on. "Here. Work this lever on the slide and—"

"No. You keep it. I never liked guns to begin with. Since this thing started I've seen enough shooting to last a lifetime."

"Not the gun, but the man behind it who's good or evil, to like or dislike. All right. Anyway, where's the stuff?"

"Here." Stakowski—unbelievably—just reached into the outside pocket of his sportcoat and took out a long, rather fat velvet maroon jewelry box, passing it over.

Alyard dropped the little pistol into his right hip pocket and gingerly opened the jewelry box. It was lined with grey foam rubber inside, a french-fitted niche cut for an ampule approximately three inches in length and perhaps a half-inch in diameter. Rounded at one end, squared off with a screw-in cap at the other, the ampule was made of some heavy-seeming sort of glass. "What the hell does this stuff do? I mean, just in case I drop it or something, I'd like to know what symptoms to expect."

"I don't know. But I know it's fuckin' deadly. There's enough in there to kill off a small city, from what I was told."

Alyard looked once more at the ampule, then carefully closed the case. Under the circumstances, he couldn't think of a better place for it than his pocket, so he put it there. "How many followed you?"

"Three."

"Whose people?"

"Albanian secret police, I think. I don't know. Could have been KGB. I gotta get outa here. You got what I need?"

Alyard crossed his legs, taking off his left shoe, twisting the heel, then turning it over. Three small, perfectly faceted blue-white stones tumbled into his palm. It would have been easy to give Stakowski only two, because Stakowski would have had no way of knowing what form his escape money would take. And Stakowski would most likely never get out of Albania alive. "These are for you. If you're careful—I'll give you the names of the right fences in Durazzo—you'll have money to spare. There's a lot of smuggling in Albania. It's a long coast. You shouldn't have trouble." He was planning to use a smuggler himself to cross the Adriatic, but that was none of Stakowski's business. He gave Stakowski the diamonds. This was a rich operation. "Here." He reached into a breast pocket and took out a small notebook, careful to open the rings rather than rip out the sheets, handing them over to Stakowski. "The first five appointments are the names of the fences you can try. The last appointment breaks down into the name of the man you should contact when you feel things have cooled down. He can get you across the Adriatic, then. They said you knew Bright's Shorthand Alphabet. Work the characters from back to front using numbers and then apply the numbers to the appointment names from the middle outward. If there's an even number of characters, disregard the middle one to the right. Work left to right all the way through. Got it?"

"Disregard the double on the right and work left to right all the way through. All right."

"Then you'll need this." Alyard went into his pockets again, taking out his wallet, giving the special packet of leks to Stakowski. "Should be enough dough to see you through until you can fence those stones. And take your gun back. You're the one who's more likely to need it."

"I don't want it. Get rid of it yourself if you don't want it."

Alyard nodded. Rather than making an issue of it, he could drop it in a trash can somewhere and, if Stakowski had led the KGB or the Albanian secret police to his door, however incriminating a gun might be, it might save his life, too. "Fine. Good luck, huh?"

Alyard extended his hand.

Stakowski took it, Stakowski's hand clammy with sweat. "Thanks, man."

"Look me up when you get to Italy, huh?"

"Yeah. Gotta. I owe you a drink."

"You got it right there." Alyard walked Stakowski to the compartment door, let him out and glanced up and down the corridor as he did. There was a woman with an ill-fitting grey coat, grey-steaked brown hair partially covered with a babushka. Alyard closed the door. . . .

The train was slowing already and Ephraim Vols—it had been Volshinski once—started running, sticking his fedora down low over his eyes so it wouldn't catch in the wind and sail off. Wave after wave of arctic fronts had been bombarding Europe since late fall, and by now he was used to the constant cold temperatures and snow. In the British Isles, he had heard, there was even now a terrible blizzard. He had liked Great Britain, serving out almost exactly halfway through a standard-length "illegal" tour there but having to get out when the project he had been working for just over three years went suddenly very sour. Instead of a rebuke, he had been given a promotion. Once he had no longer been an illegal, he had divorced his wife. To have done so before would have made him seem suspicious to his superiors and invited disaster. He saw his two children when he could, had been with them in Moscow when the man from Derzhinsky Square had come telling him that he was needed. Then a solitary flight to Albania and the rapid determination that the viral agent had been gotten out of the research complex. But the only personnel close enough to be of any use had been Albanian secret police, the English term assholes the best way to describe their ability level. And the man and the ampule of the viral agent had been lost. Then there had been a gunfight and the fellow Wilton Vironcek (whom he an hour afterward had found out had been a double worked by the GRU against U.S. Central Intelligence) had been killed and the damned viral agent lost again. This time to a man Vols had seen several times in Moscow, David Stakowski, the CIA resident.

The rear door of the last car was opening and Vols quickened his pace. The Western concept of jogging for physical fitness was certainly paying off tonight. He reached the rear car and jumped, hands coming for his hands, and he was on the platform, losing his footing for an instant on the slippery metal, but then catching himself. "I am all right," he said, at last seeing the face. He had thought the hands had felt strangely soft.

It was Anna, a half dozen last names supplied over the years, but the first name all he was ever certain enough to use. "Ephraim."

He embraced her briefly, already feeling the sweat starting under his heavy winter coat from the exertion of the run. "Is Stakowski aboard?"

"He has transferred the ampule to another man. The conductor says he travels under a Swiss passport and is named Thomas Rheinhold. I think he is American."

"Let's see then."

She opened the door and there was a wide shaft of yellow white light and he stepped through after her, closing the door behind him, trying to force out the sound of the metal wheels clacking over the metal rails. Vols opened his coat. He looked at Anna. He laughed. "You look twenty years older."

She laughed, retying her floral-print scarf under her chin. "The dye in my hair washes out. Maybe I can show you after this business. And the coat is three sizes too large."

"I must get this infernal thing back to Moscow after it's over. Can you come to Moscow?"

"I could."

"Come, then. I can show you how to make a Christmas tree. It won't be that long."

"You?"

"When I was in the West, I picked up some of their customs. The religious festival aside, it's a wonderful excuse for a winter vacation for a few days."

"All right."

"Who's watching him?"

"Two of the three men you sent, Ivan and Piotr. I sent Vassily to keep an eye on Stakowski."

"Good girl." None of the names were real, but then Anna probably wasn't her real name either. He detested confusion, so had told her his real name the first time they had shared a bed together.

"Don't you have some girl in Moscow?"

"I have several girls in Moscow, but none of them like you. Believe me or not, but it is true."

"Should I trust a man who is skilled in disinformation techniques?"

"Yes." He smiled.

"I think so, too." She smiled. "Come on."

He started after her down the corridor and they passed through three cars until they reached the one she said the dubious Swiss businessman was aboard. She knocked on a compartment door and it opened. It was Piotr, as Anna called him. Anna stepped inside, Vols after her, Piotr putting away his revolver. Certain officers in the KGB and their respective functionaries, at the discretion of the officer, were allowed considerable latitude in their selection of items of personal equipment. Vols was one of these and allowed his men the same privilege. So much of Russian equipment was inferior to the best available in the West.

"So, Piotr. You have been listening to him?" There was a suction-cupped listening device on the wall at his left.

"The fellow has not said a word. But, of course, he is alone now," and Piotr smiled. "But the funny thing is he seems to be breathing very hard."

"Yes. It is harder to deal with crazies, isn't it. Where's your friend?"

"The compartment on the other side. I don't think Ivan would have heard anything either."

Vols lit a cigarette, threw down his winter coat and took the pistol from the coat pocket, then stuffed it in the waistband of his trousers under the front of his sweater. "And you couldn't get it going in time to hear what was said between him and Stakowski?"

"No, Comrade Major."

"Let me have a listen." He walked over and took the earphones from Piotr. The sounds of heavy breathing were odd, but perhaps the fellow they were monitoring had had as little sleep as he. Vols had ordered that all conversations for the mission be in English since very few Albanian secret police personnel understood English and he didn't wish complications. "Where are the Albanians?" He surrendered the earphones to Piotr.

"I gave them some money to buy a bottle of vodka and told them to guard the first car so the Americans couldn't—" Piotr started to laugh "—couldn't reach the engine compartment and—what is the word—hijack!—couldn't hijack the train."

"You are insane, but it is a humorous idea at that."

"What will we do?" Anna asked, taking off her coat, leaving on the scarf. Underneath the coat, it was the old Anna. Great figure, breasts upthrusting proudly against the heavy sweater, the perfect swell at the hips beneath the trim waist, the gorgeous legs the coat had all but hidden.

"I think we talk with Mr. Stakowski. Is Vassily in radio contact?"

"Yes."

"Reach him, Piotr. Find out where Stakowski is."

Piotr started working the hand-held radio. Anna started back into her old-lady coat, Vols helping her with it. "Thank you."

"You stay here with the listening device, Piotr. Anna and I will talk with Mr. Stakowski."

"He is in the second car. But remember, Comrade Major, the Albanians are in the first car."

Vols nodded and started out of the compartment, entering the corridor first, holding the door for Anna, then closing it behind them. He looked at the door to the compartment where the so-called Swiss businessman was as they passed it, tugged at his sweater to make certain the Walther P-5 was covered sufficiently, and followed Anna into the next car, through it, on to the next car, where there were no compartments, only seats, most of which were unoccupied, none of the few riders seemingly awake, then through it.

"This is the second car, Ephraim," she told him as she stopped on the platform between cars. He froze with the wind blowing, almost envying Anna the ugly-looking coat.

"Go in first, walk past him and find someplace to sit. I'll follow you in a minute."

"Be careful. He should be armed."

"I'll be careful. He's a fancy gatherer and nothing more, not a field agent. Go on."

She went inside, Ephraim Vols hanging back, hugging his arms across his chest against the bite of the wind. He looked at his watch. In less than an hour, they'd be in Durazzo station. He was tempted to find out what he could from Stakowski and then let the courier Stakowski had given it to off the train, follow him and pick the time and place to recover the viral material. He certainly had enough men (and, of course, Anna) to meet the task.

"Fuck it," he said in English, tired of waiting in the cold and wrenching open the door, going inside, the suddenness of the warmth almost stifling to him.

He saw Stakowski, seated alone, wearing a trench coat, both hands in the coat pockets. One of the hands could be holding a gun, he told himself.

Anna sat beside an old woman, chatting it seemed from the movement of their lips. Vassily was nowhere to be seen, logically at the other end of the car on the outside. Poor fellow.

Vols decided to try the soft approach. He left his hands at his sides and walked straight up the aisle, toward Stakowski, the American not yet looking up. Vols stopped right in front of him, smiled and said, "David! Of all things!"

Stakowski looked up. "Vols—"

"We've met a few times. I hadn't thought you'd remember. May I join you? I'm traveling with some friends." He sat down opposite Stakowski, reached into his trouser pockets and found cigarettes and a lighter, the American watching him intently, fear etched in his eyes.

"I don't have it."

Vols smiled as he exhaled. "Now that's a silly thing to say,

David. I mean, really. What if I were just traveling with some friends and didn't know anything about the little ampule you got from Voroncek? Wilton was a clumsy spy, as I'm sure you'd agree. But he had a certain audacity. Which almost paid off for you and your people. But, I'll tell you what, David. You tell me all you can about the Swiss businessman or whoever he is that you gave the thing to, and I'll let you off the train with an hour's head start. I can't promise you more than that, actually. Bit sticky for me at that, if you get my meaning. But, for old times' sake, I'm willing to extend myself."

Stakowski's voice trembled when he replied. "Go to hell!"

"That's the spirit, David! Now, between you and me, I'm not really an atheist as I should be. I believe in God, Heaven, and, well, in my line of work, I certainly hope there isn't a hell. But I'm willing to risk a hell after death. But, the question before you, David, is, are you willing to risk a hell before death? Because we can make that. I mean, not me. I'm not into extracting information from people. But let me tell you, some of my associates are bloody rough on uncooperative sorts. Talk and you get that hour's start, David. And if you do get caught, I'll go to bat for you and pull some strings in the right places and make certain they just swap you back for someone right away. One of our johnnies is always getting caught at something or another in your country. So, what about it?"

Stakowski didn't speak.

Vols laughed. "Damn! You drive a hard bargain. All right! You win!" The cigarette was between his lips and he spread both palms outward toward Stakowski.

"What?"

"I'll tell you where to get a boat—tonight. Or this morning, I should say, that'll spirit you to safety right across the Adriatic up to San Marino where you were going in the first place. But, you've got to promise you'll never breathe a word of my complicity in the thing. It'd be bloody awful for me when it came time for May Day bonuses!" And he laughed. Stakowski laughed. "Well, what do you say, David?"

"What'll happen to Alyard?"

"That the fellow's name?"

"Thomas Alyard."

"Well, we'll make a big flap over it, of course, but he'll be traded out rather quickly. Instead of you. What about it? We have an understanding?"

David Stakowski's eyes looked on the verge of tears and there as a puerile smile on his face. "You mean what you say, Vols?"

"Yes, I do. And I'll tell you something else. There're Albanian secret police on this train. I could tell you horror stories about their incompetence, believe me. The fact of the matter, basically, is that all of us are rational. You, me, this chap—Thomas Alyard?"

"Yes."

"CIA?"

"Yes."

"Hmm. But you see," Vols said, lowering his voice into a conspiratorial whisper as he leaned slightly forward, smoke exhaling through his nostrils, "this ampule of virus or whatever. I mean, my people will be careful with it. Just as yours would be. But I hear it's rather nasty stuff, if you get my meaning. Shouldn't want these Albanian secret police fellows to get their hands on it. Bunch of positive twits. They'd probably open the bloody thing and, well, it might well be over for everyone on this train and for some miles around. Ugghh," and he shivered, not faking the reaction.

"What do you want to know?"

"Good man." Vols nodded. "Right then." He decided on asking something easily enough verifiable. "What name is this Alyard chap traveling under?"

"Thomas Rheinhold. Swiss, as I said."

"And what's his status. I mean, is he a reasonable sort of fellow? Is he armed?"

David Stakowski's face soured. "I armed him. I picked up a gun when I took the ampule off Voroncek. I mean, you know I'm not that kinda guy, Vols. But I was scared."

"Shouldn't blame you a bit, David. But what about this gun?"

"I gave it to Alyard. He didn't want it, but I made him take it."

"What sort of gun?"

"I don't know. It was an automatic of some kind."

"Right. What's his escape plan?"

"He told me to wait it out for a while until the heat died down, then get out of the country." Vols didn't push and ask how, just let David Stakowski keep talking. "He didn't get specific, but I bet he's got somebody to smuggle him across the Adriatic."

"Likely correct, David. He didn't mention any names? Anything more specific?"

"No. There wasn't any reason for me to need to know."

"Well, there you go. Good to see this Alyard chap evidently knows what he's about. Make it easier to talk sense with him. Now. You wait here until the train stops. Won't be all that long, now, and I'll make certain you walk out of the station with me. Then you get to that boat we talked about and your end of this whole affair is done with."

Stakowski audibly sighed. Vols felt sorry for him. There was no way that Stakowski wouldn't wind up in the hands of the Albanians, but he would try to do what he could to get him as quickly as possible back to Moscow. The treatment would be considerably more humane. He told Stakowski sincerely, "Thank you for your help, David," then stood up.

He caught Anna's eye and she nodded that she understood and he walked out the door, shivering as he crossed from one car to another, hurrying into the warmth. A half-hour remained until they pulled in at Durazzo station.

As he passed the compartment where Ivan was listening he knocked and entered, Ivan wheeling toward him with a gun in his hand. "Relax." He closed the door behind him for an instant, leaning against it.

"Yes, Comrade Major?"

"Meet me in the corridor in sixty seconds."

"Yes, Comrade Major."

"You're too formal, Ivan." He let himself out, passed Alyard's compartment and let himself in to see Piotr. "Come with me."

Piotr nodded.

As Ivan came into the corridor, Vols could see Anna coming down the corridor.

Vols gestured with his thumb toward the door, Piotr taking the right side, Ivan the left. Anna held back, a Walther like his own coming out of her purse. Piotr and Ivan had their guns drawn as well.

Vols knocked on the compartment door. "Mr. Alyard? My name is Ephraim Vols. I'm a friend of David Stakowski."

There was no answer.

"I'm coming in, if I may. I'm not here to harm you."

He glanced to Anna, then Ivan and Piotr.

Vols licked his dry lips and turned the door handle.

"Shit!" He started under his sweater for the P-5 automatic, crossing the compartment in two strides, the compartment window cut out neatly just inside the frame, his breath making steam as he exhaled. He leaned out into the slipstream, gun in hand. He heard the excited voices of Ivan and Piotr. He thought he heard Anna laugh.

He saw nothing but darkness, drew his head inside. "Up on the roof. Be careful. If he's up there, corner him and one of you come back. Quickly!"

He looked at Anna. She showed no evidence of laughter, except in her eyes. "This American or Swiss—"

"He's American. CIA."

"He's very good."

"Probably got off the damn train when I got on." He closed his eyes, shook his head. He opened his eyes. "Heavy breathing when he was sleeping!" And he looked again at the cut-through window and cursed his own stupidity. He folded his arms around Anna and he embraced her.

"I still think you're a marvelous secret agent," Anna cooed.

And Ephraim Vols started to laugh. . . .

Thomas Alyard, the PPK in his fist, moved through the windward edge of the woods just a hundred yards or so from where the tree line broke into the open snowswept pastures beyond. He had used the fourth diamond, the one given him just in case, locking it into his nail clipper when the train had slowed for no apparent reason back some miles ago. It had been cheap glass, thank goodness. He doubted the improvised cutter would have done nearly so well on good old American safety glass. He had cut out a handhold that he had knocked out with the butt of the PPK, scarring the plastic grips and nearly breaking them, then kept one gloved hand through the handhold while he'd cut out the rest, then juggled the glass adroitly enough to get it inside rather than letting it fall out and crash. But by that time, the train had picked up speed again and he had doubted whether he would be able to jump from the train. Without killing himself.

But the train had slowed again for a grade and he had decided it was then or never and clambored through, held on, thrown himself outward, prayed. His suitcoat had torn, but he had thrown his overcoat out ahead of him and pulled it on over the torn jacket. His suitcase had gone with the overcoat, and once he had made it deep enough into the tree cover, he had changed into the heavy sweater and pulled a second pair of trousers on over the ones he already wore. The neck scarf had gone up over his head and ears to guard against frostbite. But he had still felt silly tying it under his chin. An extra pair of socks on his feet and then another pair over his shoes, the trouser bottoms bloused inside this outer pair to keep the snow at bay. And then he had started on. There was no need for a compass with the tracks and power lines to guide him. He knew where he was going, coming at it from the opposite direction. A once privately held farm with an abandoned barn, a car inside it. If he could get the damned thing started with the cold.

The barn with the car had been for a British operation that had been scrubbed—how the CIA had found out about it from SIS was something he hadn't been told. But the car was his only way out now, his only way to the boat waiting for him in Valona that he hoped would still be able to get him across the Adriatic. And he had to be there by dawn when the fishing fleet went out or else he'd never get out at all.

Something had gone wrong. He had sensed it in more than David Stakowski's manner, more than Stakowski's words.

As he forced his way partially over and partially through a snowdrift that rose to his waist, he patted the little maroon box with its deadly cargo.

If there had been KGB on the train, then when the train had slowed it had slowed to pick up someone who was responsible, in charge. That was the only thing that fit. And Alyard couldn't risk a battle with the ampule on him. A bullet could punch through the little protective box and rupture the ampule. And then the horror would be unleashed.

Alyard kept going, despite the numbing cold.

Chapter Three

He let his bags drop to the floor. His left foot kicked back slightly and contacted the door and he slammed it shut. His eyes moved across the cabin. It wasn't as spacious as the apartment he'd leased month-to-month in the overpriced foreigners' ghetto a few blocks from the Vatican, but it was furnished better.

Abe Cross lit a cigarette and walked toward the window, reminding himself consciously that it was a porthole and to think of it as that. It faced the dockside and he saw virtually no movement as he looked out. But at this time of the morning he hadn't expected any. After all the years in the Navy, he still felt very little at home aboard a ship. In the SEALs, he had spent most of his time running, swimming, lifting weights and shooting, then teaching the men under him how to do the same.

The *Empress Britannia* was owned by the same company that owned the hotel. The *Empress Britannia*'s lounge pianist, it had been explained to him by the hotel manager, had a personal problem.

"Drinking?"

"Yes. I suppose it doesn't matter to tell you."

"It's an easy problem to get when you spend your nights in a bar from sundown until closing."

"I've seen you drink maybe twice, Mr. Cross." She had smiled, pushing a lock of blonde hair up from her forehead with the back of her left hand, the nails bright pink and immaculately manicured.

"I'm a secret drinker." He'd grinned.

"No you're not."

"Let's say I had the problem once and some friends helped me out of it."

"You're lucky you can still drink. I mean, if you don't mind my saying that?"

"I agree. So, what's my unfortunate fellow pianist's dilemma have to do with me?" He'd lit a cigarette. He kept himself to less than a pack a day these days.

"I've been watching you." She smiled and her cheeks flushed a little. "I mean, that sounds, well . . . anyway. You're good. Very good. You could be playing concert halls instead of lounges."

"I like the people in lounges better." He'd smiled.

"The *Empress Britannia* sails tomorrow evening on the tide."

"Better than under it, I guess."

"Look. I'm trying to offer you something."

"All right. You want me to take over for the guy who has the problem."

"Right. The *Empress* is continuing on to New York, then through Panama to California and up to Alaska and across to Japan. It should be quite a voyage. First class all the way. I can offer you five hundred more a month, and of course all of your expenses will be paid, so except for cigarettes and incidentals, you'd make out quite well." And she had laughed. "And with your eye for the ladies, those last words of mine you could take literally. Lots of pretty girls with nothing but money to spend on a handsome lounge pianist."

"You're too kind."

"Do you want to do it? You'd have to get on board right this evening. Or morning, I should say. You'd have rehearsals starting at noon."

"Rehearsals?"

"You'd also accompany Doris Knight."

"Any relation to Doris Day?"

She'd laughed, her eyes sparkling. "No. It's a stage name. Kind of silly, I suppose. But she's a good singer, I'm told. Does a lot of forties and fifties songs already in your repertoire."

"The arrangements would be different."

"I hadn't thought of that.

"Nice cabin. The whole lot. The company needs you," she told him. "You'd make big points with the management. Maybe enough to get you out from behind that piano if that's what you're after."

"I don't know what I'm after. I'll do it on one other condition."

"What's that?"

"What are you doing after closing tonight?"

"Mr. Cross!" And then she had smiled again. "Nothing. What do you have in mind?"

He'd explained that to her at some length afterward, which had been part of the reason he'd gotten in so late. It was five in the morning now and he looked at his watch. His now erstwhile employer had let him off early from the piano bar to help him get packed. Or, he reflected, stubbing out his cigarette, that was one way of putting it, however crudely.

In seven hours, a rehearsal with a singer he'd never heard with arrangements he'd never played, and this Doris Knight would probably resent him anyway, taking over for her cashiered accompanist.

Cross shrugged out of his windbreaker and started to undress, trying to remember in which bag he'd packed his alarm clock. He could cop six hours if he was quick.

Chapter Four

"So. What is it you want, General Argus?"

Argus was a thin-faced man, lantern jawed, brown eyes that alternated between looking wicked and looking bored, but always penetrating. In his mid-fifties or so, a high forehead under immaculately tonsored hair washed at the temples with grey, Argus struck Darwin Hughes as the sort of man who still had the proverbial hex on the dames, as they used to call it.

"Mr. Hughes. Let's put our cards on the table, shall we? You wouldn't have come if you hadn't already suspected what I wanted."

"Put your cards on the table then," and Hughes thumped his open palm against the little round table between them. They were two among perhaps a dozen patrons in Whiskey Hollow, Hughes insisting on the nighttime meeting in a public place, Argus acquiescing with not a great deal of reluctance. It was here that Feinberg's arm had been slashed. Hughes wondered if what had happened here during a barroom brawl had sealed Feinberg's doom in that plane over the desert? Or was there any sort of thing as fate at all?

The country music group was between sets, the late crowd not yet in and no rush to continue. It wasn't the Neal James Band tonight as it had been that night, but instead a group he had never heard of and doubted he would like as much. But he hadn't come for the music anyway.

"The mission you and your associates carried out. The surgical strike. I'm not going to apologize, Mr. Hughes, for the rather shabby treatment you and your men got. But, if you accept my proposal, I can promise you it will never happen again. Colonel Leadbetter's superior is out of the picture now. Entirely. I have the full authorization of the President and both the House and Senate leadership. I needn't caution you that what is said between us tonight should go no further.''

"No, you needn't.''

"All right. Let's be blunt, then, Hughes. You and your people did a great job. We fucked up. Maybe cost that Feinberg fellow his life because of it. What I need to know is this: Can you get together with Cross and Babcock and reassemble your team? Can you work with us again?''

"Nothing personal, General, but you're full of shit. That's the rather distinct advantage of being a civilian, one of many if I may say so. But when a general is full of it, you can tell him so. No. I'm not setting up Cross or Babcock or anybody else for what happened to happen again.''

"Are you aware, Mr. Hughes—well, certainly you must be. Terrorism is an on-going concern, and the problem will only get worse before it gets better. What you and your men did—''

The waitress came over and Hughes smiled at her. "Another round of beer for y'all?''

"The same as last time?'' Argus asked Hughes.

"Fine, although I might not be here long enough to finish it.''

"Hmm,'' Argus smiled evilly. Argus looked at the waitress. "Then two of the same please, thank you.''

She smiled back and left.

Hughes drained the last of his beer from his glass, Argus doing the same.

"I'm not getting involved again.''

"You already are involved, Hughes. Just like every free man and woman is involved. But you're lucky. Unlike most people, you have the opportunity to do something rather than just sit and talk about—''

She was back fast with the beers, took the empties, reassured them the band would be starting another set, then left. Argus held his beer in his right hand, but didn't sip at it.

"What you and your men did gave the enemy a severe shock. They haven't recovered from it yet.''

"That's nice.''

"You didn't blanch at the word enemy, Hughes.''

"I know who you mean, General.''

"But they will recover. And sooner than anyone expects, terrorism will come home. And then we'll really need a small, elite force like yours.''

Hughes sipped at his beer, put it down. "I don't have such a force, General Argus."

"But you could get them back," Argus said emphatically, leaning forward across the table. "What I'm offering, Hughes, is a chance to be your own man. You'd be able to reject any assignment you felt your people couldn't or shouldn't handle."

Hughes let himself smile. "You can't offer me a free hand, General. You don't have a free hand yourself. It would work out the same. We'd step on somebody's toes or somebody'd get cold feet and we'd be left out in the cold again. Like last time. And besides, there's another concern which may not have occurred to you, General. But it's occurred to me. We got away with it last time, more or less, without anyone seeing our faces, knowing our identities. That'd grow old rather quickly, wouldn't it? Let's say we did go to work for you, even under the conditions you suggest. It would be just a matter of time until the enemy, as you put it, discovered our identities and went after us. Then what? A man can't live on the edge twenty-four hours a day forever and call it living."

"Hear me out, Hughes. I've thought of all that. Nobody except Leadbetter knows all three of your identities except the President and myself. What if it stayed that way. For all the gripes you may have against Leadbetter, he tried to take care of you. He wouldn't betray you. And there's nothing the outside could learn that would link him to you as the controller for the previous mission. And your secret would be safe with the President, certainly. The President asked me to consult Leadbetter concerning your identities. Leadbetter wouldn't even tell me. The President drove to Leadbetter's house and asked him, personally. That's the only reason both the President and myself have your name and the other two, the only reason I have any of the details of the last mission. You see, Leadbetter got caught in a trap. He never had the authorization he thought he had, so when his superior pulled the plug, he had nowhere to go. I've got the authorization. And not just the President's, as I told you, but congressional leadership from both parties. The rug can't be pulled out from under you. And, if it is, it'll be pulled out from under me as well. I'd be your coordinator, not your controller. I'd take the mission requests, run them by you, and if it's a go, get you anything you needed for mission support. And we can take care of the identity situation."

"How?"

"All three of you die."

Hughes knew better than to choke on his beer, but it was a touch-and-go thing for a split second. "And why would we be doing something like that, General Argus?"

"Blind identities with no link to your expertise, your background, anything. Since you and your men would be on call at all times because of the very nature of the work, we make the entire operation blind."

Hughes put down his beer. "Spell it out."

"We have the Justice Department Witness Relocation Program work out new identities, tailored for each of your needs, nothing in them to suggest who you once were. We could do the same thing through the CIA, but they'd smell a rat and all we'd need was some interdepartmental memo going into the wrong hands and the whole thing could be blown. So, the Justice Department. Then all record of the establishment of the new identities is destroyed. The three of you would never see one another except when you were working a job for us."

"Us?"

"Me. The President. Yourselves, whoever. You'd come to the rendezvous separately, your identities unknown to all personnel involved, leave on the mission, return for debriefing and be returned to your false identities with no one the wiser. It'd work, Hughes. And you can make it work."

"I'd have to talk it over with Cross and Babcock. It's not the sort of decision I'd make on my own even if I could."

"Then you'll consider it, sir?"

"Yes, I'll consider it. But I'll need to present it to Cross and Babcock. If either of them doesn't go with it, the idea is off. They were the best men for such a team when I picked them and that hasn't changed. There should really be a fourth man."

"I'm allowed the three of you. No one else. No one else can be trusted enough to be brought in. If you need a fourth man and you think I could be of some assistance, I'll be there. I've got Airborne and Ranger and Special Forces behind me. My military record'll be open to you. And obviously, if it ever came to that, regardless of my rank, you'd be the mission commander. You'll try, then?"

Hughes sipped at his beer. The band was coming out for its next set. They looked like young kids. "Where's Cross and where's Babcock?"

"Abraham Cross was in Rome, playing piano at a hotel bar. I

assume he's still there. Lewis Babcock's involved with something in Chicago. I'm not sure what, exactly. He's taken up private practice of the law again, but went to Chicago very suddenly about three days ago. We're trying to look into it.''

"I'll look into it. I'll need to talk with Lewis first in any event, because without Lewis's help I wouldn't have a prayer of convincing Cross. And with Lewis's help, my chances won't be that much better in any event. Where in Chicago?''

"I have the address locked in my office safe. I can get it to you in the morning. I have a plane waiting at Clark County Airport near Athens to take me back to Virginia. Call you at nine?''

"All right.''

"I'll order the immediate transfer of twenty-five thousand dollars into your checking account to cover your travel expenses. It'll be there by morning.''

"I'll give you the number,'' Hughes began.

"No need, sir. I already have it. I'll try to dig out more information on Cross if that'd be helpful.''

"Not at this stage. But I have one question. How do we die?''

For the first time, Brigadier General Robert Argus burst out laughing.

Chapter Five

Lewis Babcock's feet were freezing and he stomped them against the pavement just like he'd seen the cops on the beat do when he'd been a little boy. Maybe it had helped them, but it hadn't helped him.

Behind the brick fence before which he stood in the snow and the wind lay a community within a community within a community. It was Madison Park, an exclusive residential enclave within Hyde Park on the South Side of the city of Chicago.

There wasn't a gun in his pocket, but he wished there were. Once already a private security patrol car had stopped, the searchlight on the side of the car catching his face. The two security officers had gotten out of their car, approached and asked politely—more politely than usual, he imagined when they saw that the black man they were gently rousting wore expensive clothes— why he was waiting here, if there was any trouble.

He had given them a convincing, premeditated lie. "I'm a friend of the Collins' and my brother was picking me up, but he must be running a few minutes late. Must be the damned weather." He had shot his cuff dramatically and studied his Rolex wristwatch intently, long enough for them to note the expensive timepiece, thus adding to the impression that he was respectable. He had learned that to some people, it mattered not at all who you were, but merely how much you were worth; that was the measure of respect.

"Mr. and Mrs. Lawrence Collins?"

"No. I don't know a Lawrence Collins. Albert Collins."

"Thank you very much, sir." One man had nodded to the other and both had returned to their car, killed their light and half skidded, half driven away.

Babcock had checked for a name in the complex beforehand, anticipating that his presence would be questioned.

He had waited some more and this time he checked the time with genuine interest. If Cleophus Butler didn't show in another five minutes, he would give it up.

And then the car came around the corner, the glare from the headlights catching the falling snow, the headlights washing across the opposite side of the street and then settling down along the middle, cars parked end-to-end on both sides, some of them so heaped over with snow it looked as though they hadn't been moved for days or longer.

The car slowed down.

For the umpteenth time, he wished he had a gun in his overcoat pocket.

The car came to a full stop. He heard a power window cracking ice as it began its rolldown, then after a second heard a voice from the darkened interior of the Cadillac asking, "You Lewis Babcock?"

"I'm Lewis Babcock."

"Get in the car, brother."

"You Cleophus Butler?"

"Get in the car, man, or the car leaves without ya."

Babcock shrugged his shoulders under his coat and started toward the curb, climbing the precarious hillock of frozen slush and snow, skidding down, balancing against the hood of a Lincoln Towncar, then onto the street. He stopped beside the open front window. "So?"

"Get in."

He heard the click of a doorlock going up and he reached for the front-door handle, opened the door and peered inside. Under the dome light, he could see a skinny, acne-scarred face a few shades lighter than his own, the hair obscured with a knit cap that was full of lint. The man—face, clothes—didn't go with the car, which was new, even smelled that way as Babcock slipped in on the passenger side and slammed the door shut against the cold, his eyes scanning the rear compartment before he did so to make certain he wasn't getting in over his head. He heard the lock button click down closed, studied the outline of face and hands and shoulders in the greenish light emitted by the dashboard. And now the new-car smell was mixed with something stronger, body odor. The mixture, with the heat blowing full on, was more than mildly nauseating.

"Mr. Butler. Ernie's wife Thelma said you might be able to shed some light on what was going on."

"Women talks shit a lot, man."

Lewis Babcock said nothing.

"What you to her? Some kinda private eye—or maybe she you private ass?"

Now Babcock spoke. "Thelma and Ernie are old friends, Mr. Butler. If it matters, I'm a lawyer and when I heard about Ernie's difficulties, I offered my assistance, realizing full well that Ernie could never have done the sort of thing of which he's accused."

"You sound white."

"You don't."

The car was starting to move, Babcock feeling the hairs starting to stand up on the back of his neck, something he had discovered was not merely the invention of some writer of fiction.

"Where are we going, Mr. Butler?"

"I got some friends that always grooves on meetin' outa town brothers."

"That's a charming offer, but I'm afraid I can't meet your friends now. Perhaps some other time. But my schedule's rather tight. Ernie's pre-trial hearing is the day after tomorrow."

"Just sit back and enjoy the ride, lawyer. And watch you ass or you won't live to enjoy nothin' else."

"Indulge me in a question," Babcock said casually. "Do you know what really happened to the cocaine Ernie and the other police officer were transporting to Eleventh and State?"

Cleophus Butler just started to laugh, the Cadillac picking up speed. Lewis Babcock had parked his rented Ford near the high school a few blocks away, and he suspected where Butler was taking him. "Do you know, Mr. Butler?"

"I know. But nobody gonna tell you, Oreo. One more dead pig don't matter shit to me."

Lewis Babcock said quietly, "I see," then threw himself across the seat toward Cleophus Butler, his left hand slamming Butler's head against the rolled-up window, his right hand grabbing for the wheel. Butler shouted an obscenity, Babcock slamming Butler's head into the window again, harder this time, his body weight going against the man so his left foot could reach the brake. The Cadillac was rocketing forward, sideswiped an anonymous half–snow-covered sedan, ricocheted away from it and peeled away the fender of a Mercedes. Butler's hands were grabbing at him, Babcock's left elbow smashing back into the face, Babcock hoping he'd missed the nose, not wanting Butler dead.

The Cadillac swerved left, half climbing another car, Babcock finally having the break as he cut the wheel right, the Cadillac half falling from the other car, Babcock throwing his body weight down on the brake, the Cadillac skidding now, out of control, body slamming another car on the left with its rear end, wedging itself tight totally blocking the street as it shuddered once and stopped.

Babcock grabbed for the key, killing the ignition, pocketing the key. Butler was starting to stir. Babcock, on one knee on the seat, hands at Butler's throat, shook the man violently. The face was a mass of blood but Butler was still conscious. "The life of Ernie Hayes matters to me, motherfucker. Who stole the cocaine, iced Ernie's partner and set him up for the fall? Talk!" Babcock backhanded Butler across the nose, spreading it over onto Butler's left cheek, Butler crying now. "Who?!"

"The Devil's Princes, man—all right?"

"Who in the Devil's Princes?"

"Randy Jones, Tyrone Cash and Balthaszar Roman—all right!"

Babcock started patting him down, finding the bulge of a gun, ripping it from Butler's waistband. "Why? I mean, fine, all that cocaine. But why set up Ernie?"

"You pig buddy busted Tyrone maybe a year back and Tyrone got his ass kicked. And when he started crazy-talkin' that Randy Jones's sister told the cops on him, Tyrone went after Randy's sister with a belt and got him a coupla licks on her face until you buddy pulled him off her. Then Tyrone went after you buddy with the bat, and that's when he got his ass beat. All right?"

"What about Randy Jones? Didn't he do anything about this Tyrone going after his sister?"

"Shit, man, nobody mess with Tyrone. Randy's sister a whore anyway, man."

Sirens were in the distance and they might be for this, Babcock thought. There were lights coming on in some of the buildings on both sides of the street. "They still got the cocaine, Butler?"

"I dunno, man!"

Babacock backhanded him again. "They still got it!?"

"Yeah—yeah—too much to dump on the street too quick."

Babcock let him collapse into the seat. "I'm leaving. You tell the cops or your pals in the Devil's Princes you told me anything, even mention you ever heard of me, and I'm putting it out on the street you spilled your guts on the Princes and Tyrone and all the rest of his bad asses, right? And you know what'll happen to you. Understand?''

''I never seen ya, man.''

Babcock kept the gun; it felt like some kind of a .25 automatic in the darkness. He slid back across the seat and tried the door. It still opened and Babcock stepped out into the snow and the cold. He hunched his shoulders down, pulled his collar up, thrust his gloved hands into his pockets still holding the gun. He'd dump it at the first likely looking trash can. . . .

Seamus O'Fallon watched the sun rise. It would only last for a few seconds, and then the sun would be lost in the deep grey overcast. The headaches had kept him up the rest of the night after the attack on the RUC barracks. They had driven to the harbor and taken the waiting launch northwest, slipping between Ireland and Scotland, the seas poundingly heavy with the storm, and the yacht that had been waiting to take them aboard precious little more comfortable until it had gotten underway. Then the swells hadn't been so bad. But by then the headaches had returned and there had been no sleep for him.

Young Martin had been up all through the night as well, throwing up. O'Fallon could hear the head going each time it was flushed.

The first time, Seamus O'Fallon had done the same. But for a different reason: too much whiskey celebrating. If young Martin made it through this next one and still kept his balls, O'Fallon thought, then Martin would be one of them truly. But the problem was, of course, that none of them would make it out alive from this one. The British would never let them. But all the blood would be on British hands, not theirs.

He lit another cigarette with the butt of the last one, cupping it with his hands against the wind, the deck rolling beneath his feet, spray washing up here on the wind as they would hit into a wave, but not as badly as it did over the prow. It was cold, he knew, but he didn't feel it. The headache took care of that and everything else.

Chapter Six

Abe Cross stared at himself in the mirror as he brushed his teeth. He'd actually gotten up, felt semi-awake, and it wasn't even eleven forty-five yet as he sneaked a look at the Rolex on his left wrist. He spit out the last of the toothpaste, rinsed, then dug around in his Dopp kit for the dental floss, found it and took a piece and began working it between his teeth. This Doris Knight sounded like a real winner, with a fakey name like that. And she would be ticked that her regular pianist had gotten the axe. Probably fake blonde hair, fake fingernails and falsies and a voice that sounded like a parody of itself. He shrugged his shoulders, finished with the floss.

Naked, he walked out of the small but adequate bathroom and toward the bed. There had been no time to unpack and he rummaged through his things to find clothes—underpants, a pair of black socks, a black long-sleeved knit shirt, black slacks. He wondered if there was a dress code for persons who worked for the line aboard the *Empress*. There'd be one for evening, of course. He didn't have to wear some kind of god-awful uniform, did he? He stuffed his feet back into the black loafers he'd worn the previous night and went over to the dresser, ran a comb through his brown hair a few times and snatched up his cigarettes, his cabin key, his lighter and his little Swiss Army Champion, pocketing all. "Handkerchief," he muttered, rummaging through his things again, finding one and stuffing it in his pocket. There was no need for wallet or passport and he had been told that all his meals were included in the deal so he didn't need money. Cross grabbed up the black leather satchel in which he carried his music and let himself out.

Unlike earlier that morning when he had come aboard, the

corridor bustled with activity, stewards and housekeeping staff moving in and out of cabins open and unoccupied. Sailing tonight, there would be much to do, passengers due on board any time throughout the afternoon he guessed. When he'd been making his way to his cabin, he'd spied a coffee shop and had logged away its location for future reference. He made his way toward it now, hoping it would be open for the convenience of the crew.

He took the elevator up to what he hoped was the right deck and exited, orienting himself, aiming himself in what he hoped was the right direction. After a moment's wandering, he found the coffee shop. It was closed. "Shit." He shrugged, consulted the deck plan in the glassed-over metallic frame near the coffee shop doors and found the Seabreeze Lounge. A glance at his watch again showed that it was five to twelve anyway. If this Doris Knight person was already on the prod over him, he didn't want to make it worse. He despised working as an accompanist even for four sets a night.

The Seabreeze Lounge doors—big etched-glass affairs with brass-ringed fake portholes somehow set in the upper third, the etching showing fantasy dolphins and palm trees and curling waves—were open wide, but no real seabreeze would be possible here because it wasn't an open deck amidships, and one had to content oneself with staring through Plexiglas. Tenders bringing baggage and stores aboard were all there was to be seen.

Cross entered the Seabreeze Lounge. It was the nice thing about being a pianist. Pianos were so big they were easy enough to find. This one—a concert grand with glass sides and glass top, looking for all the world as gaudy as something the great showman Liberace would have used in Las Vegas—was on a raised stage at the far end of the double-football-field-sized room, glass doors like the ones through which he had entered nearby to it, but closed. A mirror-backed bar ran along his left as he approached the piano, tiered rows of tables on his right. He was crossing a tiled dance floor.

The colors here, glistening blacks and silvery greys and subdued pinks, were classic art deco, as were the idyllically slender nudes with chignoned hair who posed in miniature splendor holding up discreetly sized lamps as though they were something vastly more important than they were.

Two shirt-sleeved men were working behind the bar, bottle counting and filling, two women helping them, drying and polishing glasses. There was no sign of Doris Knight and there had been no easeled announcement beside the lounge doors of her performing.

He approached the piano.

A woman's voice—kind of raspy sounding—called to him and he turned around. "You the guy who's replacing Lenny Brooks?" It was one of the women behind the bar.

"If he was the last pianist, then I'm the guy."

"I'm Helen."

"I'm Abe. Good to meet you, Helen."

"If you want some coffee or some sweet rolls—you know, Danish?—just go through those doors. Doris isn't here yet."

He looked where the red-haired woman pointed. Portholed doors, but mahogany colored, at the end of the bar nearest the piano. He set his music down against the lip of the stage and headed for the doors, shooting Helen a wave, going through the swinging doors. It was a kitchen. Apparently the lounge served late-night meals. It wasn't large enough for much of anything else. But there was an urn of coffee and an urn of hot water, beside the latter a bowl of tea bags. And there were Styrofoam cups and napkins and there was a tray covered with white linen napkins. He lifted them back. Fresh Danish that even smelled good. He took a Styrofoam plate and two rolls, avoiding any with nuts or coconut, and some coffee. There was no sign of cream or milk for the coffee, only sugar, which he never used.

He heard the doors behind him and turned around.

Whoever she was, she was exquisitely lovely. A veil of dark brown hair the same color as his own hung to her bare shoulders, parted in the middle and softly waved. Touching at the edges of her shoulders was the top of a bell-sleeved off-white peasant blouse. It was tucked in at the waist of an almost ankle-length navy blue skirt with a single fold at the front. She wore white, textured stockings and flat-heeled brown shoes. When she spoke, her gently throaty alto sounded at once sexy and innocent. He thought he must be dreaming.

"There's milk and cream in that first refrigerator. Or at least there was this morning. I'm an early riser whenever I get the chance."

"Thanks." Cross nodded, still looking at her, realizing he was holding the plate he'd made for himself in one hand and his coffee in the other.

"You're the pianist, Helen said."

"You're not—"

"Doris Knight?" She laughed and her laugh sounded like a carillon ringing. "They told me Doris got all upset that her pianist was canned. Maybe that's to her credit. Loyalty, I mean. She threatened to quit—at least that's what they told me—and they let her. I'm her replacement."

"That's why there wasn't a poster outside. . . ."

"Um-hmm! I guess they're making it now. I'm Jenny Hall." She walked toward him and extended her right hand, a smile lighting her face and her green eyes, her wide, pretty mouth upturning at the corners and making little things like dimples in her cheeks.

Cross stood there balancing his food and his coffee, then set them down and took her hand. "I'm Abe Cross."

"I heard you play in London—one of the hotels. I can't remember. I was spending the night there, leaving the next morning. I remember you because you were so good."

"You're sweet to say that." He realized he hadn't let go of her hand. He didn't want to.

"Can I have my hand back? I mean, you can hold it again if you want." She did the laugh again and it had the same effect.

"Only if you promise." He smiled.

"I promise."

He let go of her hand. She tossed her head to get her hair back from her face. He noticed delicate-looking gold-pierced earrings. There was a thin gold chain at her throat. "Wanna take some coffee in there and try a few songs, Mr. Cross?" She nodded her head toward the Seabreeze Lounge and did the thing with her hair again.

"It is after twelve," she told him, turning back the cuff of her blouse and reading a ladies Rolex. It was plain except for a Jubilee band of alternating stainless steel and gold links.

"Only if you call me Abe."

"I'll call you Abe if you'll call me Jenny."

"Deal." He extended his hand and she laughed, then took it. "I'm gonna use any excuse I can get to touch your hand again. Just figured to be up front about it."

"All right. I like that."

"You're the most marvelously beautiful girl I've ever seen. Except, maybe, in a dream."

She actually blushed a little and her eyes cast down. "You're still holding my hand."

"So I am." And he let her fingers drift from his. "Would you like some coffee?"

"Okay."

He poured a cup for her. "First refrigerator, you said?"

"Uh-huh. How'd they get you to replace the pianist?"

"Hotel I was playing at is owned by the same people who own the *Empress Britannia*. Made me the proverbial offer I couldn't refuse. Or something like that. Cream in your coffee?"

"Milk."

"Right." He poured milk from a little metal pitcher into her cup first, then his own. "They catch you between engagements?" He thought better of it after he'd said it.

"I was going back to the States anyway. I've been doing club dates in France and Germany and Italy for the last eight months. I figured it was time to go home. How about you? Going all the way up to Alaska and over to Japan with the *Empress*?"

He put the milk away. She took both coffees and he took the plate with the Danish, held the door for her to pass through. "I think so. But that could always change. I don't have a family or anything." Why had he said that?

"I have an older sister and a younger brother. Our parents are gone."

"I'm sorry to hear that. I was just about to ask if there were anymore at home like you, though. But younger brothers never interested me and the older sister couldn't be as beautiful as you."

Jenny Hall laughed. "She was always the pretty one. Blonde hair. She was captain of the cheerleaders in high school. I never even made it on the squad." There was a hint of sadness in her voice. She set the coffee down on a small table behind the piano and just looked at him.

"If you'd been on the cheerleaders, it would have been the only high school with enough team spirit to beat the Chicago Bears. Trust me on that." He didn't sit down at the piano yet. "Want a roll?"

She just looked at him, startled.

"I mean a Danish." He grinned.

She looked down at her shoes for a second and he thought he saw her smile. "Do you always come on to girls like this?" she asked after a moment.

His mouth was half full of danish. He shook his head, swallowed, almost choked. "I've never met a girl who looked like you. Sounded like you. Smiled like you." He took another bite of his danish and she sipped at her coffee, blowing across it first like a child might try to cool a cup of hot chocolate.

Cross finished the first Danish—pineapple and light as air—and took a swallow of coffee. It wasn't all that hot. He'd forgotten the napkin, so wiped his fingers clean on his handkerchief. "Don't want sticky keys," he told her. "Do you play piano?"

"I can pick out a few things. But I don't play very well. I played in the high school band and kept up in college."

"What instrument?"

"Then promise you won't make any jokes about it. You've got to," she insisted.

"Promise," Cross agreed.

"The flute."

"I can see where flute jokes might be awkward on the ear. I'll keep my promise." Cross adjusted the seat—his predecessor had apparently been shorter than Cross's own plus six feet—and flexed his fingers, then tried a few arpeggios to check for tune. He had imagined that with all the subtle movement of a ship and the constant humidity of the salt air, there might be a problem with the tune. But it was more than acceptable, almost dead on pitch. "What can I play for you?"

"Why don't you just play something your way and I can get your style before you try to catch mine. It was just when I came to Europe that I heard you in that hotel in London."

"I know the perfect thing. 'You Go to My Head'?"

She smiled as she said, "I know that," and Cross wondered if she really knew it like he'd meant it.

Chapter Seven

General Argus was as on time as a Swiss stopwatch. At precisely 9:00 A.M. Eastern time, the telephone rang and Darwin Hughes, fresh back from a longer than usual run, wiped the towel draped over his neck across his face as he picked up the receiver.

"Hello."

"You wanted a way to reach your friend in Chicago. Well, I've got that for you. Got a pencil?"

"Right here. Yes."

Hughes copied down a hotel address and two phone numbers. From the hotel, it was obvious that Lewis Babcock still believed in going first class.

"Got it?"

"Yes. I've got it. Know what he's up to?"

"If you feel comfortable about your line."

"Comfortable enough for this I think."

"All right," Argus began. "Nine days ago, two Chicago police officers were assigned to transport a substantial street value's worth of cocaine to Central Police Headquarters at Eleventh and State Street. It had been seized in a raid the night before. The car they were driving never reached Headquarters. It was found a couple of hours later. The cocaine was missing of course and one of the officers was dead, shot six times in the chest with the revolver left on the seat beside him. The revolver belonged to the second officer. He was found wandering around the West Side, no memory at all of what had happened, his gun missing of course. He was arrested and there's a pre-trial hearing on first-degree murder charges and a number of other charges scheduled for tomorrow. The second officer is a friend of your friend."

"How does it look for the second officer?"

"Just common knowledge and newspaper and television coverage is all I have. And the general consensus of that is that the second officer was part of a conspiracy and things went wrong and that's why he got caught. He's already been suspended and departmental charges have been filed. According to the press, he's guilty as sin."

"And what about my other friend?" Hughes asked.

"Nothing on him yet. Dropped out of sight, but we may get a lead as soon as we're able to contact his employer. Where can I reach you, Hughes?"

"Chicago. I'll call you from there. Thanks." He hung up, raised the receiver again as he flipped through the Rolodex, then dialed his travel agent. He hated getting gouged on airline tickets. "Hello. Is Millie in yet? . . . Right. This is Darwin Hughes. I'll hold." Lewis Babcock had always struck him as a crusader, and there was nothing wrong with that. "Millie? Darwin Hughes here. I need the first available flight out to Chicago. Maybe out of Athens and transfer at Charlotte? . . . Right. I'll need a couple of hours to get ready and get myself to Athens. . . . Well, do the best you can. And it will be round trip, but if it's a matter of saving a few bucks and leaving later, I'll spend the extra. . . . Right. I'll hold on." He daubed at his perspiration with the towel again.

She got him a flight and a ticket price that sounded ridiculously high, but under the circumstances he couldn't hold out for anything better. He looked at his Rolex. "Yes. I can make it. But I know I'll be running behind. Can I prevail on you for a favor, Millie? . . . No. . . . Could you meet me at the airport if it's at all possible? Meet me with the tickets?" She said she could and not to tell anybody because it might set a dangerous precedent. He doubted he knew any of her other clients anyway, gave her a credit card number and told her "Thanks," then hung up.

It wasn't even half past eight in Chicago because of the time difference and he dialed the hotel number and asked for Mr. Lewis Babcock's room. The Hilton operator tried the room and said there was no answer. He asked for the manager, got the assistant and told her that it was urgent he speak with Mr. Babcock. It concerned a death. He held the line while a bellboy was sent up to knock on Mr. Babcock's room door and another sent to page him in the hotel restaurants in case Mr. Babcock was having breakfast. After seven minutes, the assistant manager came back on the line and told him there had been no luck finding Mr. Babcock. Could they take a message? Hughes told her that the death was rather close to Mr. Babcock and that he—Hughes—wouldn't want Mr. Babcock to hear of it from anyone but him. Then he made a reservation, giving her a credit card number; she graciously handled it all personally. He said good-bye and hung up.

The next call was to the other number. A woman, young sounding with a pretty voice, answered. "You don't know me—"

"I won't talk to any reporters—"

"I'm not a reporter. I'm a friend of Lewis. He may have mentioned me. Darwin Hughes is my name. I tried Lewis at the hotel and didn't have any luck. Is he at your place?"

"No."

"You're the wife of Lewis's policeman friend?"

"Yes."

"Is it as bad as the news media says, Mrs.—"

"Mrs. Hayes. Thelma Hayes. Ernie's in terrible trouble, Mr. Hughes. And he wouldn't do a thing like that. He's been a wonderful husband and father. He's been honest all his life and the man they say he shot was a good friend. They were on the same bowling team, and had been partners in the same patrol car for the last three years. That's why they gave Ernie and Mike—"

"Mike is the dead man?"

"Yes. That's . . . that's why they gave Mike and Ernie the cocaine to take to Eleventh Street. Because they knew they could be trusted. It was a lot."

"I understand it was, Mrs. Hayes," Hughes told her. "Do you have any idea where Lewis is?"

"He's out trying to help Ernie and us, that's all I know."

"All right. If you hear from Lewis, Mrs. Hayes, tell him I called and tell him I'm flying in this afternoon and I made reservations at the same hotel he's staying at. I'll try to help as much as possible. I'll call you from the airport. Will you be at home, Mrs. Hayes?"

"Yes."

"Then I'll call and perhaps by that time you'll know where I can link up with Lewis. And don't worry. Good-bye." He hung up. Why had he told her not to worry? He started stripping off his sweatsuit as he walked toward the stairs. . . .

* * *

Thomas Alyard had his story straight if anyone asked. He'd been driving and his Fiat had developed engine trouble, which was why he was walking along the beach toward Brindisi. The reason wasn't anything near the truth, but he wasn't about to tell a casual inquirer or an Italian policeman that he had just a short while ago left a fishing boat that had smuggled him out of Communist Albania with a vial of the latest in bacteriological warfare developments in his pocket.

He had given the fisherman the fourth diamond, as he didn't anticipate having to cut more glass. Back in Italy, his credit cards would get him farther than an unset diamond anyway. There was an airport and he could call in, then fly from there to Rome, even if it meant chartering an aircraft. He wanted the thing in his pocket gone into someone else's hands. That it hadn't been more difficult getting out of Albania meant only one thing to him: The KGB was taking this personally, which meant that sooner or later, David Stakowski would be caught and forced to talk and then the KGB would be after him. They would, of course, already be looking for the Swiss businessman, Thomas Rheinhold, but Rheinhold had ceased to exist as soon as the smuggler's fishing boat had gotten into Italian territorial waters, the passport going over the side along with all the other identification except the driver's license and American Express card.

Alyard had a story for that one too. He was an Italian citizen—he could fake the language well enough and excuse the accent by saying he had spent much of his time abroad—and why would an Italian citizen need a passport in his own country? A little outrage could do wonders.

He kept walking. . . .

The sun was strong and the wind was bitingly cold here along the beach. He had been looking out to sea while the other man had been talking with his subordinates. And now that the subordinates had been dismissed, the man was talking to him. The Albanian secret policeman was becoming pronouncedly annoying. Finally, Vols looked him square in the eye and said, "It should be sufficient for a loyal Communist to know that this Thomas Alyard or Thomas Rheinhold is an enemy of the state. Information such as you ask me for is on a need-to-know basis, as you well know. You have no need to know. It is enough that he is an enemy agent and that he is wanted for questioning in Moscow. Now. Who would have taken him across and where would he have been dropped, since your people obviously have lost him?''

The Albanian glared at him. ''If we had been told earlier, Comrade Major, of this man's importance, he would not have slipped through our security net.''

'' 'Net' is a very good term for it, Captain. A net has holes in it, just like your security. I told you he was a fleeing enemy agent. That was all you needed to know. You lost him. Now I must get him back. As simple as that. You can best serve the state now by providing me with information. The names of any likely persons who would have risked smuggling him out with the fishing fleet and were possessed of a fast enough boat to get away from the fleet, reach Italy and be able to return without being missed. I will especially be interested in any returning boats from the fleet which didn't catch the usual amount of fish or any fish at all. And, if you have such information, and as a policeman I would assume that you might, where is the most likely spot that Alyard would have been put ashore. Near Brindisi? Where? The female agent I'm working with will be in charge and one of my men will be with her. The other thing you can do is keep your hands off David Stakowski.''

''He might have much valued information, Comrade Major.''

''That will be for the ears of my superiors in Moscow. If you need to be informed of this via official channels, that too can be arranged. The point is, you have work to do and so do I. The optimum method then is for us both to be about it. For the good of the state, of course.''

''Brindisi is the most likely spot. Smugglers can be supplied there, our informants say, with Western goods. We bend every effort to stop them, Comrade Major, but . . .''

Vols smiled at the Albanian secret policeman. ''In my country, American blue jeans are very hot items on the black market. Yet, when the security of the state is at stake, we will sacrifice pursuit of blue-jean smugglers for the higher good. I suggest that you follow our example, Captain.'' He turned and started walking up the beach. But he looked back over his shoulder and called to the policeman who still looked after him, ''Remember! The woman is in charge!'' And under his breath, Vols added, ''You bloody ass.''

Chapter Eight

The telephone call he had made from Brindisi had not been encouraging. Stakowski had been captured and it was evident that the KGB had made him—Alyard—as the courier for the ampule. He was speaking with the chief "wizard" who had contrived what so far had proven to be an unpleasant comedy of errors. "The firm doesn't think our interests would best be served by your immediate return to Rome. Our branch here has been in contact with the home office and we think extending the road trip would be advisable since our other salesman has come down very seriously ill. Even though you have his samples, I don't think you can cover the whole territory yourself, Tom. We have an experienced man available who can help you. He's from the home office. If you can meet him and give him the extra samples you have, he can take a lot of the burden off your shoulders. And let me say, so far you've done wonderfully."

"Well, gee, thanks, Mr. Fleege. If you really think I should."

"Ohh, there's no doubt about it. I could see you coming down with the same thing our other man got if you don't watch yourself closely. There's a lot of it going around. Especially in your area and here in Rome. No. The wise thing, believe me, is to get together with the guy from the home office, unload those extra samples and then—well, you've been doing so well—why not take a few days off? Just lose yourself in the countryside and relax, guard your health at the same time? Everybody here thinks it's the best thing to do, Tom."

"Well, Mr. Fleege, if you really think so. Where should I meet this guy from the home office?"

'We're not sure when he's coming in, so he'll find you if you check in with our district warehouse on the coast."

"All right. Will he have my vacation check?"

"He sure will. Bringing it from the home office with him. Hey, and Tom?"

"Yes, Mr. Fleege?"

"You have a good rest now. And don't overdo things. Want you back ready for work."

"Okay. Did you make those arrangements about my place that I asked?" It was the best lateral way to ask about Appalonia; had she been told he was away on business, not just sleeping around?

"Yeah. Everything's fine there. Took care of the cat for you, Tom, just like you asked."

Cat; funny. "Well, give my best to everybody at the office then. And thanks for your help."

"You bet. Take care." The line went dead. The warehouse on the coast was an emergency safe house just outside Naples. The guy from the home office could be anybody. But the check would be flight money, maybe a weapon and a quick setup on what the true picture was. And he—Alyard—was to give this guy the samples, meaning, of course, the thing he'd smuggled out of Albania. And there was KGB trouble, a lot of it going around. He shook his head, looked at his wristwatch. The chartered plane would have to take him to Naples now. And that was dangerous, because how many people matching his description would be chartering airplanes? The KGB could check on that very easily and follow him straight to Naples. But, apparently, getting rid of the ampule was the thing of vital importance now. And once he no longer had it, if the KGB were really hot on the trail, the heat would be transferred to somebody else's shoulders.

He left the telephone booth and started back for the charter office. . . .

It was just less than two hours since his conversation with his controller in Rome. He had taken a cab rather than sprinkling his name around at the small airfield outside of Naples by renting a car. Add to that, he was exhausted, having traveled nonstop since he had left Rome, catching no sleep at all except for about forty-five minutes on the plane which, after awakening, had actually made him feel worse. He had given the driver the address of one of the newer suburban hotels and left the taxi, made himself disappear into the lobby, found the coffee shop and had a sandwich, then left the hotel, taking another cab and giving still a second blind address. Another hotel. Here, he immediately changed taxis, giving a totally false address, giving the driver the correct address only after they had driven some blocks and Alyard had satisfied himself that they were not being followed.

The "warehouse" was an apartment building out of a complex of three, very expensive and breezily Italian in appearance. To be on the safe side, he had entered one of the other two buildings and waited in the lobby until the taxi had driven off, then walked around the fountain-dominated courtyard to the middle of the three buildings, entered the building and rung the manager's apartment.

A voice came back on the intercom, barely intelligible and perhaps a little drunk-sounding. "Is this Mr. Fabrizzi?" he asked in English.

In English, heavily accented, he was told that it was.

"I'm a friend of Mr. Jacobsen. He left word I was to use his apartment? My name is Ivy. Lauren Ivy." The first name for the contact exchange was intentionally neuter sexually in the event a female required use of the safe house.

"Are you the person Signore Jacobsen told me about?"

Alyard answered as he was supposed to. "He called you from St. Moritz, didn't he?"

"A moment, Signore." The buzzer for the door lock actuated and he passed through into the little sitting room–lobby. He lit a cigarette, staring at the plastic plants and the fake oriental rug. The little pistol he'd gotten from Stakowski was stuffed in his trouser waistband under his jacket and he left his overcoat and his suitcoat unbuttoned just in case he would need it.

After several moments, a man in a flamboyant floral-print shirt who looked to be girdled into expensively cut slacks, a cigarette hanging out of the corner of his mouth, came through the elevator doors.

"You are—"

"Mr. Ivy. Signore?"

"Fabrizzi. Here is the key. Third floor. Turn to your left out of the elevator."

"Thank you." Alyard nodded, taking the key in his left hand so his right would be free to get at the gun if needed. He was beginning to feel naked wandering through Italy carrying this ampule of whatever god-awful thing it was. Fabrizzi returned to the elevator and held the door as Alyard picked up his suitcase and followed him. They rode in silence to the first floor, Fabrizzi getting out, Alyard nodding to him, Fabrizzi never nodding back.

Alyard left the elevator at the third floor, the fourth floor by American reckoning, and found the apartment. The key fit, which boded well, and he let himself in. He almost urinated in his pants.

"Thomas Alyard?"

The black man in the immaculately tailored blue suit had some kind of large military pistol pointed at him. Alyard didn't speak.

"I got my key in Langley, Virginia. My name's Thomas, too. Thomas Griffeth. The code phrase is 'I ate at a very disappointing restaurant last night. Can you recommend a good place for dinner?' And then you say—"

" 'I know just the place, but the prices are outrageous. Do you like veal?' "

" 'Veal is my favorite if it's prepared properly.' "

Thomas Alyard relaxed. "What did you come for, Mr. Griffeth?"

"The little item you got from Mr. Stakowski, before his misfortune."

"Put the gun away. It's yours. Anything to drink in this place?" He was glad to be rid of it. . . .

Darwin Hughes had avoided the hassles of transhipping a firearm as luggage, assuming that he probably wouldn't need one in Chicago and that, if he did, the Chicago policeman, Ernie Hayes, could probably tell him how to find one.

He reached into his pocket and took two dollars out of his money clip and tipped the bellman, taking his key and security locking the room door. He had asked at the desk if Mr. Babcock had been heard from. Mr. Babcock might have come in, but hadn't checked at the desk.

He sat on the edge of the double bed and dialed Mrs. Hayes. "Mrs. Hayes? This is Darwin Hughes, Lewis's friend who called this morning. Has he checked in with you? . . . I see. Well, I'm in Chicago staying at the Hilton. Same floor as Lewis, actually. . . . Thank you very much. Airline food isn't that great, I'll admit. And a home-cooked meal would be wonderful just now. . . . Yes, I've got a pen." He ripped a piece of paper off the message tablet and took the Cross pen from his jacket pocket and copied her address. "You're sure it's not putting you out, Mrs. Hayes? . . . Wonderful then. I'll see you in an hour." He hung up. He tried Lewis's room again as he'd had them do from the lobby. There was no answer. He dialed the hotel operator and placed his promised call to Robert Argus. "General. Darwin Hughes. I had no idea this was a personal line."

Argus's voice came back a little more tired sounding than it had sounded hours earlier. "We tracked down your other friend. He went to Naples last night. He took a job as lounge pianist on a vessel called—wait a minute—yes, the *Empress Britannia*."

"I sailed on her when she was brand new. Where's she headed?"

"New York, then through the Canal and to Frisco and then up to Alaska and across to Japan."

"There's no sense trying to contact him aboard the *Empress*. Let him come to New York. This thing with my other friend will take a little time anyway, and as I told you, I'll need his help to persuade our piano-playing friend."

"The ball's in your court. Do as you see fit, Hughes. If you need any help, just dial this number. It follows me almost everywhere I go."

"Poor fellow. But, thanks; I'll remember that."

Argus hung up and so did he.

Hughes started opening his tie and collar, glanced at his Rolex as he did. There was time, if he hurried, for a quick shower. . . .

The Devil's Princes had, in the last five years, inherited the mantle of "largest street gang in Chicago," largely because of their finances and their business practices. Their financial success came from their virtual monopoly on cocaine along the streets of the city's south side, and their early recognition that crack was the wave of the future. Their business practices amounted to one principle: ruthlessness. If anyone interfered in their operations, he was immediately killed in the most unpleasant manner possible, as a warning to future meddlers.

Lewis Babcock had spent the better part of the morning researching this material from the archives of the *Chicago Tribune*, taken an early lunch at a little basement place that served a mound of roast beef and a small loaf of bread and let the customer utilize his imagination and the horseradish to do the rest. The healthiest beverage on the menu had been beer and so he had had one. He'd retrieved his rented car and driven along the shore of Lake Michigan to the address the newspaper accounts had cited as headquarters for the Devil's Princes.

Suspicious looking men in clothes darker than their faces had hung around the front of the place—D.P.S.A.C. all that the lettering on the storefront window revealed—and he had driven around the block once to be certain he had the correct address. Finally, he had parked his car across the street from the Devil's Princes Social and Athletic Club, grateful it was only a rental vehicle, and walked across toward the front door not really knowing what he expected to do. But he needed some feel for the place.

He approached the door, half expecting one of the guards outside to stop him, but none did. He tried the glass door and it opened easily and he went inside. There was a pretty, light-skinned girl behind a receptionist desk at the rear of the converted store front, carpeting and expensive office furniture and potted plants that had not been visible through the venetian-blinded windows. He stopped in front of her desk.

"Can I help you, sir?"

"I was hoping you could. My name's Lewis Babcock. I'm interested in a moment of Mr. Tyrone Cash's time."

She smiled good-naturedly. Apparently he had echoed an often-made request. "I'm sorry. Really I am. But Mr. Cash never sees anyone without an appointment and he's not even in. I could take a message for him, though, and make certain he gets it."

"You're very nice," Babcock told her almost sincerely, assuming she was giving him a standard run-around. But she was nice-looking. "Tell you what. Let me leave my card. I'll just put where I can be reached in Chicago on the back here." He took a card from his business-card case and turned it over and took a pen from his pocket and scribbled the address of the hotel, putting down the room number next to his own. "Would you tell Mr. Cash that I'm representing Officer Ernie Hayes, unofficially, as a friend of the court. And I'd like to discuss some information I've recently obtained with him prior to my introduction of the material at the pre-trial hearing tomorrow. If he could get back to me tonight, I'd really appreciate it." He handed her the card.

"I'll be sure he gets it." She smiled.

"Some men have all the luck," he told her, turning back toward the door and walking out.

He crossed the street, but instead of walking to his car, he walked to the telephones at the corner, outdoor kiosks, only one of the three operational, the earpiece cigarette scarred and so dirty he held it only next to his ear, not against it. He called the hotel. "This is Mr. Babcock in 807. I'm expecting a message from a business associate and, stupidly, I gave him the wrong room number. If someone asks for me in room 809 could you just ring my room instead?''

"Certainly, Mr. Babcock. I have an urgent message for you from a Mr. D. Hughes.''

Babcock's blood ran cold and it wasn't the chill of the wind or the slushy pavement around the phone kiosk. "What's the message? Read it to me, please.''

"Yes, sir. 'Please get in touch immediately. Am staying here. Gone to Mrs. H.'s for late lunch. Hughes.' That's the message, sir. Is there any reply?''

"No—no. I'll contact Mr. Hughes personally. Thank you.'' He hung up. "Shit,'' Babcock murmured, indulging himself in a rare obscenity. . . .

Thelma Hayes, looking pretty and very domestic, opened the door after just one ring. She wiped her hands on her apron, smiled and said, "Lew. We were all worried about you.''

"Everything's fine, Thelma.'' He embraced her briefly and walked past her, slipping out of his coat. At the dining room table, Babcock saw him, a forkful of spaghetti half to his mouth, face lighting in a smile. The eyebrows cocked in his high forehead, so dark-seeming compared to the salt-and-pepper grey of his hair, more salt than the last time. His face was long, only thin-seeming because of its length, his ears large-seeming because of the close-cropped hair. The chin was strong, prominent. The mouth—long and thin—spread and curled upward at the corners in a smile, revealing even, white teeth, seaming the vertical lines in his cheeks even more deeply. "Mr. Hughes.''

"Mr. Babcock. I must say, your friend Mrs. Hayes is an artist with spaghetti. You know it's one of my favorites. I can see why it's so imperative to assist her husband from his predicament. If the poor man is used to this, its unavailability must be unbearable.''

Lewis Babcock looked at Thelma Hayes. Her black eyes were pinpoints of uncertainty. And then Babcock smiled at her. "He's an old friend. And he really is a connoisseur of spaghetti. Could I have a little?'' He wasn't really hungry, but Thelma had been a wife and mother since graduating high school and marrying Ernie, and normalcy was what she needed now, he guessed. Her face brightened and he had guessed correctly. "Kids still in school?''

"They'll be playing over at their aunt's house—Ernie's sister Marge. She'll drop them off around six.''

"I'm looking forward to meeting them. If not tonight''—Hughes smiled—"then soon, I hope. You must let me take you and your husband and the children—and Lewis too, of course—out to dinner. Doing even ordinary things with small children can be such an adventure."

"Sure." Thelma Hayes left for the kitchen. Lewis Babcock left the arched entrance into the dining room that lead off the hall and approached the table. "Why are you here, Mr. Hughes?"

"Well, lad, I'm here to help. And to get your help."

"To get my help," Babcock paraphrased slowly. "Like the last time?"

"No. Not quite like the last time, Lewis," Hughes said evenly, his diction perfect, despite his background as a Texan, his speech almost faintly British sounding. The well-modulated voice and careful diction Babcock had long before put down to Hughes's childhood hearing problem. Corrected fully—the man could hear as well as anyone and better than most now—it would have necessitated a careful attention to the details of speech to speak so perfectly with part of the developmental years lost to him. The slight British intonation Babcock attributed to Hughes's early World War II experiences working with the British when Hughes had been the youngest man ever chosen for the wartime Office of Strategic Services, or OSS. The hearing problem had reaped one ancillary benefit for Hughes: He was a faultless lip-reader. "I'd had something I needed to discuss with you, then learned through an associate that you were here endeavoring to extricate Officer Hayes from this cocaine thing. I thought I might speak with you and also be of some minor assistance. Kill two birds with one stone, so to speak."

"If anyone could kill two anything with one stone, you could. Where's Cross?"

Hughes smiled. Cross had become something like a son to Hughes in the short time the three of them and Feinberg had worked together. "Abroad the *Empress Britannia* working as a piano player in a lounge. I imagine he's having a wonderful time. He'll be in New York in several days' time and I thought we could speak with him there."

"We?"

"I'll confess to an ulterior motive, Lewis. In seeing you first, that is," and Hughes grinned broadly, daubing at his mouth with a napkin, standing as Thelma Hayes entered from the kitchen.

"Sit down, Lew. I was just about to offer Mr. Hughes a glass of wine. Would you like some?"

"If you're having some, yes," Babcock told her.

"My sentiments, ma'am," Hughes told her.

"Both of you sit down. This isn't formal. I can tell neither one of you are married, standing up every time a woman comes in with something from the kitchen."

"I was married, as a matter of fact. I have a daughter your age or a little older," Hughes told her.

"That's hard to believe—I mean, looking at you."

"Compliments are always graciously accepted."

Hughes's wife had died, Babcock knew. But not how. Hughes's son and daughter-in-law were dead as well. He looked at Hughes. There had been little happiness for this man, his daughter-in-law the victim of a terrorist hijacking, his son a suicide, unable to live with it. Babcock wondered if he could have lived with it, either? But Hughes had, in his way.

Thelma Hayes left the room, presumably to get the wine.

"May as well sit down before the lady chastises us," Hughes said, gesturing toward a chair. Babcock took it. "Your friend Officer Hayes. He is innocent, of course?"

"Of course. And I finally got the evidence to prove it."

"What did I hear you say?" Thelma Hayes said as she reentered the room, her voice brightening.

Both Hughes and Babcock stood, Hughes helping her with her chair, saying, "Allow me," and expropriating the wine bottle and the butterfly corkscrew. "These are the best kinds of corkscrews, you know. The others were designed to Attila the Hun's specs, I think."

"What did you say about my husband?"

"I've got conclusive proof, but it wouldn't hold up in court. Not the way I obtained it."

"Black-bagging it, were you lad?"

Babcock shook his head violently. "No! It was worse than that. I essentially beat it out of Cleophus Butler."

"Cleophus Butler? What's a Cleophus Butler?"

Thelma Hayes answered. "An informant. He's on the edge of a lot of stuff, Ernie told me. Ernie thought he might be able to help with some clue or something."

"He helped a great deal, actually. But not willingly," Babcock told them. He recounted for them—minus the gorier details in deference to Thelma Hayes—his experiences with Cleophus Butler in the automobile the previous night. "So, we know who took the cocaine, why Ernie was set up—"

"Then why can't we go to the police, Lew? Ernie's got a lot of friends on the force and—"

"Cleophus Butler could deny he ever said it, could tell a lie out of spite that would only further implicate Ernie, or could just clam up. And even if he did testify, his character is dubious and the best we'd have is something the prosecuting attorney could label as hearsay evidence, inadmissable in court. But I set something in motion that should help. I need you, Thelma, to gather up some things and let me drop you at Ernie's sister's place, just in case."

"But what if Ernie calls?"

"We'll have to risk that. If he calls and you're not here, he'll probably call his sister's house anyway. I think I can predict with a fair degree of certainty what will happen if anything does, but you being here alone with the children could be tempting fate." He looked at Hughes, Hughes's face impassive. He knew him better than that. Hughes was simply waiting for him to reveal what was necessary to Thelma and reveal the rest later, exactly his intent. "If it goes the way I hope, we'll have all the evidence we need by the time Ernie's pre-trial hearing starts tomorrow. And with Mr. Hughes arriving, that's just more help on our side, Thelma. Trust me on this."

Hughes filled the three glasses with the red wine. "I propose a toast, if I may be so bold," Hughes began, raising his glass. "To Officer Hayes's vindication and the reuniting with his lovely wife and family."

Thelma Hayes forced a smile. Lewis Babcock raised his glass. "Let's drink to that, indeed!"

He downed his wine. Without looking at the label, he could tell it was definitely New York State. . . .

Thomas Alyard stepped out of the shower. After his contact had left, taking the ampule with him, he had fallen asleep on the couch and slept there for several hours, having no idea of what time he had originally nodded off. Hunger had started to gnaw at him and he had investigated the larder before showering. Much as he had anticipated, it was fully stocked. Beer in the refrigerator, wine and an assortment of hard liquor under the counter and enough food for six men for a week. Alyard had no intention of finding five friends, so anticipated he was adequately stocked to ride things out for a few weeks before returning to Rome. By that time, the ampule would be safely out of harm's way and the research necessary to duplicate its contents and therefore negate its potential strategic value would have begun.

He toweled himself dry. There was a good supply of towels and the apartment was even equipped with a washer and dryer and soap for when he ran out.

The man to whom he had given the ampule—he was consciously trying to forget his name even though it was probably anything but his real name—had assured him that despite the fact the KGB and Italian Communist sympathizers would be watching every way out of the country, he had a foolproof way to get it out safely. The man had joked that it wasn't very fast and he didn't relish traveling that way, but "any port in a storm," then laughed resoundingly.

Alyard tried shrugging off the memories.

He had no robe and never slept in anything but his skin, so he took a dry bath towel and wound it around his waist kilt fashion. He picked up the gun he had been given along with a supply of money and a new set of identity papers, passport and credit cards. He had brought the gun into the bathroom with him just to be on the safe side. It was a Beretta 92F, the new American military pistol. He had used them before and, if the gun were typical, he could hit what he aimed at with it. He had given his contact the Walther PPK Stakowski had given him, wanting the gun ditched in case it could be traced to anything. He had also given his contact the remainder of his identity materials which linked him to the Swiss, Thomas Rheinhold. The thing to do, always, was to think of the loose ends.

Alyard entered the kitchen. Appalonia was a marvelous cook. But, he doubted he would starve, having cooked for himself for many years before she had come along. He began planning. For the first week, he would stay in the apartment. But he wouldn't be a couch potato, despite the ample selection of tapes for the VCR and discs for the CD player. He'd been promising himself to get back in shape and he knew just the right sort of workouts he could employ to tone up, despite the fact there was no equipment. A knowledgable man could utilize chairs, door frames, all of that.

As he started opening cans, he started working out his schedule. Up in the mornings at eight. A good workout, then a shower, then catch up on his reading over breakfast and afterward. Another workout at— There was a knock at the door.

Thomas Alyard snatched up the Beretta and turned toward the

sound, his back to the counter. He wasn't about to answer the knock. There was supposed to be no one coming to contact him. He crossed out of the kitchen and halfway across the living room, giving his towel another tuck. He had sucked in his breath so hard when he'd heard the knock at his door that he'd almost lost it.

The knock came again. And now he could faintly hear a voice. He came closer to the door, standing beside it but not in front of it so he could hear. ". . . Fabrizzi. There is an important message for you, Signore Alyard." What the hell was the apartment manager doing shouting his real name along the corridor for everyone to hear. "This is Fabrizzi. There is an important message for you, Signore Alyard. The telephone in the apartment, she don't work."

Alyard licked his lips. He didn't budge.

"Here. I slide it under the door, Signore." An envelope slipped under the door. "Good-bye, Signore."

He waited a long time, watching the face of his wristwatch, feeling the sweat start under his armpits, spread to his palms, feeling it like a cold wash on the soles of his bare feet. He gave it a full five minutes before he bent down and reached for the envelope. As he tugged at it, there was a loud hissing sound and a grey-white cloud belched from under the crack toward his face, engulfing him. He staggered back, punching the Beretta toward the door. He felt the towel slipping again and automatically reached for it, and then . . .

Thomas Alyard's head ached and he was cold. He opened his eyes and realized he was naked and lying on—the dining room table?

Three faces stared down at him. "Mr. Alyard. Don't get up. It'll only make the headache worse. My name is Ephraim Vols. I'm telling you my real name because this is very important. I'm a Major with The Committee for State Security of The Soviet. Are you thinking clearly enough to know what that means?"

Alyard thought he nodded, but when he moved his head, the pain engulfed him again and his eyes closed against it. He could hear the man's voice—Vols?

"Get this man a blanket, Piotr, before he freezes to death, naked like this."

"Yes, Comrade Major."

"Vassily. See if you can find something to drink. Look in the kitchen. A nice glass of whiskey would be pleasant. And remember, after all the time I've spent in England, when I say whiskey I mean what you or Piotr would call scotch. Check with Piotr and see what he wants. And get something for yourself.''

Alyard opened his eyes again. The face was looming over him. ''I'd offer you a drink, Mr. Alyard, but I'm not sure it would be wise to mix alcohol with so much of the residue from the gas still in your bloodstream. After we've gone, I'd say give yourself a few hours of sleep before you touch the stuff. Just friendly advice. Take it or leave it as you will.''

''Thanks.''

''Glad to see you can talk, at least. I'm not sure what's in it, but we used it once before and I got a whiff of it. Bloody awful smelling and even that one sniff gave me a headache for an hour or more. Ahh, Piotr!''

Alyard had closed his eyes again, and now felt a blanket being draped over him, a draft that chilled him to the bone as it settled.

''Once you're up to it, just let me know and we'll help you off this table. I apologize for that, but when we let ourselves in, you were closer to the table than the couch and I wanted to make certain you still had a pulse. Problem when you go playing around with chemicals with human beings. Everyone's so different. What will put one man to sleep might kill somebody else.''

Alyard opened his eyes again. Vols's face was pleasant looking. He even smiled faintly, like a benign father or a physician. His eyes were a washed-out blue and he had sandy brown hair and was light complected. If this Vols fellow had worked in England for the KGB, with his speech, his manner and his appearance, he would have seemed the typical man on the street.

A shorter man—Vols was apparently on the tall side—handed Vols a tumbler and Vols sipped at it. ''Decent.'' Vols nodded. ''KGB safe houses are usually stocked with terribly cheap liquor. I think it's from maturing with vodka. There's a difference from brand to brand, of course, but it's not so noticeable as it is with whiskey or bourbon or rum. But the CIA always goes first class, doesn't it?''

Alyard didn't say a word.

''You're wondering how we found you. Well, it wasn't your fault, so relax on that. Mr. Fabrizzi has worked for us for years, usually just filling us in on who used the safe house here and the like. But this was rather on the important side. You should have heard the flap it caused on Derzhinsky Square when it was learned the Americans of all people had stolen the ampule. I mean, that's the sort of theatrical thing one expects from the British. Right out of one of their thriller novels. Secret agents and all of that. Don't go contemplating avenging yourself on old Fabrizzi, by the way. He'll be long gone and out of your reach by the time we're through talking and that headache's worn off.''

''Not to introduce a note of discord, but you're not getting shit out of me. And anyway, I don't know anything.''

''Ahh, but you do, Mr. Alyard. I hate sounding so depressingly formal. Do you prefer Thomas or Tom?''

''Whatever.''

''That's an odd diminutive for Thomas—a joke, Thomas. Feel like sitting up yet?''

Alyard started to try, fell back, felt hands catching him so he wouldn't knock his head, at last sat up. He felt stupid, naked except for the blanket sitting in the middle of the dining room table. And he felt more vulnerable than he ever had in his life. Which was, of course, what they wanted; he knew that as surely as he knew that he was.

''Let's get Thomas off the table and into a chair or someplace comfortable. Ahh! That reclining chair.''

Alyard felt strong hands on him, getting him into a standing position for a moment, the blanket falling away and he was naked. And then the blanket was wrapped around him and he was helped to the recliner and helped to sit. All that was missing was them tucking him in and singing him a lullaby.

He closed his eyes against the pain in his head, then opened them again. Vols was perched on the arm of the couch, holding his whiskey tumbler and staring down at him almost sympathetically.

''First up. Let me apologize for barging in like this and taking over your flat. But soon as you've helped us with a few details, as I mentioned before, we'll be off packing.''

''Going far away?''

''Good—packing. No, but I may, yes, depending on how far the ampule has gone. You see, Thomas, you and I have a lot more in common than you'd suppose. I mean, certainly, we're on opposite sides. You fight for truth, justice and the American way and all, and I fight for the slimy tentacles of Communism and repression and all that rot; but, both of us have roughly similar jobs and we're both caught in the middle on this. Are you a friend of David Stakowski?''

Alyard didn't respond.

''Well, in any event, we've packed David off to Moscow by

now, I suspect. He'll get a severe talking to and spend a few weeks in prison somewhere until this is all sorted out, but then he'll be sent back to your people in some sort of trade. But, and this is merely personal observation, but, you might think of assigning David to more or less standard intelligence duties. He's really not very good at this cloak and dagger sort of thing. Just a bit of advice.''

Alyard didn't say anything.

''As I was about to say, you and I do have one thing in common. We're trapped in the middle. I mean, you didn't steal the ampule with the virus. And it wasn't stolen from me. You were sent in when David botched things up on his end, and I was sent in when the security people at the facility and the Albanians botched things up on their end. We're both rather like clean-up men or something, Thomas. I'll find the ampule regardless, but I could use a bit of help from you. I don't expect you to talk freely, of course. We're both professionals. I'm going to give you a shot of some new type of truth serum just developed. It's perfectly safe, but I don't think it would have mixed too well with alcohol either. And if I were you, I'd turn this rather disappointing experience into something positive. The truth serum is very new and once you've awakened, I'd rush off to a chemist and look up getting some blood drawn before it's completely metabolized so it can be analyzed. Could be a real coup for you and ease the career-dampening effect this might have otherwise.''

''What the hell kinda guy are you?'' Alyard couldn't help but say it.

Vols smiled, genuinely it seemed. ''I'm a patriotic Soviet citizen doing my duty. Over the years, I've found that sadism and other mental quirks can make a chap lose sight of things. If I'd been specifically told to scorch the earth of anyone involved in this, then you'd be dead as soon as you talked. But, lucky for both of us, no such instructions were passed down. Killing you would achieve absolutely no purpose. And the last thing anyone in our business should want is more of the David Stakowskis in the ranks. Incompetents are dangerous. We both know that. Now, if you're feeling up to it, let's have the left arm. And don't struggle. There are three of us and you're not exactly in fighting form at the moment at any rate. Broken needles are unpleasant. By the way?''

''What?''

"You're not allergic to peanut oil, are you? I understand that's one of the components of this new truth serum. I have some of the old stuff, but that'll only delay me and prolong things for you and the results will be the same."

"No. I'm not allergic to anything that I know of."

"Lucky you! I have a terrible time with evergreen pollen in the late spring. Piotr, you hold his arm. Vassily, swab that spot with alcohol first, then administer the injection." Vols took a swallow of his scotch. "And by the way, no need to worry. This is a spanking-new needle. We've been very cautious with that sort of thing since all this AIDS flap started. Go ahead, Piotr."

It was like living in a nightmare where everything was so totally insane and yet it was impossible to escape. He let them give him the needle. Stakowski had caused it all with his incompetence and if he resisted, all he'd get would be a broken needle in his arm and they'd try again.

Vols asked him to count backwards from one hundred and Thomas Alyard did as he was asked. It only seemed natural. . . .

The car's heat was too high and Darwin Hughes reached over and turned the fan down to its lowest setting. The door opened and Lewis Babcock slipped behind the wheel. "I turned down the heat a little. It was stifling in here."

"No. Thelma's always been a little cold-blooded. You know?"

"Women are more sensitive to temperature changes but have greater tolerances for the extremes. Now. What have you set up, Lewis?"

"What have you set me up for?"

"You mean, why am I here? It's a long story." Babcock threw the car into gear. Hughes looked up at the house and waved to Mrs. Hayes, who was watching from a yellow lighted window, the drapes drawn back. "I was approached by a Brigadier General, a man named Robert Argus. He has Presidential authorization as well as authorization from House and Senate leadership on both sides of the aisle to reactivate us. The three of us. He swears up and down that what happened last time wouldn't happen again."

"He's talking out of his hat."

"Probably so, lad, but you must admit the possibilities would be intriguing."

"Well—and I appreciate you helping out here, regardless of your motivation—but you can count me out. I've started setting up a practice. I'm going to start a real life."

"I'll tell you what, lad. Why don't we put aside this matter until we've resolved the matter at hand. What's on tap for tonight?"

"I set myself up for the Devil's Princes to come after me. A guy by the name of Tyrone Cash is behind what happened to Ernie. Cash and two other guys—Randy Jones and Balthaszar Roman—were in it with him. They're the top guys in this street gang. Big cocaine and crack dealers. Got a reputation for killing anybody who gets in their way. That's why I set myself up. If they run true to pattern, they'll come after me. Only place they'd know to look was the hotel. But to be on the safe side, I wanted Thelma and the kids out of the house."

"Does Ernie's sister's house present that much better an alternative?"

"Best we've got."

"Could have tried a hotel."

"Ernie's brother-in-law's a cop. I checked. He's gonna be home tonight watching a football game."

"Assuming they're safe then, you set it up for these gentlemen with the picturesque-sounding names to come to the hotel and kill you?"

"Right." Babcock nodded.

"What exactly did you do?"

Babcock quickly told Hughes about the visit to Devil's Princes' headquarters earlier in the day and the invitation he had left, including the false room number and then setting it up to have the incoming calls transferred to his own room.

"That's wonderful except for two things: First, the hotel operator, unless she's busy, might give them the correct room number in the event they need to call you again; and second, what about the poor slob in the target room?"

"It was the best I could do on the spur of the moment. I figure I can do something about the people in the other room. I'm not sure what just yet. And with you here—you said you're on the same floor?"

"I'm the poor slob in the next room."

Babcock started to laugh and then so did Hughes, although he didn't know why. Neither of them had a gun and it was likely that the delegation from the Devil's Princes would.

Chapter Nine

Abe Cross finished with his bow tie. He refused to consider a clip-on, so he contented himself with an imperfect but sincere knot.

When he had first started playing in the London hotels after the surgical strike in Iran was behind him, he had purchased a tuxedo off the rack. But after he'd felt secure enough in what he was doing that it appeared he would be doing it for quite some time, he had had three tuxedos custom tailored, three not an inordinate number since he needed to wear one every night with the places he worked. He had one white dinner jacket as well, just for necessity since he had always thought they made the wearer look like a lost waiter without a tray.

He found his cigarettes and lighter, grabbed up his music case and started out of his cabin. For the first time in a long time, the prospect of working was not just tolerable, but exciting. Jenny Hall was what excited him. He'd found that her arrangements were quite compatible with his own style of playing and, when he improvised a little, she not only didn't complain, but would vocalize along with it. Her voice was another matter. It was a perfect blending of alto timbre and a range which got her comfortably into soprano. And when she hit those notes, the higher ones, it was something he couldn't describe.

He wondered if he was in love.

The corridor was crowded and passengers were still arriving, stewards carting unbelievably stacked luggage carriers out of the elevators and into cabins, so many people moving about that twice he had to let an elevator pass before there was room enough for him to squeeze aboard.

"Do you work here, young man?" He turned his head and saw

a pair of pretty blue eyes behind him under a crown of soft grey hair. She reminded him of his aunt a little.

"Yes, ma'am. I'm Abe Cross. I'm playing in the Seabreeze Lounge."

"Ohh! The piano! I love the piano, don't I Fred?"

Fred was apparently her husband, who looked at once bored and embarrassed but nodded that she did, indeed, like the piano.

"Well, I tell you what." Cross smiled. "When you come down some evening and catch me play, just ask for something you'd like to hear and I'll bet I can play it."

"Do you know 'I'll Be Seeing You'?"

"My mother was a big fan of Liberace. I can play it. But I don't have a candelabra, I'm afraid." For that matter, he didn't have a brother named George, either.

The elevator ride mercifully ended and he glanced at his Rolex as he made his way along the corridor—should it be called a companionway? he wondered—toward the Seabreeze Lounge. He entered from the enclosure-protected side as he had at noon. Now there was an elaborate easel set-up with a poster announcing the "vocal magic" of songstress Jennifer Hall. They didn't know how right they were about the magic part, he thought. The publicity still inset into the poster didn't do her justice at all but still looked good enough to eat. At the lower third of the poster it said something about the "inimitable piano styling of Abe Cross," which made it sound as though he took pianos in for a wash and a set. The lounge was already filling up and as he started for the piano, he heard a familiar voice, Helen the barmaid. "Want something?"

"Ice water'd be terrific. Thanks."

"Man, you are different from Lenny Brooks."

He didn't know what to say to that. He stepped up onto the smallish stage and started laying out his music. He heard a voice behind him, a man's, totally unfamiliar. "Mr. Cross?"

"Yes," He quickly added a 'sir' after he saw the uniform. He guessed he'd been expecting somebody who looked like the guy from "The Love Boat," but the captain of the *Empress Britannia* was a short, stockily built man with a thick head of dark hair so brown it was almost black, streaks of grey at the sides, the sideburns short and pure white.

"I'm John Milewski, but I answer to the name Captain." He extended his hand—it was the size of a five-pound ham and had heavy black hair on the back—and smiled. "I understand you play terrifically. I have spies everywhere." And then he grinned. "And I also understand you were a Naval officer. Correct?"

"That's right, Captain. I was a lieutenant."

"Dry land or water?"

"A little of both. I was a SEAL Team Leader. Last duty station was in the Med. But that was a while ago."

"Annapolis?"

"Nope. Navy ROTC."

The grin widened still further. "Good. Annapolis men can be a pain in the ass. I know. I was one. Have a drink with me later, all right?"

"That'll be my pleasure, sir."

"Well, good luck, tonight. Won't be seeing me around much until after we shove off and we're out of Naples harbor." He cocked his head like some sort of salute and strode off.

Abe Cross returned to laying out his music. Helen showed up with the ice water. He checked his watch. He didn't have to start for another ten minutes according to the schedule given him that afternoon, but he decided to get off on the right foot just in case the captain did have spies everywhere.

He took some of the more popular Beatles songs, in a medley alternating the faster ones with the slower ones, the focus of the medley the song "Yesterday," measures of it used to segue from one song into another and to cover key changes. He glanced at his watch again when he was through. It had killed twelve minutes. He noticed the grey-haired lady from the elevator and he did a long, complicated sounding but easy enough run which led into "I'll Be Seeing You." He glanced up as she sat down and she looked positively sweet as she smiled at him. He segued into "I'll Get By," and then decided on a slightly different attack before he started having people coming down with hyperglycemia attacks. Movie tunes were always popular and at once unexpected. He did "The Magnificent Seven" and "High Noon."

A gorgeous blonde whose breasts and the top of her dress were slowly but steadily parting company it seemed, came up to the piano and gave him a big smile and slipped five bucks into a glass Helen the barmaid had put out and asked him if he could play any Barry Mannilow and he told her he could. Fred, the little old lady's husband, came up, apparently having seen the donation from the blonde, and started slipping a ten into the glass. "Those were on me. Tell her I said so," Cross told the man.

"Thanks, fella."

"Anytime." He had learned to play on one level of consciousness and carry on conversations, even once or twice make change.

After about twenty minutes, Helen came by and asked if he needed anything and he asked for an ashtray. As he lit up a Pall Mall, he started playing "Set 'Em Up Joe," the cigarette hanging from the left corner of his mouth. It was the wrong brand of cigarettes, he didn't own a porkpie hat, and he wasn't Sinatra, but Abe Cross kept playing the song anyway. . . .

He hadn't gotten rid of the PPK. It was smaller than his own gun and easier to carry around aboard the ship if it came to that. But there was no reason to suppose that it would. He moved through the engine room now, along a section of pipe which brought steam to the turbines, which in turn cranked the screws. He'd been tapped for the job by the people at Langley for one reason. The ampule couldn't be transferred by military aircraft because the military might somehow get wind of it and want it for their own biowarfare studies, he'd been told. And it couldn't be transported by civilian aircraft because the airports would be watched. Even though he had always worked the Orient whenever he'd done any out-of-country things, it was always possible that someone would recognize him from a file photo or something.

There was an ancillary problem with moving the ampule by aircraft at any event. A virus, he'd been told, it might be something which could infect when vectored in air. If some catastrophe were to take place on a seagoing vessel at least, the worst that could happen was the ampule going down. He had placed the ampule and its maroon container inside a waterproof, air-cushioned bag just in case of that.

He was told that no one would suspect that such a valuable and dangerous item would be taken out the slow, old-fashioned way, by ship, anyway. The reason he'd been tapped for the assignment was that he'd spent two years in the Merchant Marines before finishing college and was qualified to pass himself off as an experienced man below decks. He didn't relish the idea of taking a cruise this way, but it was all in the line of duty.

He had packed his good clothing and changed to worn Levi's, a work shirt and even a peacoat and watchcap, taken his spurious seaman's documents and reported for work, the job arranged for him in advance before he had even reached Italy. He had asked why a cruise ship rather than some merchant vessel. He had been told it would be less suspicious. That hadn't rung one hundred percent true to him, but he had learned that information was often withheld for the supposed greater good of the mission.

He found an easily identifiable junction of pipes, yellow ones meeting red ones. He set about finding a suitable location in which to stash the ampule. . . .

Ephraim Vols had not come to Italy prepared for a cruise at sea on a luxury liner. But the information the truth serum caused Thomas Alyard to reveal had led him inexorably to the conclusion that a cruise it must be. Through the description and name given him by Alyard, he had worked through contacts in the Italian Communist party to learn that a man of different name but identical description had chartered a plane from Rome to Naples less than twelve hours before. Fabrizzi's description of the man having matched identically to Alyard's, Vols had assumed it reasonably accurate. The man had rented a car at the airfield and returned it at his hotel, after which he had checked out leaving no forwarding address. A description gotten from an awakened desk clerk at the hotel had indicated that the American—another name used at the hotel—had left wearing blue jeans and a seaman's jacket. On a hunch, Vols had telephoned a source in the longshoremen's union and, after an hour's wait, been phoned back. Two black seamen speaking English and matching the same general description had signed aboard vessels leaving Naples harbor that night. One had given the name Nigel Hornsby, spoken 'like an Englishman, like you,' and joined the crew of the *Herculaneum*, a merchant vessel leaving for Marseille and Cardiff. The second, giving his name as Alvin Leeds, had taken work below decks on the cruise ship *Empress Britannia*.

Vols had taken the only course of action open to him, since he had kept his word and left Thomas Alyard alive and well. He had ordered the man called Piotr to fly to Marseille and the man called Vassily to go on to Cardiff, each man with the same directive. If the black seaman leaves the vessel, kill him if necessary but first find out if he has the ampule. Each of his men had an injection kit similar to his own, the truth serum marked as insulin so it could get past airport security checks.

Something the longeshoremen's union contact had said about Alvin Leeds had made Vols determine to pursue Leeds himself. The job had been waiting for Leeds, held for him. That was not entirely unusual, but unusual enough to make a connection.

There had been more telephone calls then. Arranging passage

on the *Empress*, rousting a sympathizer who ran a men's clothier—Vols had brought nothing with him to Italy except a change of underwear and socks, one clean shirt and his toothbrush and electric razor.

As a passenger, his luggage would be subject to search and any real weapons were impossible to bring along. But he could always improvise. Three suits and a tuxedo hastily altered and an appropriate number of shirts, ties, underpants (he never wore undershirts) and other necessities and a set of expensive luggage to help him look the part of the tourist (and because he liked real leather and had been looking for an excuse to get it past his expense reports)—he felt he was set. A last-minute call to Anna in Albania; David Stakowski had killed himself in his cell, the Albanians failing to keep the suicide watch Vols had ordered through her. Orders to Anna to fly to New York City where the *Empress* would first dock so she could take the ampule into an escape route that could be arranged while she awaited his arrival. And a promise to Anna that after this was over, they would still see to that Christmas tree he'd promised to show her. A taxicab to the docks, through the inspection points, his luggage taken away to be brought on board.

The "All Ashore That's Going Ashore" gong already sounding, people waving vigorously from the decks to the docks and from the docks to the decks, Ephraim Vols ascended the gangplank and boarded the *Empress*. The first officer welcomed him aboard and the recreation director assured him he'd have an exciting trip.

He hoped not too exciting. The call made just before his call to Anna had given him encoded specific details about the contents of the ampule. And if he hadn't talked to Anna, felt the reassurance of her calm, he would have become ill.

Chapter Ten

When they stopped at the K-Mart, Lewis Babcock had asked, "Why do you want to stop here?"

"Lewis. Hotel rooms offer some potential for improvising weapons, certainly; but when we have such a vastly richer opportunity open to us, we'd be fools not to take advantage of it. Wouldn't we?"

As they had driven from Ernie's sister's house, Hughes had worked up a list. He tore the list in half now and gave one half to Babcock. "Remember with the steak knives, not the ones with serrated edges. Right?"

Hughes went through the store as methodically and as quickly as he could, purchasing a small crowbar, brass-headed carpet tacks, a claw hammer, ammonia, several pressure-sensitive wall switches, a hundred feet of electrical wire, black electrical tape, extension cords and—he counted himself in luck this time of year—an electric fan. The fan was on sale. He located Christmas tree lights. He found two pairs of safety goggles and two pairs of white workmen's coveralls in more or less correct sizes.

Babcock was already at the checkout counter, looking as though he felt slightly stupid. "You have everything, Lewis."

"I even found your water pistols. They were on sale."

"Good. I hate spending too much for something," Hughes enthused.

Out to the car with their purchases and a quick ride downtown, traffic at the hour relatively light for such a large city.

There were a few stares as they walked through the lobby, especially directed at the unbagged box for the electric fan, Hughes felt.

They checked Hughes's room. There had been no messages

and nothing was disturbed. Each of them armed with a steak knife, they entered Babcock's room. No messages and nothing disturbed there either.

"You mind telling me what all this junk is for, Mr. Hughes?"

"I'll explain as we go, Lewis. First, check the water pistols that their good and tight and try to judge how true to aim they are at under a dozen feet. Use the shower as your backstop, And" —Hughes smiled—"if it's all the same to you, Lewis, I'd love the one that's shaped like a Luger. The green one."

"You're joking."

"No. And I haven't gone senile, either, Lewis. Hurry with that accuracy test," and Hughes began unpacking the fan. . . .

The green plastic Luger-shaped water pistol, Babcock had told him, shot a foot low at twelve feet and six inches to the left.

Darwin Hughes sat in darkness in a straight-backed chair in the far corner of his room, alone, the water pistol on the table beside him and alongside it, one of the pressure-sensitive switches, the switch bridged off the wall outlet beside the door leading into the corridor. Leading from the wall was an extension cord, which was connected to the two strings of Christmas tree lights over the door.

In the almost total darkness, he could read the luminous face of his Rolex perfectly well. It was 4:00 A.M. If the Devil's Princes were ever going to come, they would come within this next hour. If they didn't come, he would have lost an entire night's sleep for nothing and poor Ernie Hayes would be bound over from his pre-trial hearing and face a frame-up that he might never escape short of the kind of drastic measures that Hughes's brief meeting with Hayes's wife had confirmed Hayes himself would never condone.

The green and red Christmas lights came on.

Hughes took his fist and pounded once on the wall which adjoined Babcock's room. Two knocks came back, meaning that Lewis Babcock as well had seen the signal indicating someone had come through the emergency stairs exit door. The blue and yellow lights would have indicated someone coming down the hall from the direction of the elevators. Earlier in the evening, dressed in their K-Mart coveralls, they had pried up the carpet where it was seamed between the elevators and their rooms, doing the same thing just near enough to the emergency stairwell as well. Using a razor-blade knife to cut out the padding, they had inserted the pressure-sensitive light switches beneath the carpet in the niches cut to receive them in the padding. Running his electrical wire to the wall and then under the carpet edges to their rooms, he had a primitive but effective intruder alert system installed.

While there had still been considerable traffic in the corridor, every few minutes or so the lights from the direction of the elevators would come on. He would automatically click them off with the switch beside him on the nightstand. Once it had passed 2:00 A.M., he began taking the more infrequent lightings more seriously, waiting with his improvised weapons ready just in case it were the real thing.

It hadn't been yet.

But this was the first time the lights had signaled approach from the direction by the emergency stairs.

He shut off his green and red lights, assuming that Babcock would have done the same. He had guarded against one of them falling asleep by installing the lights in both rooms. However this turned out, Hughes somehow felt the hotel people wouldn't be terribly happy with their carpets.

There was a series of knocks on the wall. Hughes signaled back they were understood. To his feet, he moved quickly and silently across the room, his water pistol in his right hand.

The series of knocks had indicated someone was entering the room Babcock occupied.

Hughes's right fist balled on the Luger-shaped squirt gun. He pulled up his safety goggles from beneath his chin.

There was the sound of the safety chain next door being ripped out of the wall.

Hughes worked his own chain off and stepped into the corridor as the first scream came. A tall, thin black man wearing a nylon stocking over his head for a mask wheeled toward him, a .45 automatic in his right fist. Hughes fired for the man's eyes before the .45 could come on line, the startled man screaming something unintelligible as both hands went to protect his eyes, Hughes's body slamming him to the floor.

Hughes could hear the sound of the electric fan now and then, someone shouting, "My eyes. Motherfucker!" Hughes's right knee smashed up into the base of the downed man's jaw, putting him out. Hughes's gloved left fist grabbed up the .45, his right hand sweeping over the slide to chamber a first round if one weren't already chambered.

He was through the doorway, shouting, "Lewis! Me!"

One of the men was down on the floor, rubbing his eyes and screaming, the other man locked in combat with Lewis Babcock. There was a .45 beside the man rolling around on the floor and Hughes caught it up in his right fist as he passed him, crossing the room in two strides, upping the safety of the .45 automatic as he laced the pistol across the side of the third man's neck. The body slumped to its knees. Lewis Babcock sagged back against the wall. "I can't believe it! This idiocy worked."

Hughes grinned. "Turn off the electric fan, will you. I'll catch a draft."

He walked over to the other man, satisfied himself the situation was static for ten seconds and went into the hallway. He grabbed the semi-conscious man out of the corridor and dragged him inside the room, then closed the door. The chain was ripped from the wall but the door was otherwise functional.

"Lewis. Call the lobby and complain you heard some people making a terrible racket, looked into the corridor and saw them getting into the elevator."

"Right.'

Hughes dropped to one knee beside the man who was still rubbing his eyes, crying now. "The tears will do you good, my friend. Get that pepper out of your eyes better than anything else. Let's get rid of this stocking over your beautiful face." Hughes tore the stocking away. A milk-chocolate-skinned black man in his late twenties or early thirties.

"Pepper?"

"You didn't notice the fan? When you and your friend entered the room, my associate Mr. Babcock turned on the fan—all the way to high. We had twenty pounds of finely ground black pepper in nice neat little one-pound plastic bags. Just shake the bag open in front of the fan and you have an instant blinding pepper storm that even penetrated these things." Hughes held up the stocking. "But not these." And he tugged his goggles down to his neck. "Guns make a lot of noise and might interrupt our discussions up here. These don't." Hughes produced one of the steak knives and held it to the man's throat.

"Hey, man—"

"What's your name?"

"Ahh—"

"Tell me your name." He pressed the knife against the tip of the man's nose.

"All right—all right! Balthaszar Roman, man!"

"Balthaszar? Ever called 'Balls' for short?"

Balthaszar Roman actually grinned.

"Sometimes, yeah."

Hughes moved the knife and pressured it against Roman's testicles just enough so he'd feel it. "If you don't very shortly tell me what I want to hear, your pals will never call you Balls again. Understand?"

The man's upper lip glistened with sweat. He nodded vigorously.

"All right. We're public-spirited citizens. Who pulled the trigger on Officer Hayes's partner, Mike?"

Balthaszar Roman licked his lips. "I can't—"

"I can understand a man of scruples. I'll wager you won't even cry out when I saw your nuts off." Hughes increased the pressure with the knife.

"Tyrone! Tyrone did it, man."

"Tyrone did it. Is Tyrone with us, Balthaszar?"

"He was in the hallway man!" Balthaszar Roman's eyes were still streaming tears from the pepper and perhaps from the realization of what he had just said.

"Ahh. Now. Another question, Balthaszar. Is a Mr. Jones with us, too?"

"Yeah, over there."

"And Tyrone decided he wanted vengeance on Ernie Hayes because of the affair involving Jones's sister, correct?"

"Ernie Hayes kicked the shit outa Tyrone when he went after her like that with the belt."

"Why would officer Hayes have done a thing like that, now. A clear-cut case of police brutality if I've ever heard it, Balthaszar. You should have lodged a complaint."

"Man—"

"Shut up, Balthaszar. That's so you can listen very carefully. Now. If Tyrone killed Officer Hayes's partner, how did officer Hayes wind up just walking around dazed when he was picked up?"

"We stopped the car with a garbage truck we stole. Hadda snow plow on it. Hayes banged up his head on the steering wheel."

"Lewis?" Hughes called out.

"There was a big bump on Ernie's head."

"You're doing wonderfully well, Balthaszar. Now. What happened next?"

"Tyrone had it figured we'd smoke Hayes and his partner, but then with Hayes unconscious and his partner kinda that way, Tyrone says he got himself a better idea. Ya know?"

Hughes smiled. "No. But you'll tell me, I'm sure. What happened then?"

"Tyrone says he's gonna fix Ernie Hayes good. We throw Hayes in the car Randy was drivin' and Tyrone—he takes Hayes's gun and smokes the other pig with it. Then we dump Hayes in some alley, man."

"What about the cocaine, Balthaszar?"

"Gimme a cigarrette, huh?"

"Bad for your health. Almost as bad as not answering my questions." And Hughes prodded him again in the crotch with the knife. "Where's the cocaine?"

"Princes owns a junk yard over on South Michigan."

"So?"

"There's a fifty-four Cadillac. Red with black upholstery. What's left of it. He got the coke in the trunk inside the spare."

"That's very inventive, Balthaszar."

"Look, man—lemme go now, huh?"

"Balthaszar, you have two simple choices You can become a public-spirited citizen too or you can have serious problems."

"Man—I say shit 'bout Tyrone, he gonna burn my ass he hear."

Hughes looked at Lewis Babcock. "Lewis. When Tyrone makes his break for the door—"

Tyron Cash was up from the floor, breaking into a dead run. Babcock picking up the straight-backed chair and smashing it across Cash's back as he made for the door, putting him down.

"You see, Balthaszar, Tyrone heard every unkind word you said about him. Now, those two choices again. Either go to the Drug Enforcement Agency people with your story or go out on the street. If Tyrone doesn't get you, I will. Lewis?"

"Yeah?"

"My little tape recorder still running?"

"It certainly is."

"Aww shit."

"Precisely." Hughes and Babcock had assessed the situation while installing the improvised alarm systems in the hallway. Counting on getting Tyrone Cash to talk about himself and still keeping him in one piece might have proven impossible. And, if Randy Jones was either so hopelessly loyal or terrified that he wouldn't step in when his own sister was being beaten with a belt, Jones might prove intractable as well. That had left Balthaszar Roman, the one with the least violent reputation of the three and probably the easiest to intimidate.

"Here's what you're going to do. I have a friend who did me a favor earlier this evening. I called him up in Washington and asked if he could get a squad of DEA personnel to station themselves across the street discreetly all night. He called me back and said that he could. I told him to tell them that a man wearing white coveralls would walk out of here and come and speak with them. Now, you can either do that, Balthaszar, in which case you'll be given the fairest treatment possible and protection from your friend Tyrone and the rest of the Devil's Princes, or you can just walk outside and try to hide from Tyrone, whom I will promptly let go, and me."

"Man!"

"You have a very limited vocabulary. You should read more. When you've made your decision, if it is to cooperate with the DEA and tell them everything, I want the entire thing with Officer Hayes explained first. Before that pre-trial hearing tomorrow."

Hughes stood up, staring down at Balthaszar Roman. "Do you wish to be given a nearly new pair of coveralls or do you wish to die?" Hughes looked over toward Tyrone Cash. The gang leader was stirring on the floor. "Next time Tyrone wakes up, if you haven't made up your mind, I let him go. If you have, I'll hold him for the drug enforcement people. So what'll it be, Balthaszar? DEA or D.E.A.D.?"

"Gimme the coveralls. Shit!"

Lewis Babcock started to laugh.

Chapter Eleven

Seamus O'Fallon had felt better throughout the day and had finally gotten some sleep, the headache just a low throb that he could easily enough control.

They sat around a small table in the master's cabin, the rough seas calmed enough that it was possible to keep a cup of coffee nearly full on the long table and not have to hold onto it to keep it from spilling. Young Martin looked green still, but what better color for an Irishman. O'Fallon smiled to himself. And it could have been sea sickness.

They were listening to the BBC overseas broadcast.

The death toll from the bombing of the RUC barracks was only a disappointing one hundred and two confirmed. But, there were still five unaccounted-for bodies and several of the injured were listed as critical.

When the broadcast was over, O'Fallon said, "Martin. There's a good lad and turn off the radio, will ya now."

"Yes, Seamus."

Martin turned off the radio, one of those things made to look like the old-time cathedral radios but thoroughly modern and very expensive.

"Well, lads," O'Fallon began to the dozen men seated at the table. "We coulda done better with the bombing if we hadn't had to do it so hastily. But, on the bright side, the bloody Brits'll barely have time to catch their wind before we do the next job, they will."

"Seamus?"

It was Patrick Kehoe speaking, a burly young fellow who was as fine a man with a knife as anyone O'Fallon had ever seen. "What is it, Paddy?"

"What is it we're after doing out here? You can be tellin' us now, sure."

"Ahh, that I can, boyo. We're engaged in a great endeavor, we are. When I talked about this one, I said chances were none of us would come back alive outa it, didn't I now."

"For fact you did, Seamus," Paddy Kehoe responded enthusiastically.

"Well, the truth of it is now that I think none of us will ever touch the dry land again unless they overpower us and carry our bodies home. And the likelihood of that happenin' is real remote, it is."

"What are we up to, Seamus?" Young Martin asked.

"It began when a fine fella, a son of the old sod if ever there was one, told me, 'Seamus. Could you and the lads be after usin' my fancy boat?' And I says, 'Well, might be a nice thing for an outing with the ladies and the little ones, for sure.' And then I got to thinkin', I did. And I asked this fine fella—a Yank he was and a regular giver to The Aid and a helper many's the time when we needed somethin' real special like a LAWs rocket or somethin'. So, I says to him, 'Would ya be after offerin' us a crew to boot?' And himself, he says, 'Sure.' Well, lads, the opportunity was too much for the O'Fallon to resist, it was. And me mind started cookin' up on somethin' nobody done to the bloody Brits for a long time. And, would any of ya be after guessin' what it might be I thought up?"

There was dead silence except for the subtle throb of the engines and the creaking of the vessel around them.

"Well, then I suppose it's me that'll be tellin' ya, now. I says to myself, 'O'Fallon. How could we hurt the bloody Brits real bad and at the same time get ourselves publicity all over the world for the cause? How could a handful of stout-hearted lads such as ourselves do somethin' that might really force the Brits out? And then it came to me—like somethin' in a flash, it did. I was walkin' along and me mind was driftin' to thoughts of Mary McKeown and takin' a roll in the covers and then the inspiration comes on me. We hijack us a British ship. One of them humongous floatin' hotels they suck up to the rich boys with. 'So fine,' I says, 'O'Fallon.' But it had to be a special boat, it did. Any you lads remember how that one tooth of mine was hurtin' the devil outa me?"

"I remember, Seamus!" Sean Dougherty announced. "You

was worse tempered than usual, you were, Seamus!'' Everybody laughed and so did O'Fallon.

''That's the truth of it, Jack. But I was there polishin' my arse listenin' to all the drillin' noises and all and tryin' to get it outa me mind, I was. And I picked up some silly woman's catalog or magazine. I started lookin' through. And there, right in front of me eyes, was what I wanted all along. Me tooth even stopped hurtin', lads. And that's the Lord's own truth, it is. But I seen the tooth puller anyhow.''

''What was her name, Seamus?'' Paddy asked.

''The *Empress Britannia*, lads.'' The cigarette in the corner of his mouth was nearly out and he lit another with the butt.

Chapter Twelve

So far, there had been no sign of the black seaman Alvin Leeds or whatever his real name was. And it was at once too late and yet too early to go prowling about the vessel in search of him. A first-class cabin had been all there was available and, he confessed to himself, a first-class lifestyle was something he could easily get used to again. When he'd lived in England, he'd been there under the guise of a technical writer, a freelancer with a generous expense account. The generous expense account had provided for good clothes, nice weekends in the country, the whole capitalist milieu. The woman who had been assigned to pose as his wife—she'd died six months after returning to the Soviet Union—had been fun to be with, enjoyed the radically altered lifestyle as much as he.

He sipped at a vodka martini and listened to the pretty girl singer. Ephraim Vols had developed a strong liking for American music when he'd done his service in Great Britain, and this young woman not only sang the best of it with aplomb, but the pianist who was doubling as her accompanist had a wonderful touch at the keys.

He brushed a speck of lint from his new tuxedo.

She was doing a medley of Judy Garland songs, but with her own style and flair.

He lit a cigarette. The process was simple, really. He had until they were a day or so out of New York to set the thing up. He would get hold of Leeds and somehow get the truth serum into him and obtain the location of the ampule from the man. Vols doubted that in this case killing could be avoided. The logical thing was to somehow get Leeds's body over the side just before they hit New York so the missing crewman wouldn't be noticed until after the passengers had gotten off and through customs. Getting the ampule through customs might prove interesting in itself, but he'd cross that bridge when he came to it. And besides, Anna would be there to work out an escape route—he hoped not to Cuba because he couldn't stand people like Castro— and she'd probably attack the customs problem for him. And, there was always the possibility that Alvin Leeds wasn't the American agent, but he'd wagered that Leeds was and his gut-level reactions were rarely wrong.

Vols tried putting the thing out of his head, his eyes scanning the crowd of listeners. There were plenty of unattached women, it appeared. His eyes kept going back to the pretty young woman who was singing, this Jennifer Hall. He wondered, a little more than casually, if she and the pianist—a good-looking fellow in a rough and tumble sort of way—were an item.

There was only one way to find out; and, the more he blended in with the ordinary life of the vessel, the more unnoticed he would be.

She finished with "Somewhere Over the Rainbow," if that was its proper name, and the audience burst into applause. Vols stood and applauded loudly, others standing to applaud as well. The pianist stood and applauded for her too. And Ephraim Vols smiled. The girl actually seemed to be blushing.

Where, these days, did one find a girl who did that?

A waiter was trying to pass and Vols pulled a bill from his pocket. "Please ask the young lady if she'd be good enough to join me for a drink, would you?"

"Certainly, sir."

Vols sat down and remembered his cigarette. The pianist had taken a break as well and Vols watched as the pretty girl was stopped by the waiter. The waiter gestured toward Vols's table. The girl and the pianist exchanged a hurried remark and then both of them started toward his table. Perhaps they were an item at that.

Vols stood as they neared. "I must congratulate you, Miss Hall. You have such a beautiful voice. Of course my invitation for a drink is extended to your accompanist as well. Mr. Cross, is it?"

"Hi," Cross said, extending his hand. There was strength in the hand, Vols thought absently. From playing the piano with such vigor, perhaps.

"Please. Join me. Both of you. I'm traveling alone and there's a certain melancholy the first night at sea."

He watched the girl as she looked at the man. The man's eyes seemed to shrug. "If Miss Hall's willing, I'd be happy to," the pianist answered.

"Bravo! Please. Sit down. Order whatever you'd like."

Vols hailed a waiter and the girl ordered a gin and tonic, the man a Michelob, an American beer. The man lit a cigarette. Vols lit a fresh one. "Have you two been working together long? That's a stupid question. You work together so well, the answer is obvious."

The girl laughed. The man exhaled smoke. "We just met this morning. Abe's the replacement for the pianist who usually worked on the *Empress*, and when the pianist left, the singer left. I was returning home and I was asked to sing my way across."

"Well, dash! That's amazing. You must have a natural musical affinity."

"Maybe we do," she answered.

"You, Mr. Cross. I can imagine how it must be to capture all the nuances of a song in the way Miss Hall works. You must be a true musical genius."

"My mother, then my aunt, they made me study piano. So I guess I've been at it long enough to get the hang of it. Thanks."

"I should be thanking you—both of you—for such wonderful music. I know where I'll be spending all my evenings while aboard!"

The drinks arrived. Abe Cross. There was something in the name that reminded Vols of something, something he'd read or been told about. It wasn't something official, work related, or he would have remembered it easily. His memory worked that way. "Mr. Cross. I know this is beastly rude, but your name. I know I've heard it somewhere before."

"Could be. Small world sometimes."

"Cross—something struck me strange about it—I've got it. My word."

"The airline hijacking, right?"

The girl looked at Cross, startlement in her eyes.

Vols waded in. He didn't know why. "He's not a hijacker, my dear. He was a victim. The only survivor, if I recall."

"You recall okay," Cross said, taking a sip of his beer. "But that's water under the bridge."

"What happened?" Jennifer Hall asked.

Cross looked uncomfortable. Again, Vols waded in. "It was a terrorist thing, if I remember correctly. Nasty business. And painful to talk about too, I'd think. Forgive me for mentioning it. I had no desire to bring up unpleasant memories. My job requires a lot of memory work and it sometimes filters over into my private life."

He'd given Cross a ball to run with. Cross took it. "What do you do? I mean, you know what we do." Cross smiled.

"Yes. I suppose that's only fair, isn't it? I'm a journalist of sorts." He was using the old cover with the new identity because there hadn't been time to construct a new cover. "I'm terrible! I forgot to introduce myself. I'd say I really did need this holiday." He laughed, the girl singer and the pianist laughing too, the tension easing a little because of his faux pas. "I'm Andrew Comstock. And I am a journalist. Technical writer, really. If you'll keep it under your hat—the attention would keep me from getting my work done—I'm engaged in a piece on ocean technology and this is a bit of a working holiday. I'm catching a flavor for the assignment and·getting some information on how ocean-going liners are run these days. Before I print anything, of course, I'll ask the line's permission."

"Sounds cool," Cross observed.

"Are you going all the way to Japan, Mr. Comstock?" Jennifer Hall asked over her glass.

"No, don't I wish, though," Vols answered. "As a matter of fact, I booked passage to San Francisco only. I couldn't pass up the Panama Canal and all that." He extinguished his cigarette. "I have a capital idea. And I know you'll tell me if I'm overstepping my bounds here, but I find myself famished. Would you both care to join me for a bite to eat. This was your last show."

"I am hungry."Jennifer Hall smiled, looking up at Abe Cross.

"There's a method to my madness, I'll confess. I love the company of a pretty girl and, if memory serves again, Mr. Cross, you were some sort of officer in the United States Navy, weren't you?"

"Some sort," Cross said, sipping at his beer again.

"Mind if I pump you a few moments for some technical jargon and what-have-you? Make my job terribly easier. Really it would."

Cross hesitated a moment. "All right. I could use a sandwich or something."

"Outstanding, as you Americans say."

"Yeah. We say that all the time."

"I'll signal the waiter."

Vols had remembered something else during the course of the conversation, the reason he'd remembered the hijacking incident in the first place. The solitary man to have gotten away was later revealed to have been a SEAL, the American equivalent of his own country's naval Spetznas.

Was the replacement of the ship's pianist just a coincidence? Or was this Cross fellow here for a purpose? "Ahh. We'd like three menus, please—but just to read." The girl laughed, but the pianist—Cross—didn't laugh at all.

Chapter Thirteen

Lewis Babcock threw the brass doors of the Dirksen Federal Building open, the pre-trial hearing dismissed, all charges dropped against Ernie Hayes. The icy wind stabbed sharply at him through his overcoat. But, for some reason, it didn't bother him as much as it had on the way in, despite the fact that someone overheard in the corridor outside the courtroom had been talking about the temperature having dropped outside and the wind being higher.

Darwin Hughes was standing on the corner, having left the hearing room as soon as the judge had announced dismissal of all charges, Babcock having seen him go but unable to join him, Thelma hugging him so hard. Babcock quickened his pace so he could join Hughes. Thelma had said, "Please. If he's leaving or something, give him the biggest hug for me."

"If you're the Lone Ranger, I guess that makes me Tonto," Babcock said over the wind, Hughes turning around. "Thelma told me to give you a big hug, but I don't feel like being arrested on a morals charge."

"You're in better spirits, Lewis."

"I'm in better spirits. I didn't think it was going to work that well, if at all. We even got that stuff disconnected without the hotel being any the wiser."

Hughes smiled. "Their carpet will probably start rolling up a little one of these days soon and then they'll find those switches. But, we'll be long gone. I'll make a donation to charity in their name."

"I think you already did. I would never have thought of that in a million years."

"Same idea, though. You would have toughed it out and had to go after the cocaine. I just eliminated a few steps."

"It was good working with you again, Mr. Hughes."

"I'd like you to keep working with me, Lewis. A lot of people need help. Like your friends Ernie and Thelma. Only in circumstances even more desperate. We both know that. This General Argus has given us the opportunity to change things a little. There'll be a lot of heartaches in it, Lewis. Jobs we can't take because there isn't a solution, jobs we may take and screw up, lives lost. But I really believe we can accomplish something. Otherwise, I wouldn't have considered it."

"They'd track us down, Mr. Hughes. We were lucky the first time—all of us except Feinberg. They never got our faces. We start doing this on a regular basis, the inevitability of them learning our identities is unquestionable."

"That can be fixed, too, Lewis. The question is"—and Hughes smiled that big smile of his that deepened the lines already etched there, made his eyes light up—"are we interested in trying it all again? It's a great sacrifice. There's no denying that. But how many men are given the opportunity to really put things right?"

"You really think we could? I mean, really have any effect?"

"I really think we could, Lewis. We did already."

Lewis Babcock told himself, Hughes is way into his fifties, can't keep doing this forever. Probably the team would only have a few missions and—if any of them made it through alive— disband. And maybe Hughes was right. He usually was.

Babcock pulled the glove from his right hand, feeling his flesh instantly start to tingle with the cold, extending his hand to Hughes. Hughes pulled off his right glove and took Babcock's hand. "God help us, it's a deal," Babcock told him.

"Yes," Hughes said almost like a groan. "God help us indeed."

Chapter Fourteen

It was the first night after passing through the Straits of Gibralter and the tour director had organized what she called a Colossus of Rhodes party, apparently a regular event on the cruise because all the barmaids in the lounge were wearing little things that looked like mini-skirted togas and there were plastic Romanesque columns on either side of the stage. "Do you guys know any songs that would fit in?"she had asked in her sweetly sincere manner, her blonde curls tossing as she battled her eyes and thrust her hands into her skirt pockets meaningfully.

"Gee, I dunno," Cross said.

" 'Three Coins in the Fountain'?"

"That's a great idea, Jenny."

"I can play that. Got a nice arrangement of it," Cross volunteered.

"When Lenny was playing for us, he used to do this. And I hope you will," the woman began earnestly.

"He used to do what?" Cross countered suspiciously.

"We have this toga costume and—"

Jenny Hall laughed. "I bet you've got pretty knees."

"You'll never find out that way," Cross told her, smiling. Then he looked at the tour director. "Felicity. I like wearing Levi's. But I haven't worn Levi's since the *Empress* sailed because I know you guys have a class image you've gotta keep up. And I can dig that. I show up every night wearing a tux. Don't hear me complaining. Tonight I'm wearing a tux, too. Either that or Levi's. No toga."

"Okay, already, if you feel that strongly about it."

"I have this kinda off-the-shoulder thing," Jenny said almost too quickly, as if she were trying to avoid a fight. As she

92

described the dress to the tour director, she did funny little things with her hands across her body, designed apparently to show where the dress did this and that.

"Oh, that's wonderful. You'll look heavenly in it," Felicity had said. She'd blown them both a kiss—it was a habit with her—and left them to rehearse.

They'd concocted arrangements for a couple of other songs that might fit in and Cross had tried his arrangement of the theme from *Ben Hur*, something he hadn't played in a while but liked and used to throw in on some of his movie-tune medleys.

And then he'd flat out asked her. "Tonight. After we're through. Will you sleep with me? I mean, if we can avoid Andrew Comstock?"

She hadn't answered.

"I beg real good," he had said.

Jenny Hall laughed. Her voice became businesslike and clinical and at once funny, her eyes sparkling. "Why do you want to sleep with me?"

Cross started ticking off reasons. "You're the prettiest girl in the world, I listen to your voice and it sends chills up my spine, I see you come on stage and I start getting a hard-on, you're fun to be with, a good listener, intelligent, thoughtful and by the time we hit New York, I'll probably ask you to marry me. You want more reasons?"

"That's enough."

"Got a date, then?"

"Yeah." She'd smiled.

Cross had bought her a Coke and taken her back to her cabin. She napped in the afternoons for an hour or so to relax before getting herself ready for a performance. He wished they could nap together, but neither of them would be any better slept for it. He'd gone to his own cabin, stripped and plopped down across the bed, trying to sleep. That hadn't worked. He got up, redressed and started walking the *Empress* from stem to stern. The captain buttonholed him and offered to buy him a cup of coffee. Cross settled for orange juice.

"I'll come right to the point. I've been hearing really great things about you, Mr. Cross. And Miss Hall as well. I don't usually get involved with this stuff. I let the tour director take care of it—"

"Look, Captain. No disrespect, but I don't care what Felicity wants. I'm not wearin' some damn toga."

''Toga? Oh, the Colossus of Rhodes party tonight. Naw. She used to be able to pull that crap with Lenny Brooks, but then he was afraid of losing his job and I somehow get the feeling you're not afraid of much of anything. No, I wasn't about to ride your ass over some silly thing like that. I just wanted to know if you'd like the job playing piano on the *Empress* on a permanent basis? I mean, you've got naval experience. It could lead to something better. A lot better. You know what some of my ship's officers get paid?''

''No idea.''

''A lot, Mr. Cross. And this is a growing company. Solid future. Think about it for a while. I'd like to have you aboard with me.''

''That's a great compliment, sir. Thank you. And I will think about it.''

They'd talked Navy stuff for another twenty minutes and then the captain's beeper had gone off and he was needed someplace else. But he picked up the tab for the coffee and orange juice.

Cross had returned to his cabin, tried again to sleep. He'd all but asked Jenny Hall to marry him and been offered a steady job. It was enough to keep any man awake. Finally, he'd gotten up, shaved again, showered and all the rest, then gotten dressed.

He'd arranged to meet Jenny for dinner in the Crow's Nest restaurant and when he saw her there, already waiting, she looked lovely. The dress she wore was just slightly off-white, more than slightly off the shoulder, at once seductive and demure, like something a Greek goddess would have worn. But as he touched her shoulder when he passed her to sit down, the touch was warm.

Over dinner, small talk, neither of them mentioning what had passed between them earlier. And then it was time for Cross to start playing piano and she stayed behind to finish her drink.

It was harder playing tonight than it had ever been, his mind elsewhere and his concentration forced. And then it was time for the first show and he almost missed a segue just thinking about her.

They sat together and talked about everything and nothing between sets for him, and then he was on again. Then she performed again and he started seriously wondering if he'd make it through the third performance without dragging her down onto the stage and ripping her dress off.

He forced his mind to focus on other things as his fingers

moved across the eighty-eight. He had heard nothing at all from Hughes or Babcock after the surgical strike into Iran. Cross wondered if they'd gotten back together to do something else insane, but doubted that. Hughes was probably off training the SAS or the SEALs to be tougher or something. And Babcock. Babcock had been a character. Health nut, top physical shape, "Mr. Culture." But a good guy. He was probably living with some gorgeous black girl and taking up the law practice he'd never had time for. If he ever did see Babcock again, he had to try him at chess at least once more. The man was sharp.

His attention drifted and he started studying the newest variation of the audience. One face from the third-show crowd was missing—Andrew Comstock. "Thank you, God," he murmured. Comstock and his late suppers and his insatiable desire for information were enough to drive him—Cross—crazy. And Cross hadn't missed the way Comstock looked at Jenny. Which proved Comstock was just as normal as the next man.

Cross looked at his watch.

It was time. He did the intro and took the microphone and spoke into it. "Ladies and gentlemen. The *Empress Britannia* is proud to present someone who sings as good as she looks . . ." It was not the standard introduction, but he'd felt like saying it. "Direct from her triumphant tour of Europe, the incomparable Miss Jennifer Hall!" He put down the microphone and started applauding, then realized embarrassedly that he'd forgotten to shut off the thing and his clapping must have sounded like thunder claps to the lounge crowd. And then she was on stage.

Jenny blew him a kiss and smiled as she took the microphone and he started playing. But she signaled him not to. He stopped. "Ladies and gentlemen. I just had to say this. This man—this man right here, Abe Cross. He's gotta be the best pianist I ever worked with. And a wonderful guy. And not bad-looking himself. Let's give him a big round of applause, please!" And she put the microphone under her arm and turned toward him and started applauding. He did what he was supposed to do, stood up and took a short bow and then sat down and began playing her first song, "What's New?"

What was new was that she loved him back. . . .

They chose his cabin for the night. Andrew Comstock had, mercifully, never shown.

Cross turned on the light and shut the door behind him. He'd straightened up a little before his shower and, with the help of the daily maid service, it didn't look bad. "Shouldn't we both sit down and run a medical and sexual history on each other?" she whispered as he took her in his arms.

"I'm okay if you're okay."

"Yeah. I'm okay. Now that you're holding me. I really did think you were never going to ask."

"I didn't know what you'd answer. Funny thing if you're a guy is, well, you want her to say yes, but not too easily. And then you're ticked off if she says no. You can't win."

"Who wins, then? The woman, you think?"

"Nobody wins that way." He drew her closer to him, his fingers touching at her hair, at her cheek, drifting down across her shoulders. "What do you do to yourself? Your skin's so soft." He kissed her shoulder. "And it tastes so good, too."

Her hands touched at his face and he lowered his face to hers and touched her mouth with his, his hands hard against her back and moving down to her rear end, her hands massaging his face and neck and starting to tug at his jacket as he kept kissing her.

As he moved his hands again, his left hand catching at the fabric of her dress to pull it up, she slipped away from him and backed across the room a little. "There's so much you should know about me."

"I know. You're secretly left-handed. I already guessed that. If you tell me you're just the result of a cunning sex-change operation, I hope you know I'll kill myself."

"I'm not left-handed. And I am real. And if you killed yourself, I think I'd do the same thing. I love you."

He walked toward her, slipping out of his jacket and throwing it on the chair. "It'll get all wrinkled."

"I've got two more."

"You really—"

"Yeah. I wanna marry you. I can always go get the captain."

"He's asleep."

"Tomorrow?"

"Maybe."

"Why only maybe?"

"Maybe I won't be any good in bed." She smiled.

"Somehow, I don't think that'll be a problem."

" I don't think it will be either." Her hands moved behind her to unzip, and his arms closed around her and he held her hands there and kissed her hard on the mouth. Then his left hand tugged the zipper down. She'd already gotten the little hook and eye thing open. She stepped back from him and shrugged her shoulders and the dress fell. He guessed it was one of those things with a built-in bra, because she wore none, the nipples of her pretty breasts hardening as the palms of his hands frictioned against them. The dress caught at her hips for the briefest second, and she moved her hips and the dress fell the rest of the way. There had been an ankle-length white silk slip under it and she hooked her thumbs in the waist of it and pushed it down. Nothing but panties on, she pressed herself close against him, her hands at his tie, undoing it.

"I thought this looked rumpled enough to be real."

"I'm glad I didn't have my pants off when you said that."

The tie was opened and she started working at his shirt buttons. He had never liked studs. His hands cupped her breasts as she opened his shirt, her mouth touching at his chest, her fingers knotting in the hair there. He drew her closer to him, arching her back, kissing her neck, then moving his mouth down, touching at her nipples.

She pulled back again. "Take them off me, please." He dropped to his knees and pulled her panties down and her arms closed around him, drawing his head close against her abdomen. "I do love you," she whispered.

He stood up. She still had stockings on, the kind that magically defied gravity and stayed up on the thighs. He'd get to them. Cross swept her up in his arms. She kicked her high heels off and he carried her over to the bed. She was a tall girl and, regardless of how easy it looked when Clark Gable had carried Vivien Leigh up the staircase, carrying a full-grown woman in your arms was never that easy. But he put her down on the bed, without showing her that she'd been anything but light as a feather, then started out of his clothes. Another thing in movies was that guys never wore socks or underpants when they had to dress or undress in a hurry, and though Cross hadn't thought about it that much, he'd never thought he looked his romantic best struggling his socks off.

He threw the rest of his things on the chair and picked up her dress and laid it across the back of the chair.

"Thank you," she told him.

"I was always polite. Even as a kid." Cross found the light switch and flicked it off, noticing she was watching him intently.

"You can see where they got the term horny," Jenny whispered, giggling a little, as the lights went out.

He got into bed beside her and took care of the stockings, throwing them away, then slipped between her thighs. "Do it now," she whispered. "There's a lot of night left to do it again."

"All right," and Cross felt her hands guiding him as he kissed her.

Chapter Fifteen

Most of his time in the Navy hadn't been spent aboard ship, but he'd spent enough time to know when a vessel the size of the *Empress* stopped. The *Empress* had stopped.

Abe Cross, his right arm asleep under her, slipped his arm from around her shoulders, her head from his chest, and sat up, massaging his arm to get the feeling back. With the porthole curtains closed and because of the constant westward movement of the vessel, he had no real circadian rhythm sense of what time it was. He looked at the luminous black face of the Rolex Sea Dweller on his left wrist and squinted his eyes to get in focus. It was 4:00 A.M.

Unless it had been a faster trip to New York City than anyone had anticipated, there was trouble.

Cross swung his legs over the side of the bed, realized he had to urinate badly, and stood up.

He stumbled across the cabin to the head and hit the light switch. There was no light. He urinated anyway, didn't bother flushing and left. He found the chest of drawers and opened the top drawer, shuffling around inside until he found the two items he wanted, a pocket-sized mini-Maglite and the larger, three D-cell version. He turned on neither but instead walked to the bed.

Cross sat on the edge. "Jenny. Wake up. Do it now. Wake up, darling."

"Ohh, that sounds nice—'darlin.' " She rolled over. He kissed her eyelids and she opened her eyes. "What time—"

"It's about four A.M. The *Empress* is stopped and there's no electrical power. With these cabins so soundproofed, I don't know what's going on. You get dressed in something. I've got a

99

pair of sweat pants and a hooded sweatshirt you can get by with. The pants have a cord you can tighten to adjust the waist. Might look silly with your high-heeled shoes, but a lot more practical than your dress in case there's something up. Now hurry. Will you need a flashlight to find the head?''

''No, no, what—''

''I don't know what's wrong. Go to the bathroom and I'll find your underpants for you and get that sweatsuit. And you were wonderful.''

''So were you,'' and she hugged her arms around him tightly for a second, then slipped out from under the sheet, his eyes accustomed to the darkness now, her slender, long-legged body looking like a wraith moving through the darkness.

He cupped his hand around the head of the smaller flashlight until he had the beam focused for pinpoint use and then searched the floor for her underpants, found them and her stockings too in case she wanted them, then put them on the bed. He went to the closet. He took down the sweat pants and hooded sweatshirt and put them on the bed for her as well. He went to the dresser again and found himself a pair of underpants and skinned into them. He took two pairs of socks, put one pair on the bed for her and sat down, pulling on the other pair. ''Abe?''

''I've got your things for you—you're probably better off with a pair of my socks. They're on the bed,'' Cross told her, patting her fanny as he crossed the cabin again to the closet. He found a pair of Levi's and pulled them on. His track shoes. He stuffed his feet into them, telling himself he'd worry about tying them later. A black knit shirt. He couldn't tell in the dark, except that he owned no other color at the moment.

He pulled it on over his head and went back to the dresser. He took out the one-and-three-quarter-inch Safariland Garrison strap. It had the standard Garrison buckle that could be used in conjunction with the belt as a flail if needed. He started threading it through his belt loops.

There was time now, Jenny still dressing, so he dropped to one knee and tied a shoe, switched knees and tied the other one.

And then there was a knock at the door.

''Probably somebody from the crew. But hide on the other side of the bed, just in case,'' Cross ordered.

''All right, what's—''

''I don't know.'' He went to the door, took off the chain— they didn't hold against even a moderately powerful person who knew how to use his body weight anyway—and as he opened the door, he shifted the larger aircraft aluminum bodied flashlight into his right hand, ready to use it like a nightstick.

There were panic lights on in the corridor, the kind that ran off batteries, and he could see clearly the face of the man just outside the doorway. "Mr. Cross. I'm afraid I lied the other evening when I said I was a journalist. I'm really with British Intelligence. Is Miss Hall with you?"

"Yes. Come in," Cross told him. It was Andrew Comstock and there was a flashlight in his right hand and a look on his face that in the grey light seemed to combine both fear and determination. "Jenny. It's Mr. Comstock," Cross announced, starting for the bed. He grabbed the blanket off it and walked back toward the door, giving it to Comstock. "Roll it up and slide it against the base of the door. It'll block light from getting out under the crack and slow up anyone trying to force the door. Is that part of the problem?"

Comstock—or whoever he was—took the blanket and started stuffing it against the bottom of the cabin door. "That is part of the problem. Are you with CIA, Mr. Cross? I rather suspected you might be."

"Why?" It was Jenny Hall, coming around the bed, who asked the question.

"There's at least one American agent aboard this vessel whom I know of. That's why I was sent. I was in the area and your country's people asked my country's people to help out, NATO or something. All I know is the chap's got something stolen from the Russians. On my end, we weren't told if the Americans were sending in another agent to shepherd this chap themselves. I was just ordered to hang around and see if any help needed to be rendered. And now the *Empress* has been stopped. Some sort of terrorist group. Could be Russian-inspired. They have their dirty fingers in a lot of pies these days. There!" And he stood up, the blanket wedged against the bottom of the door fully. Cross turned on the big Maglite.

"Well, you secret agent guys always have guns and stuff in your exploding attache cases, right?"

"I was just about to ask you the same, actually," Comstock smiled. "Could you avert the light a smidge?"

Cross moved the flashlight's beam downward.

"Terrorists?" Jenny Hall said, incredulous sounding.

"I couldn't sleep and I pulled on these clothes and went for a turn around the deck. Hadn't felt myself all evening. Why I missed your performance, actually. And suddenly I heard some commotion up on the bridge and then searchlights came on going over the water and there was this yacht lying just off the port bow. I heard what sounded like a few silenced shots from the bridge and then I saw some of the people I'd seen the last few days about the ship. A couple of crewspeople and a few passengers and God knows who else. But they had guns and two of them were moving the captain between them and they had guns pressed against him and his hands looked bound behind him and there was a black sack over his head."

"Aww, shit," Cross snarled. "Sorry for using the 's' word, Jenny." He sat on the chair, feeling Jenny's dress starting to slip off the back of the chair, catching it. She was beside him, took the dress, folded her arms across her abdomen, hugging it to her. "How many?"

At least a dozen came up over the side from the yacht. Carrying things that looked like explosives."

"Why did you come here?" Jenny asked.

"I remembered a bit more about Mr. Cross than I let on. The articles that appeared following that airline hijacking. They said the lone survivor, Lieutenant Cross, was suspected of being a Navy SEAL. Frankly, the whole story about being the substitute piano player smelled a bit. So, I put two and two together and assumed Mr. Cross was the CIA chap."

"I'm not," Cross told him.

"Damn," Comstock hissed.

"There's a gun hidden in my cabin, if we can get to it. And we have to find the man traveling as Alvin Leeds."

Abe Cross just looked at Jenny Hall. "What?"

"It wasn't the piano player thing that was contrived. It was the singer story. Doris Knight was asked to quit so I could take her place."

Abe Cross just closed his eyes for a moment.

Chapter Sixteen

The Englishman seemed to know his stuff; Cross gave this Andrew Comstock devil his due. "They were speaking English, if you call it that. I made them as being Irish. And that could be bad. They're about as fond of we British as the Mid-East terrorists are of Jews. And there're a goodly number of British subjects aboard this vessel."

"What you said about the Russians," Cross whispered as the three of them waited at the L of the corridor.

"Russians? Yes?"

"If this CIA guy you mentioned has something the Russians wanted, could they have used the Irish terrorists to get it? I mean, hide behind a terrorist raid?"

"Good point, really, Mr. Cross. But, somehow, I have a gut feeling they didn't in this case. I think we're living through the nightmare of coincidence."

"I agree," Jenny Hall added.

Cross peered round the corner and saw nothing. Jenny's cabin was in that direction, about half the length of the corridor down. "Run for it?"

"Agreed." Comstock nodded.

Cross took Jenny's hand and pulled her with him, breaking into a dead run. He'd made certain that she took her key out of the little beaded bag she'd used as a purse so there'd be no fumbling in front of the cabin door.

They kept running, Cross looking back, Comstock right behind them, running well. "Here! Here it is!" Jenny announced to Cross unnecessarily. She shoved her key into his hand and he thrust the key into the lock, opened it, shoved her inside and waited for Comstock, then pulled the door closed after them.

Cross shone the larger of his two lights low across the floor. Her portholes weren't curtained. "Get those curtains closed," Cross ordered. Jenny took one, Comstock the other. Then Jenny went to the closet, using the mini-Maglite, Comstock packing the bedspread along the crack between the cabin door and floor.

"I'll be just a second. Gotta change and get my gun."

"Got any other weapons?" Cross asked. He knew of one, her body, and he kept putting down the urge to curse her out or hit her or kiss her. The part about not knowing which was the hardest part.

"I've got a small knife, too. I was supposed to just be around here if the Russians tried anything, never even contact our man unless they did. And he was never told I'd be here, just that this was the ship to take."

"Wise move," Cross remarked.

"Tell me, Miss Hall," Comstock began. "Is Leeds the chap's real name? I was never told, but assumed it was probably false?"

"I think it is," she answered from half inside the closet, using the darkness like a screen to dress behind, Cross imagined. "I was never given another name. I've been working in Europe for the past eight months and I'm a little out of touch with what's going on back at Langley."

"Your singing's a cover, then," Cross started rather than asked. "Kind of like Bob Culp and Bill Cosby used to do on television except you don't play tennis. Right?"

"I guess. That's a little before my time, but I've caught some of the reruns. Funny show. Okay. I'm set."

She emerged from the closet, his sweatsuit replaced by a pair of tight-fitting jeans with too-short legs that looked as though they'd been washed a thousand times and run over by a truck—evidently brand new and just in fashion. She had put a long-sleeved pullover sweater on instead of his hooded sweatshirt. And in her hands were her weapons. The pistol was a Colt Officer's ACP .45 in stainless steel. The knife was a Cold Steel Mini-Tanto.

"Let me see the knife, unless either of you are into knives more than I am," Cross began.

She gave him the knife.

"Any spare magazines for the pistol, Miss Hall?"

"Call me Jenny, Andrew. And yes. Two spares, six rounds in each, just six in the gun. And I'm keeping it."

Cross looked up from inspecting the knife. "What the hell do you do with this?'' There were divers straps attached to each of the two belt slots, the kind that gave with movement.

"I wear it sometimes under a loose shirt, all right?''

"Is Jenny Hall your real name?''

"Yes. And I really do love you,'' she told him matter-of-factly. "And I tried to tell you, well, before. But you didn't want to talk.''

He shook his head. "I know. Don't remind me. And I meant what I asked you, before, too. All right!?'' He started taking the diving straps off the sheath to pocket them. He had no way of strapping the knife to his leg or his arm, but it would fit nicely inside the trouser band of his Levi's against his skin.

"I'm sorry I interrupted you two,'' Comstock said suddenly. "I'd kept trying to tell myself you weren't an item. Oh well,'' Comstock exhaled. "Perhaps I'll catch the next pretty girl that comes along.''

Jenny leaned up and kissed Comstock on the cheek. "Sorry, you being an ally and everything.'' She laughed. And then her voice was perfectly serious. "Whatever this thing is Alvin Leeds is carrying, it's important and sensitive. We have to find him and quickly before the terrorists have the ship totally under control.''

Cross looked at his watch. "If they don't by now, they will soon enough. They've had plenty of time to do it. What's this Leeds look like?''

"Black chap about your height, and American of course; all I was told,'' Comstock volunteered.

"I memorized his face from some photographs,'' Jenny Hall announced. "But that doesn't do you guys any good. So, we all stick together.''

"Are you good with that pistol, Jenny?'' Comstock asked. "Nothing implied, of course, but I'm on the service pistol team and I've used a gun a time or two before for this sort of work.''

Cross looked at him. "I know. You're in the 'double O' section and you have a license to—''

Comstock cut him off with a laugh. "Wish we had half the budget the motion-picture johnnies have. We might be able to pull off some of that spectacular derring-do ourselves.''

"I'll keep the gun, thank you, Andrew. I've—ahh—I know Abe better than you. No offense. I mean, all we have to say you are who you say you are is that you say you are.''

Cross just looked at her, shaking his head. "Don't try saying that again.''

"Agreed," Comstock told them. "And good procedure, as well. Well then, madame? What's next?"

"Abe, any ideas?" She looked at him, her face pretty in the shadows from the flashlight he held.

"Just find the guy. If we meet any bad guys, try for their weapons if we have to brace 'em. But once we do find him, the only way off this tub is that yacht Comstock mentioned," and he nodded toward the self-proclaimed British agent. "They gotta have a radio. You can call in some help. If these guys are Irish, they'll have taken the *Empress* to put some sort of squeeze on the British. Which means they won't be blowing up the ship right away. Once we have Leeds, you and Leeds," he said to Jenny, "can get away in the yacht and get help or at least get that whatever it is away to safe hands. And," and he turned to look at Comstock, "you and I can stay behind to work from inside against the terrs. If we get that far."

"You leave with me," Jenny Hall said adamantly.

"No. I walked out on one of these parties once, and they killed everybody they held hostage. I'm never doing that again," Cross told her.

Her voice was unlike he had ever heard it. "Now I remember, too."

The memories washed through him in an instant, memories he used to see every time he closed his eyes. The Islamic Funda-mentalist terrorists taking over the aircraft, diverting it, brutaliz-ing the Jewish passengers and Arabs sympathetic to Western democracy. He had tried to help. They had found his United States Armed Forces I.D. card, then started beating him to death. He'd made a break for it, killing some of them, pursued, nearly killed again, escaped. By the time he had reached friendly terri-tory, everyone he'd left aboard the aircraft had been murdered. A pregnant girl he had gotten to know a little before everything went bad—Darwin Hughes's daughter-in-law—had been among the ones killed. Hughes's son, her husband, had killed himself in his despair. And Cross had turned to alcohol to try to forget it all when they had told him that there was no way to go after the terrorists, nothing that could be done to get justice for the vic-tims. Out of the gutter of his own despair, Darwin Hughes had called him, recruited Lewis Babcock, a boy named Feinberg and himself to strike at Iran's central training headquarters in the Elburz Mountains along the Soviet border. Feinberg had given his life. The mission had come off. And it was over as quickly as it had begun. And Abe Cross had thought it was out of his life, all of it.

But it was back again. These Irish terrorists were just like any others. Their cause was so glorious and so special and noble that they had a license to bomb department stores, shoot up school buses, kill women and children and old people. And it was all for the good of the people, whoever they were.

Abe Cross looked at Jenny, then Andrew Comstock. "Let's do it." And he started for the door, the little knife in his palm.

Chapter Seventeen

With several thousand members of the Devil's Princes at large on the Chicago streets and likely to remain so even though their leaders were all in custody and their economic base was destroyed, Darwin Hughes had thought it the better part of valor to avoid spending another night in the Windy City. And he regretted that. The Art Institute of Chicago was one of the finest museums of its type in the free world, the Lake Front, even in winter, a thing of beauty. The restaurants, the theaters. But, foregoing all of that, he had booked out to Athens, Georgia, via Charlotte, North Carolina. And Lewis Babcock had elected to spend a few days with him before settling out his personal affairs long enough to get up to New York and help convince Cross to join the team again once the *Empress Britannia* had arrived in New York.

Hughes had found himself grateful for the company, his mountain retreat a lonely place at times. He found it good to run against someone again, especially a superb athlete such as Babcock, good to shoot against someone, especially a marksman such as Babcock. And Darwin Hughes realized there was a great deal he had missed—the action.

Hughes was sitting on his porch, the weather in the mountains with rare exception perpetually comfortable. Babcock had just come back from a session on the range with the sniper rifle, the black synthetic stocked Steyr-Mannlicher SSG .308 held in the crook of his arm like a field shotgunner might carry his smooth-bore. Babcock stood at the base of the twenty-three steps. "You know, Mr. Hughes, by the end of the day, these steps get a bit ridiculous."

"I'll have the porch lowered, Lewis. Remind me in case I forget, will you? Or would you prefer the ground raised, instead?"

Babcock shook his head and started up the steps. The telephone rang, Hughes catching up his glass of tea, the ice clinking as he moved quickly, attempting to outrace the answering machine. He caught the phone just before the machine would have clicked on. ''Hello.''

''Hughes. This is Argus. Have you been watching television?''

''Quit the military, have you, and gone to work as a Nielsen polster?''

''Very funny. I assume you haven't. Turn it on. I'll wait.''

''I have a satellite dish. Any particular station?''

''Any of the networks.''

Hughes set down the phone, saw Babcock entering the great room and told him, ''General Argus is on the telephone. Evidently something's happening.''

''I thought we weren't committed until we talked with Abe Cross?''

''We're not,'' Hughes answered. He turned the power on and tuned to the nearest network channel. He recognized the face of the newscaster.

''. . . or approximately four A.M. Greenwich Mean Time, only a little more than an hour ago. The *Empress Britannia*, flagship of her line, has been described by many as the most luxurious of the great ocean-going vessels. Although there has been no formal list of demands from the terrorists who identify themselves as, I quote, 'champions of Northern Ireland liberty,' informed sources in London, speaking on condition of anonymity, say they believe the hijackers are members of an outlawed wing of the IRA with a record of violence to their credit. This may include the recent bombing in Belfast of a police barracks which has claimed one hundred and twenty-three lives.

''For those of you who may have joined us late, the *Empress Britannia*, one of the finest of the—'' Hughes cut off the television.

''Cross is on board,'' Babcock said quietly.

''Indeed.'' Hughes nodded, going back to the telephone. He picked up the receiver and said to Argus, ''I assume that's not all, what they're saying on the television. Otherwise you wouldn't have called. It sounds more like something the British would be involved with.''

''No. It isn't all there is. I'm sending a chopper for you and Mr. Babcock. I can fill you both in then. Any problems with that?''

''None. Are we moving out directly or coming back?''

"Directly would be best, for a number of reasons."

"How soon before the chopper gets here?"

"About—hang on—about another thirty minutes."

"If you're in touch with the pilot, tell him to watch out for the air currents up here. They're a bit tricky at times. Should we bring things we might need?"

"It won't be necessary. We have all that's needed."

"Splendid. Thirty minutes." Hughes hung up and looked at Babcock. "I doubt they're thinking of dispatching us just to rescue Abe Cross."

"We haven't trained."

"Well, let's hope our Irish friends haven't either then, shall we?" Hughes looked at his watch. There was a great deal to do and very little time to do it. "Open the safe and get rid of the rifle and scour up the other guns."

Chapter Eighteen

Seamus O'Fallon stood up and stretched, picked up his Uzi submachine gun and started down from the bridge of the *Empress*. Only three passengers and one crewman remained unaccounted for, only one of the four traveling on a British passport. The rest of the British subjects he had had assembled in the main lounge. He stopped on what the diagram he had memorized—kindly provided by a travel agent—had called the Beach Deck. There, on their knees, were the captain and his senior officers, wrists cuffed behind them, ears plugged with cotton and heavy black velvet bags pulled over their heads, the drawstrings of the bags pulled tight enough to make it uncomfortable but not so tight as to choke them, then tied at the backs of the necks.

He stood in front of them, looking toward the east. Soon the sun would be rising and he didn't want to miss that. The British passengers he had cowering in the lounge could wait for him. He'd waited for the British all his life. Paddy was walking up toward him, playing with one of his switchblade knives as usual. "Seamus. There's still nothin' at all on where the missin' crewman and the three missing passengers have gotten themselves. Should I start executin' hostages? Might make them change their minds about playin' hide and seek."

"Not yet, Paddy. We might be needin' all the hostages we can muster once they start in to threatenin' us with their bloody SAS bastards. A damned Brit writer, a piano player and his songbird and some negro engine wiper ain't gonna do much."

Soon it would be time for the sunrise. A headache had started, but the pills had put it to the back of his brain and he could control it there. It was only when it came at the front of his brain and the blood cast was over his eyes that it wasn't controllable at all. . . .

Cross had reasoned that the boat deck would be the place to start for two reasons. There were no elevators running, of course, because there was still no electrical power. So, they had worked their way up cautiously along one of the stairwells. It was the logical place for two reasons that formed into one: It was on the boat deck along the portside where the trap shooting was conducted in the mornings and afternoons, and where the shotguns and ammunition used were stored; if this Alvin Leeds were a clever man and wasn't armed, it would have been the first place he'd gone; and, by Cross, Jenny and the Englishman Comstock going there, there was a slim chance of encountering Leeds and a better chance (not much better, but a little) that just maybe the terrorists hadn't thought of the armory yet and weapons might still be available.

A problem standing on two legs presented itself just forward of the stairwell as Cross peered out, then quickly tucked back. "There's a guard. He's got an assault rifle. Looks like an AK."

"Damn the luck!" Comstock murmured.

"Maybe not," Cross said after a moment. "An assault rifle is gonna be a lot better than a bunch of long-tubed scatterguns and some trap loads. And if he's right here, maybe he's guarding the armory because they haven't emptied it yet."

"A regular Pollyanna, aren't you?" Comstock observed.

Cross looked at Jenny Hall. "Well? Want me to try for him?"

"You could get yourself killed, Abe," she told him, her voice just as warm sounding in a whisper.

"That means you won't tell me to, but it sounds like a good idea, right?"

"Take my gun," she advised.

"No. I've got what I need. Hang loose." Cross edged forward so he could peer just around the flange for the open watertight door which capped the stairwell. The man hadn't moved, his AK-47 slung across his back and not handy to instant use, smoke curling up from in front of him, the occasional smell of pipe tobacco on the air, the vessel still aimed into the wind.

Cross reached under his shirt and took the Mini-Tanto from its sheath. He moved the blade in his hand, wheeling it through his fingers to get its balance. The Magnum Tanto, vastly larger, was his favorite edged weapon. And, despite the size difference, the balance was surprisingly similar.

With the knife folded back, spine against the interior of his wrist, edge along the edge of his forearm, Abe Cross stepped fully into view—if the man turned around.

Cross started toward the man slowly, in his mind visualizing the sheet music from Chopin's "Revolutionary Etude," a complicated and beautiful piece he'd memorized as a child and still played when the lounge crowds were thin enough or drunk enough not to notice he was slipping in something classical. He had learned, years ago, that there was a sort of empathy struck between stalker and prey, and the prey would turn because he had felt something, heard nothing, seen nothing, merely felt it.

It wasn't working, his mind still being drawn toward the man he stalked, the man shifting uneasily on his feet, but not turning around yet. Cross tried visualizing a transposition into a minor key. He started moving again, just on the balls of his feet, the Mini-Tanto still against his forearm, hidden, his forearm almost limp at his side. The gap to the man with the Soviet assault rifle was less than eight feet, Cross pausing, inhaling, focusing his strength and all his concentration except for that portion of his mind mentally notating the transposition to the hand in which he held the Mini-Tanto. His fingertips were acutely aware of the variations in surface texture of the rubberized handle coating, reading it like a road map but written in Braille.

Four feet.

The man twitched uneasily.

Cross started bringing the piece up a minor third.

Two feet, his fingertips pressing more tightly against the haft of the knife.

He reached out, his left hand going quickly over the face and nose, snapping the head back at the neck as his right hand arced outward, the knife moving in his fingertips and the edge crossing from left to right, literally from beneath ear to ear, deep enough to sever any powers of speech, the body already dying as he held it, the Mini-Tanto spinning in his fingertips, driven downward like a stake into the heart of something despicably evil. And to Abe Cross, terrorist and evil incarnate were now and had been and would, he suddenly realized, always be synonymous.

He brought the body down slowly, looking from side to side, not bothering with untangling the sling from the dead arm and shoulder, merely slicing through the webbing, catching up the assault rifle, making a hasty square knot where he'd severed the sling, putting it over his shoulder and starting to drag the body back toward the stairwell in which Jenny Hall and Comstock were still hiding, he thought.

And then Comstock was beside him, taking some of the weight of the dead body, whispering hoarsely, "I think you terrified the girl, old man. Be understanding with her."

Cross whispered back, "You're the strangest man I ever met—and I don't really know how I mean that."

"Then I'll take it as flattery." They had the body beside the watertight door and boosted it up over the flange.

Cross looked at Jenny Hall's face. It was whiter than he could have imagined human skin to be, but the cheeks were red and flushed. But he gave her credit. Her hands trembling slightly as she did it, she dropped to her knees beside the body, blood still trickling from the wide crimson gash in the neck, starting to search the body for anything useful. The man wore combat boots. Cross untied the laces and started pulling them from the eyelets, the nylon cord laces useful potentially as garrotes.

"Two magazines for a Browning GP—High Power to you," Comstock announced. "Now, if we can only find the bloody gun."

"I've got it," Jenny announced. "And a magazine for the assault rifle."

"Swiss Army Knife—only a cheapie copy," Comstock noted.

Cross had the bootlaces free, feeling up the legs. There was a buldge and he used his knife—it needed cleaning anyway—to cut away the fabric. On the left calf there was an improvised fabric harness holding a Gerber MKI boot knife in place. He cut away the harness and took the black-handled knife and black leather sheath.

"Identity papers," Comstock said. "Name's McCarthy."

"Wonder if he's any relation to Charlie?" Cross asked without expecting an answer.

He didn't get one.

"Nothing else on him—but I haven't checked around his crotch. I see some kind of bump—and don't laugh. But I'm not going to," Jenny announced. "One of you guys do it. I'll keep watch through the doorway."

Cross did it, pulling down the zipper, feeling inside. He struck paydirt. There was a leech holster on a garter clip tucked under the front of the shirt just below the trouser band line, inside the

holster some sort of unrecognizable brand of .25 automatic.
"This is next to useless," Cross remarked.

"I agree. Keep it anyway."

Cross looked at him. Comstock had the Browning High Power
9mm in his right fist. It wasn't held menacingly or anything like
that, but Jenny had made a good point despite her syntax. All
they had to say Andrew Comstock was who he said he was was
that he said he was.

Abe Cross wondered if that were enough. . . .

The chopper touched down, Hughes ducking his head as he
grabbed up his two bags and ran for it, Lewis Babcock beside
him. There was only one actual weapon Hughes had packed. It
was one of the long-bladed Tantos. He was determined to give it
to Abe Cross or die trying to.

Chapter Nineteen

The armory door was locked. There were no signs of any other guards, nor was there a sign of Alvin Leeds, the man they were looking for. "What do we do about the lock? Shoot it off and let them know we're here?" Jenny Hall asked, almost rhetorically, her voice edged with frustration.

The armory door was located at the rear of the recreation equipment storage facility, Comstock on guard at the outer door overlooking the deck fore and aft with the Browning High Power expropriated from the man Cross had killed.

Jenny had exchanged her beaded evening bag for a leather purse about the size of a small saddlebag. "Got a lock-pick set in there or anything?"

"No. Do you know how to use one?"

"Not too well. I figured maybe you or Comstock could."

"Well, I don't know about him. But anyway, there's nothing to use as a pick. I'm sorry I went all pale as a ghost on you. I could feel it when it happened. Kind of sick to my stomach."

"You shouldn't have watched me kill the guy," he told her, studying the hasp and the padlock, the hasp ordinary enough and the padlock of average size, the kind requiring a key rather than a combination. "You're just a gatherer and a courier. This violent crap isn't your kinda work, right?" and he looked at her.

"I'm sorry this turned out this way. I mean, that you had to find out this way. You know?"

"I know. If we get out of this alive, you wanna pick up where we left off?"

"Do you think we can?" she asked.

"We can try," Cross told her, leaning down and kissing her lightly on the mouth. "We can try."

She smiled, leaned her head against his chest for an instant. "I wasn't making it too badly singing. I mean, things weren't working out a hundred percent the way I wanted them to, but they were going okay. And I was nearly through college and I still figured I'd make it, once I'd graduated and didn't just have to look around for jobs close enough to the university that I could make classes. Mom and Dad gave me a trip to Europe for a graduation present and I thought if I took it, maybe I could even line up some jobs in Europe. Well, I did. I spent three months singing in England and Italy and Greece, little places but they were okay. I came back home and kept at it. About a year later, this guy came to my dressing room after the last show. I thought he was just some guy on the make, that he was kidding. But it turned out he wasn't. The government wanted me to go back to Europe and make a series of pickups for them. Nothing dangerous, they told me. And it sounded like fun and a good excuse to go back to Europe. I really liked it there, you know?" He nodded. "I did that for them. A few months after I got back, they asked me to do it again, only in the Far East. So I went. When I came back, they offered me a job, telling me I could do the same thing I always did. But they'd help book the tours for me. And the salary they'd pay me would just make my singing that much more profitable. They sent me through training and everything, they said, just in case. I've been doing this for five years, full-time. It hasn't always been as easy as they said. But appearing before the public every night, you spend a lot on dresses and things, and sometimes there's a place that is really good to appear in, carries some weight, you know? And I couldn't have gotten in those places without the Company arranging the bookings. And the money helps. And anyway, men don't have a monopoly on wanting to do something for their country."

"I understand," Cross told her.

He looked at the lock again, then started moving about the storage room. Shuffleboard equipment, childrens' pool toys, clubs for playing miniature golf— "Whoa."

"What?"

"Wait a minute." He wasn't into golf at all, but knew a putter when he saw one. "I wonder how sturdy these things are? Let's see." He took a half dozen of the things out of what looked like an umbrella stand and started back to the locked door. The hasp was on the loose fitting side to begin with and the armory door was wooden, just a regular door. He reached under his shirt for the Gerber MKI boot knife. "This is short and stout enough it might work. Just don't stand anywhere near me in case some metal snaps. Get back."

Cross started wedging the blade of the Gerber into the gap between the mating of door to doorjamb and the hasp plate, getting it down nearly to the crossguard of the knife's haft. He took one of the golf clubs and started wedging it between the knife handle and the door. "Now, watch your eyes!" He started prying slowly, getting the feel for it, the hasp starting to buckle a little. He closed his eyes, turned his face away and threw his weight down steadily but rapidly. There was a loud crack, but not loud enough to be heard beyond the confines of the room, he judged. And he felt something impacting his right upper arm. "Aww, shit." But when he looked, he wasn't bleeding. His flesh stung. The hasp had broken off, just cheap metal. He freed the little Gerber and it looked scratched but largely undamaged. He resheathed it and dropped it in his hip pocket. There was an ordinary deadbolt lock on the door. He took a half-step back and then moved forward, his left leg snapping up and out as he pivoted on his right foot, a double kick to the door where lockplate joined doorframe. The door sprang open inwards and there was a clattering of brass parts to the floor.

"Very impressive." Jenny smiled.

"I thought so." Cross nodded.

By the light of their flashlights, they entered the armory, Cross more firmly securing the little Gerber knife. There was a single rack of a dozen shotguns, on closer inspection half of them 12-gauges and the other six of them 20s. They were all Remington 1100s. There was a cabinet with neatly stacked shelves, on the shelves boxes of shotgun shells. On the top shelf, there was an H&K flare pistol and an assortment of flares. "Find something for the shotgun shells. Put this flare gun and the flares in your purse in case we need them later." He'd been hoping against hope for something more substantial, unless this wasn't the only arms lockers. But how often did a bunch of free-spending tourists turn into bloodthirsty mutineers these days, anyway? He took the 20-gauge guns from the rack, putting them in the corner. "These babies go over the side." He started taking down the 12-gauges, pulling the magazine plugs in them one by one so he'd have full capacity. He threw the plugs away, loading one of the shotguns for himself and another for Comstock.

Jenny had a large sack, and she poured empty shell casings on the floor, loading 12-gauge boxed shotshells into it.

Cross started out, one of the loaded 12s and all six of the 20s with him. "Comstock!"

"Nothing happening. What took so much time?"

"It was a little challenging getting the door open. Have a shotgun. Magazine plug's out and it's loaded. Just trap loads. Best they got."

"I can do some damage with this."

"Start pitchin' these over the side. Just 20s and we can't haul 'em with us."

"Agreed."

Cross started back to the arms room for the rest of the shotguns and to help Jenny with the shotshells. . . .

They went back the way they came, the body of the terrorist just as they had left it, each of them carrying two shotguns, Cross and Comstock alternating at each landing on the bag of shotshells, their pockets bulging with them.

"If Leeds hasn't been taken prisoner, I'd wager he's hidden below in the machinery spaces," Comstock said, puffing a little as they reached the next landing and he handed off the bag of shells.

"You're right there," Cross agreed.

They had been checking each deck as they came to it, to see if there were signs of the terrorists moving about the vessel, ransacking. On the two decks they had passed so far, there was no sign of anyone.

Jenny went to the watertight door—it wasn't sealed—and opened it, peering through, tucking back quickly. "I saw someone. I couldn't make out who he was, but he disappeared about halfway down the corridor, maybe into one of the cabins."

"If he's a bad guy, we can use his weapons. If he's a good guy, maybe he can help. Jenny, you stay here. You stay with her, Comstock."

"You had the last one, Cross," Comstock began.

Cross smiled. "You're right," and Cross slipped through the door before anything else could be said, the Mini-Tanto in his right fist along with the flashlight, the AKM slung under his left arm, his finger just outside the trigger guard. He moved slowly, keeping as flat against the corridor bulkhead as he could. It would take forever to carefully search each cabin, but there were linen and supply closets spaced along the corridor as well. He would check those.

Cross kept moving, stopping by the first of the closets, trying the door. It opened freely and he ran the flashlight beam from side to side, top to bottom. Nothing but mops and brooms and cleaning supplies. He closed the door, quietly, at the edge of his peripheral vision seeing something, standing stock still, not moving his head so he could place what he had seen. It had been a door opening or closing. He closed his eyes for an instant. Three doors down. He opened his eyes and stepped more fully into the corridor, picking the door. It was one of the cabins. He walked toward it, punching the AKM slightly forward, ready.

Cross passed the door and stopped, tapping on it lightly with the muzzle of the AKM. The door swung open, inward.

Cross hissed into the darkness beyond, "I know you're in there. Out. Or I come in shooting." He had no intention of making all that noise, but there was no way for whoever it was inside to know that, and a strong gut feeling told him it wasn't one of the terrorist hijackers.

"All right," a man's voice came back. Cross had heard the voice somewhere before.

A tall, thin-faced man with black hair and mustache wearing the uniform of a junior officer emerged, hands up over his head. "You bastards will never get away with this," he announced in thickly German accented English, squinting against the beam of the flashlight behind which Cross stood.

"Who are you?"

"Hans Liedecker, recreation officer."

'You know much about trap shooting?''

"What?"

Cross lowered the beam of the flashlight. "I'm with the good guys. How'd you get away, or didn't they ever get you?"

"Mr. Cross? The piano player?"

"That's me. When I'm not ticklin' the ivories I'm fighting the forces of evil. What happened?"

"They brought all the senior officers to the bridge, handcuffed and hooded. They used the junior officers like myself to help them with the passenger lists. Even some of the crew were among them, the bastards. And some of the passengers, too. They had all the British passported passengers brought to the Seabreeze Lounge and all the rest of the passengers taken to the casino—aft. It was crowded in the casino, I was able to slip out using the dumbwaiter down to the kitchen below. I almost never got out of the thing''

"How are they treating the passengers? And, for God's sake, lower your hands.''

"They have segregated the women and children from the men. They have the men staying on their knees with their hands behind their necks until their hands can be tied. I don't know what they plan next.''

"What about the British passengers?''

"I don't know, Mr. Cross. I thought maybe if I got away I could make it to the arms locker and do something.''

"Any other guns aboard the *Empress* besides those twelve shotguns?''

"Just a few flare pistols, Mr. Cross.''

"We threw the 20s overboard because they were too much to carry and I didn't want to leave them behind. We've got the six 12s and all the 12-gauge shotshells. And a few other weapons. Join us.''

The German nodded vigorously. "Yes. Of course. How many are you?''

"Four, now. We're down here by the stairwell.'' And Cross, the German beside him, started back along the corridor toward the stairs. If the hijackers were segregating the passengers by nationality, they were setting up for hostage executions. Time was running down fast, too fast.

Chapter Twenty

Hughes and Babcock stood, peering down across the illuminated map of the North Atlantic, at its boundaries Europe and West Africa, the eastern United States and the northeast coast of South America. The map and the huge, circular light table on which it was placed dominated the center of an otherwise sterile room approximately thirty by thirty and built with all the charm of a bomb shelter. Shipping lanes were lighted in red dashes and airline lanes in blue. There was a red plastic X set roughly equidistant from the Azores and Gibralter. No one was in the room but them and General Argus. The helicopter had ferried them to a farmer's field where two Harrier jets had awaited them. No location had been given, but Hughes judged they had been flown north and east. His guess was somewhere in Virginia and it hadn't been important enough to ask.

On the far wall were banks of television screens, monitoring the three major networks and CNN, regular programming on the three networks preempted for special coverage of the hostage crisis in the Atlantic. But nothing seemed to be happening. When Hughes and Babcock had reunited, they were driven for approximately ten minutes to what appeared, on the outside, to be an abandoned factory, simply told to wait then, while the driver and the man with him had pulled off. As soon as the car had disappeared, a uniformed military policeman had exited the side door of the factory and bidden them to follow him to a curious passenger elevator. On the outside, it looked old and in disrepair, but inside was spotless and new. There was only one button to push and Hughes had pushed it. General Robert Argus was waiting for them when the elevator stopped and the doors opened.

"The British are going to be hard pressed to mount any kind of major operation without the cooperation of either Portugal, Morocco or Spain. The logistics would kill them and any chance of surprise would be out of the question,'' Argus said, breaking the long silence.

''The Azores are Portuguese, too, right?'' Babcock asked.

''Yes. Spain and Great Britain aren't always exactly on the best of terms, Mr. Babcock, and we understand London has diplomatic traffic with both Rabat and Lisbon right now to set something up. But they're probably hoping for the cooperation of Portugal. The *Empress* is a little closer to the Azores and there'd be less coverage of what they're doing. Nothing definite yet, but we do know the Special Air Service has been put on alert and is ready to move. You've heard the demands made by this O'Fallon, the man calling himself the leader of the hijackers?''

Hughes said, ''There wasn't time to catch anything more on the television or radio while we got ready for your chopper to pick us up. What are the demands, General?''

''Impossible. He wants the complete pullout of British forces from Northern Ireland and the Prime Minister to get on television and publicly denounce the government of Northern Ireland and pledge British noninvolvement in Irish affairs from now on. He wants the same statement read before a special session of the United Nations Security Council. O'Fallon's not going to get it. And he knows it unless he's a total imbecile. And there's evidence to suggest that this Seamus O'Fallon is just the opposite.''

''What do you mean, General?'' Babcock asked. ''You know him?''

''You have a dossier on him?'' Hughes suggested.

''We do indeed. A lot of it we originally got from the British, but they're being mum on him now. Apparently the FBI was interested in him and so was the CIA. He made some illegal trips into the United States for arms and financial support. Still a lot of people in this country who think they're helping starving widows and orphans and all they're really doing is giving money to buy Communist-bloc weapons to promote more killing. Other things to worry about than O'Fallon's past, though. He's wanted for murder, bank robbery, kidnapping, almost any major crime you can think of. He's got a reputation for brutality that closed him off to a lot of the Irish movement. Things got so hot for him in British territory that he had to flee for about two years. Just been back for under a year is the best estimate.''

''Where did he spend his vacation?'' Babcock asked.

"Good point, Mr. Babcock. No one is one hundred percent positive, but there is reason to believe he was working in Central America, based out of Cuba. We're not sure. There may be a Russian connection, too."

"There usually is, isn't there?" Hughes observed.

"Well, in more ways than one." Argus gestured toward a raised area to the right of the map table where there was a small conference table and a number of chairs. "Let's get a few things cleared up." Argus started for the table. Babcock looked at Hughes. Hughes raised his eyebrows only, then nodded in Argus's direction.

Argus sat at the head of the table, Hughes and Babcock flanking him. There was a pitcher on the table and several glasses. Hughes watched as Babcock investigated it, poured water and gestured toward another of the glasses as he looked at Hughes.

Hughes shook his head "no thanks" and looked at Argus. "What's going on, over and above the obvious, General?"

"I can't brief you any further unless you both agree to accept the mission."

"What's the mission?" Babcock asked. "You didn't fly us here to this place"— and Babcock gestured with his hands— "just so we could go after our friend Mr. Cross."

"No. I didn't. Certainly, Cross's life is important, as are the lives of all the hostages. But there's something vastly more important aboard that ship even the British don't know about, and we can only pray the hijackers haven't found."

Hughes looked at Babcock. Babcock said, "I'll abide by your decision, Mr. Hughes."

Hughes nodded, looked back at Argus and said, "We're in. Now. What the hell is going on?"

Argus closed his eyes, inhaled, opened them wide and began to speak. "The Russians have always been very interested in chemical and biological warfare. And they've done some things our scientists haven't been able to do."

"What does biological warfare have to do with the hijacking of a ship on the high seas?"

"The Russians developed a new viral strain, Hughes, Babcock. We wanted it because its potential was so devastating. It was felt that if our scientists could duplicate it and the Russian production plans were delayed, its effectiveness would be neutralized with both sides having it. No one would use it. It was being produced at a laboratory in the mountains in a remote section of Albania, where it was nice and cold in case anything went wrong.''

"What do you mean, 'nice and cold'?" Hughes snapped.

"No two viruses are exactly alike, they told me, and this one multiplies exceedingly rapidly with heat. The virus—in an ampule—was stolen and all the lab notes and tapes destroyed. The virus was smuggled out of Albania into Italy. It wasn't safe to fly it out. If something had gone wrong, like an explosion in mid-air, the virus would have been released and multiplied. And anyway, the intelligence agency handling it wanted first crack at it, didn't want the military involved and all the civilian airports and everything would have been watched by the KGB. It was decided that the best way to get it out was by ship, that no one would suspect that. The viral agent is on board the *Empress Britannia* and, if O'Fallon and his gang of hijackers don't get their demands, after they've executed some hostages, they'll carry out O'Fallon's major threat: to blow up the *Empress*. O'Fallon claims he's got the vessel mined with plastic explosives and napalm. The heat from such an explosion would trigger the virus. Airborne, it could go anywhere the winds carried it.''

"This virus, what does it do?" Babcock asked, his voice low.

"I had a hell of a time getting that information myself, Mr. Babcock. Nobody wanted to tell me. But I finally nailed it down. It's like an exceptionally virulent form of influenza at first. Once it reacts with certain enzymes in the human body, it mutates. The flu symptoms last for about twenty-four hours, but getting progressively worse. Then the virus attacks the cerebral cortex. The infected person would be dead—and most agonizingly—in under thirty-six hours. And there's no vaccine available to counteract it. One of the things our scientists would have done was to develop a vaccine in the event the Russians someday did use it.''

"How many casualties could be anticipated?" Hughes asked clinically.

"That's hard to say, I've been told. Depending on the amount of heat generated in the explosion, the altitude the plume from the blast would attain, prevailing winds. If the winds took it east, most of western Europe and North Africa would be covered, at the very least. That's what they told me. And this is all unofficial.''

"Can't the British be told?"

"I got a flat refusal on that, Hughes.''

"How many dead?" Hughes insisted.

"Millions. No one has an answer more specific."

"Idiots!" Hughes exploded. "How can anyone with a conscience play around with something like that? Are we all mad? The Russians and us, too!?"

"We didn't develop it. We were trying to defend against it," Argus insisted. Babcock's face went slightly grey.

Hughes stood up and began pacing the raised area around the table. "So, we have to get on board and kill everyone of the hijackers so there is no possibility in the slightest that the bombs can be detonated. We can possibly count on some help on the inside from Cross, if he's able and once he knows it's us. Then we have to find the ampule containing this god-awful thing. And all before the British send in the SAS for a full-scale assault which could result in the unintentional release of the virus."

"It's the only hope we have," Argus said softly.

Hughes turned around and looked at him. "Tell me about this O'Fallon. Would there be any chance we could . . ." He didn't even finish the question. It was too absurd to bother finishing.

"If we told O'Fallon, he'd use it. O'Fallon, according to the information we had on file, profiles out as a manic depressive with pronounced homicidal tendencies and some sort of Messianic complex. And then there's another factor. A specialist in neurosurgery contacted Scotland Yard about six months ago that he had treated a man matching O'Fallon's description. He'd seen the man's face again on a Wanted poster and felt obligated to call. If it was O'Fallon, he's been diagnosed as having an inoperable brain tumor, at the time given less than a year to live. O'Fallon is an old hand at the terrorist game. He knows full well the British won't honor his demands and that they'll do the only thing they can do, hit him. But he's dying anyway. If it was O'Fallon, the man's got nothing to lose."

"Except his immortal soul," Hughes commented quietly, then sat down. "What's the British posture in terms of control of the area? And will the Russians be going into the area as well? We need to know that."

"I'll get you whatever information we can come up with," Argus promised.

"Why," Babcock began, "are you sending us in? Not the SEALs? Because you can't make it official?"

"There are two CIA people aboard the hijacked vessel, Mr. Babcock. One is a man, black, like you—"

"You mean I'm black?! That's news to me," Babcock interrupted in one of his rare attempts at humor. "And I'd always thought it was just that I tanned easily!" Hughes smiled, thinking the opportunity had probably been irresistible.

"—who's traveling under the name of Alvin Leeds," Argus continued, as if Babcock had said nothing at all. "It's just a cover identity. He's traveling as a boiler wiper or something. He's the man who brought the ampule of the viral agent aboard the *Empress* and it's his job to protect it. A second CIA person was sent in at the last minute to cover Leeds, Leeds not even knowing about it. A woman named Jennifer Hall. She's a regular CIA courier and gatherer working under the cover of a singer."

"She's actually singing aboard the *Empress*?" Hughes interrupted.

"That's right—" Argus began.

"Cross should know her, at least casually," Babcock said, sounding as if he were thinking out loud. "She might turn to him for assistance if she knows anything about his background."

"Were either Leeds or the woman—this Miss Hall—armed?"

"Both of them were, Hughes. Trouble is, Leeds will think he's all alone. He doesn't know anything about her."

"What geniuses organized this thing to begin with?" Hughes asked.

"A few geniuses who may retire earlier than they've planned. That's the word from the White House," Argus told them.

"There are two possibilities only, unless anyone can think of something else," Hughes began. "And I'm open to suggestions, believe me. But, as I see it, we can do a high altitude, low opening drop near enough to the *Empress* to swim in—if weather, wind and sky conditions are right. Have to be under conditions of total darkness or the game'd be up. The only other option—and British or Russian presence, or both, could preclude that immediately—is go in by submarine and leave the vessel while it's submerged. If this O'Fallon and his gangster friends have installed any intruder alert systems on the hull or anywhere else we might bump into them. In either event, they'll make us as soon as we try getting aboard. And assuming we do get that far, how do we get the ampule off?"

Argus studied the tent he'd made of his fingers for a moment, then said, "Just a thought, but the hijackers have a yacht pulled alongside the *Empress*. Presumably how they got aboard. Probably the old routine of letting the vessel lie dead in the water and when the *Empress* stopped to assist, they came aboard with their guns. But maybe you can utilize the yacht to get the ampule off.''

"Too easy to be stopped. If I were this O'Fallon—and thank God I'm not—I'd have the yacht rigged with explosives that could be radio detonated in case any of the passengers or crew tried making a break for it. No. The yacht's out.''

"Helicopter,'' Babcock said absently.

Hughes bit his lower lip. "Wait a minute. When I was a little boy, I saw it done once. They used to pick up mail that way.''

"What are you talking about?'' Babcock asked him.

"All right. In the early days of airmail. To speed up the pickup process and sometimes because they'd pick up where there wasn't really an airfield, they utilized a system originally developed to pick up mail at railway stations where the train wasn't scheduled to stop. Modified, of course. They'd have a pouch on a tensioned line, but a little slack in it. The old biplane would come through, flying low and slow and it had a hook out at the bottom of the fuselage. The hook would snatch the pouch off the line and then the pilot would draw it up into the cockpit at his leisure and go on to the next pickup point. We could use that same system if we can set up the rig and find a pilot good enough.''

"One of those guys who lands on aircraft carriers,'' Babcock suggested.

"Better still,'' Argus supplied, "the guys who take off and land from smaller vessels—they do it in the Med a lot—with observation planes. Electronic surveillance equipment aircraft.''

"All right!'' Hughes clapped his hands together. "Forget about the submarine option unless the moon will be too bright or the winds too high. We airdrop off the *Empress* and swim up to her. Then we get aboard. We'll need a picture of this Leeds fellow and the woman CIA op. We find them and Cross, then start liquidating the hijackers until we can reach whatever area of the ship we settle on for the pickup. We erect whatever gadget it is we need and call in the aircraft by radio, then finish the wetwork.''

"Sketch out what you need,'' Argus said.

"Lewis and I'll need diagrams, photos, everything you can get on the *Empress*. And we've got to go in quickly. This madman O'Fallon will start executing hostages if he hasn't already and the SAS won't be left waiting around forever once he does. We'll need some special weapons. I can make you a list. What you can't get immediately, you might be able to hit up one of the SEAL Teams stationed around the District of Columbia for as a loan.''

"How'd you know about them?'' Argus asked him.

"I helped train them,'' Hughes answered.

Chapter Twenty-one

Argus had left the room to gather what information he could pertaining to weather in the predawn hours of the next day in the area where the *Empress* was being held, and to ascertain what information he could concerning British and Soviet submarine traffic in the area as well, in case weather precluded the preferred of the two options.

Hughes had been making a list, Babcock pacing the floor, stopping to stare occasionally at the same rerun newsreel footage of the *Empress Britannia* in happier days, before all of this, footage of the bombing of the Royal Ulster Constabulary barracks, which was linked to Seamus O'Fallon, footage of other terrorist atrocities in Northern Ireland.

Babcock turned away from the television screens in disgust. "I think people like this stuff."

"It's like a soap opera to some people, only the characters are real; but, in a way, they're not real at all. They see something that disgusts them and they say, 'Oh my God, that's horrible,' and then they flip channels and there's 'The Honeymooners' or 'I Love Lucy' and they're laughing again. And all the while, they're on the road to oblivion."

"You sound like a pessimist, Mr. Hughes."

"I'm certainly not an optimist. Optimists rarely study violence, Lewis, because in their world, violence isn't something that happens. It only happens to other people and if it ever does involve them, they sincerely expect that the rest of society will say 'Oh my God, that's horrible,' and really mean it. But of course, very few people really mean it because very few people are ready to do anything about it if it happens to someone else, let alone themselves. When a confrontational situation occurs, they are willing to sacrifice the higher good they've always preached about for a good that's even higher, their own self-preservation. And afterwards, if they've made it through alive, they congratulate themselves that they're still around to help make the world a better place. True pacifists act out of dedication to principle, right or wrong, and because of that, are at least deserving of respect. But too many people are totally lacking in principle, lacking in anything that at all gives any depth or purpose to their lives. They just live; and, when death finally comes, they feel cheated. And, of course, they have been. But they weren't cheated by death, only cheated by their lack of perception of life, cheated by themselves. Like baseball, Lewis. They missed their chance at a base hit simply because they were waiting to make a home run on a perfect pitch that on one level of consciousness they hoped would never come; and they were waiting so long, they only wound up being walked.''

Slowly, Babcock said, "You're a cynic."

"You're observant. Tell me how you can do what we do even once, let alone more than that, without being a cynic? But yet, I'm not a true cynic; because, if I were, I'd say the hell with it and walk away from it, wouldn't I? You and I, and Cross if we can get him back—we're the fellows with the buckets put in charge of bailing out the boat after so many leaks have sprung, it's impossible. And, just to make it interesting, we aren't given buckets to use at all, just sieves. And, depending on our ingenuity and endurance, we can find ways of plugging up the holes in our sieves or work faster and faster. The result will be the same. The only advantage we have is that we can say we tried to slow it down a bit. Which brings us back to the concept of optimism. Each of us doing this sort of thing feels somewhere inside himself that maybe, just maybe, with the little extra time we buy before the ship of civilization sinks, mankind may figure out how to keep it from sinking entirely. And it sounds so much nicer to say you're looking forward to the future optimistically than to just admit to all and sundry that you're an asshole.''

Chapter Twenty-two

The weapons on the equipment list Hughes had ready for General Argus were what Hughes considered bare bones, all necessities. Hughes would bring the Magnum Tanto for Cross, so only two knives were needed, Gerber BMFs, Gerber MKIIs or Benchmark TAC IIs his first choices. He allowed for no second choices. There were many fine custom-makers, his own personal favorite the blades of Weatherford, Texas, knifemaker Jack Crain, and not just because the man was a fellow Texan. But anything handmade, unless it were crafted in some yurt in Inner Mongolia, could be traced to the maker these days. And that could trace back to the man who used it.

Three Beretta 92F military pistols, eight spare fifteen-round magazines for each pistol and two twenty-round extension magazines for each pistol. The availability of the pistols he wasn't worried about. To holster the pistols and carry the spare magazines, he wanted Bianchi UM-84 rigs, the civilian version of the M-12 holster and its concurrent accessories. He needed the civilian version because he needed black. Black BDUs were already packed, for himself and for Babcock, but they'd likely do the entire operation in wetsuits since either way they went in they would get a dousing.

Assault rifles would be unnecessary considering the battleground, but H&K MP5 SD A3 integral suppressor 9mm submachine guns would be essential, each to be fitted with an Aimpoint Electronic sight. Not only were the H&K subguns reliable and efficient and silent, but they were deadly accurate for a weapon of their type.

A silent weapon of smaller overall size might be needed and, for this, Hughes opted for a Walther PP in .22 Long Rifle. There would be no time to have a pistol fitted with a slide lock or to have one gunsmithed so it would work properly with subsonic ammunition, so it wouldn't be quite as silent as it could have been. But silent enough if used with discretion.

Argus returned, sheafs of computer paper in his hands, Hughes saying to him, "Here's the list. I don't really want to accept substitutions. For the Walther .22, if you have to, get Bob Magee at Interarms on the phone and tell him it's for me. He's an old friend and it won't be the first time Bob's helped the federal government get the equipment it needed in a pinch."

"There's something you have to know," Argus interrupted, his voice oddly subdued as he almost threw the computer print-outs down on the table. "There's a new factor to consider. It may be critical."

"A deadline for the demands to be met?" Babcock asked.

"No, not yet. Feeling is this O'Fallon wants to prolong the thing as much as possible for maximum media attention. No. It has to do with one of the passengers. I just got word from the CIA that their man—they didn't give me his name—their man who got the ampule out of Albania and into Italy. After he handed it over to this other agent going under the name Alvin Leeds, he was captured by the KGB. They gave him some kind of truth serum and the best guess is he spilled everything he knew about who he gave the ampule to. He didn't know the name of the vessel, but he would have been able to give an accurate enough description of Leeds that if the KGB had somebody clever working for them on this they might have found Leeds in time to get aboard the *Empress*. And that's just what probably happened. The CIA man that was drugged—he remembered the name of the KGB officer in charge. The name was Ephraim Vols. Used to be Volshinsky. Vols or Volshinsky or whatever he calls himself is one of their best people they tell me. Very efficient and imaginative. A bad combination for us. His name has popped up as being wholly or partially responsible for some of their most successful operations in the last several years. There's reason to believe he has passed himself off as an Englishman on several occasions. It's quite possible Vols is aboard the *Empress* traveling under an assumed identity and using a British passport. He'd know exactly what that ampule contains."

Hughes said nothing for a moment, then, "That could conceiv-ably work to our advantage. I doubt the Russians are eager for this viral agent to be released over Europe and North Africa if they don't have any way of innoculating against it. Vols might realize the danger, if he's as sharp as you imply, and take steps to obviate it. Could be to our advantage that he's there.''

"But if he is," Babcock interjected, "he's not going to be too eager to see us take it off the *Empress* and hand it over to the CIA. Just gives us something else to worry about at our backs while we're trying to get the job done.''

"No, but if he is able to operate, he may be the first person we should look for after Cross. Before we go after Leeds. Vols might already have gotten his hands on it,'' Hughes told Babcock and Argus. "And if he did, his primary concern will be getting it off as fast as possible. If he doesn't think to second-guess this O'Fallon, Vols might go after the yacht as his means of escape. But at least he's a professional, and in his own interests to stay alive and retake the ampule, he might do us some good.''

"I hope you're right." Babcock nodded sombrely.

"Only one way to find out, isn't there, Lewis?" Hughes said cheerfully. "Now, about that weather report," Hughes began again. . . .

The weather was beautiful, the breeze strong and cool and the sun bright. And Seamus O'Fallon was able to hold the headache back for now, the pill having taken effect. But the pills seemed to work less and less well each time he used them. And he used them with greater frequency. Maybe the British doctor had been right and he was living on borrowed time; and the debt was about to be collected.

"Line them up over there now, lads, would ya." He gestured toward the portside edge of what his diagram told him should be properly called the Beach Deck, the line removed and the guard-rail taken down so there was nothing to prevent an incautious step plunging one into the whitecapped sea below. An incautious step or a moderately vigorous push.

A British battle cruiser had taken up position off the port bow and he was certain their binoculars would be trained on the deck and that they wouldn't miss what was about to transpire.

He didn't want them to miss any of it.

Six men with their wrists and ankles tied and their eyes blindfolded, each man wearing a Mae West. The irony of the concept of a life preserver did not escape him.

They would have parabolic microphones aimed at the *Empress*;

but, just in case, he took up the blue and white plastic battery-operated loud hailer and squeezed the trigger handle tight in his fist. "This is Seamus O'Fallon speaking, leader of this stalwart group of freedom fighters combatting, in their own humble way, the dirty heel of British oppression in Ireland. We have asked that in the interests of promoting peace and harmony in Ireland, the British Prime Minister denounce the puppet regime of so-called Northern Ireland in the electronic media, and take oath that all ties with so-called Northern Ireland are henceforth abolished, all military aid ceased and a complete withdrawal of all British forces, both overt and covert, be begun immediately. We have asked that such a declaration be repeated before a special session of the United Nations Security Council. But, alas, the warmongering British government, in a sad attempt to hold to their last vestiges of Empire by whatever means they can, however sadistic, have refused to lift the yoke of oppression. No announcement has been made. It is with great personal sadness, peace-lovin' man that I am, that this further step must be taken to show the British people and people everywhere how vile and heartless the British Government is. Lad!" And he called to Paddy and Jack and some of the others. "Shoot the poor people—and be merciful when ya do it, now. Then push their bodies over the side, will ya, now."

He kept the loud hailer fisted tight so that it would aid the Brits on their warship in hearing the screams as the six men he had selected at random from among the holders of British passports were shot to death, the submachine guns Paddy, Jack and the others had roaring for the briefest instant, the bodies collapsing, all but two of them falling over the side of their own accord, the last two helped along by some of the lads.

Seamus O'Fallon shouted through his loud hailer, " 'Tis a sad day, it is, when the British Government value wealth and power over the lives of their subjects."

He put down the loud hailer and stared over the side.

The six bodies, despite a few bullet holes in the Mae Wests, floated nicely, bobbing up and down on the whitecaps. He wanted them there as a reminder.

The headache was starting to come stronger.

Chapter Twenty-three

Hans Liedecker, the German recreation officer, held one of the 12-gauge autoloaders in each hand, Cross glancing back at Liedecker and Jenny Hall, whom he had delegated to bring up the rear. Comstock was beside him, Comstock with the Browning·thrust into his belt and another of the shotguns in both hands. Cross would have taken one himself for close range, despite the load, the shotgun not such a bad proposition. Would have taken one had he been able to find a hacksaw with which to get rid of a foot or so of needless barrel. They were at or below the waterline now, the corridor along which they moved opening onto the third from lowest level of the main cargo hold according to Liedecker.

For the past five minutes they had moved slowly and in total silence, the sounds of movement ahead of them, coming from the cargo hold.

Cross edged forward, the AKM at high port in both fists, Comstock falling in behind him, the shotgun held the same way. There was no pretty wallpaper here, no attractive carpeting, no occasional tables set with vases of attractively arranged flowers. There was a smell of diesel oil, the spotless decking beneath them grey painted steel, like the bulkheads and the overhead, and oddly Cross felt more at home with the decor, more like the navy he had come to know—how many years ago?

He kept moving, the sounds louder, men speaking English, joking, an occasional command in a louder, more authoritative voice, the commands the only things intelligible at the distance. There was something going on about an installation and setting it right. Cross thought they were probably talking about a bomb.

Large double doors, not watertight but equipped with panic

bars, lay open at the very end of the corridor, from Liedecker's briefing as they had entered this level, Cross knowing the doors would open onto a catwalk, the base of the cargo hold just below.

He continued moving forward. . . .

Some of the male passengers from among the British had passed out, others still on their knees as they were told. He had refused to allow toilet privileges and so there was a strong smell of urine, mixed with the stronger smells of fear and sweat. He would not allow the female passengers to attend the male passengers who had succumbed, but made them sit with their hands tied behind them, on the floor under the tables. The children, untied, his men had herded together and put in the bathrooms. Windowless, the bathrooms were black as pitch, the electricity still turned off at his order. Soon it would be necessary to either restore the electricity or light candles and utilize flashlights for moving about. The day would soon be ended. But darkness was another way of demoralizing his hostages. In the casino, where the non-British passengers were being held, he had ordered that conditions be slightly better. Families were still broken up and the adults segregated by sex, the children kept apart, but he allowed the men to sit too and, in small groups, the hostage passengers were allowed toilet facilities.

His fingers moved over the keyboard, the headache rising within him. Young Martin and two other men, ones O'Fallon had planted among the crew, were entering the lounge, the taller of the two other men with a body over his shoulder. There should have been no bodies yet.

"Let's see the body, Martin."

Young Martin cleared his throat.

O'Fallon sat at the piano, picking out "The Rose of Tralee." He'd taken up with a woman who played the piano and lived with her for more than a year and—so she had told him—he had a natural ear for music, even though he couldn't read a note.

"One of our lads?"

Young Martin said nothing, nor did either of the two men with him.

"Speak up, boyo."

"Tim McCarthy's dead, Seamus. Throat slit, ear to ear it was." Young Martin looked a little green about his face and his eyes shifted nervously.

"Let's have a look at him, then," O'Fallon said slowly, standing up. The man with the body over his shoulder unslung it, young Martin and the other with him helping to get the body down on the little stage. O'Fallon looked down at him. It was Tim McCarthy, all right, his face already livid and chalky grey, the blood dried where the gash at his throat was, brown and crusty, another wound visible in his chest.

"We found him in the stairwell leading to the deck where the armory was, Seamus. And the armory's been cleaned out of all the shotguns. And Tim's rifle and his pistol—they was gone, too, Seamus."

"The O'Fallon made him a grievous error, Martin. And Tim, here, he paid dearly for it," O'Fallon said slowly, dropping into a crouch beside the body and touching his right hand to the cold right cheek.

O'Fallon stood up. He looked down from the stage toward where the male British passengers knelt in discomfort. The women, tied and huddled under the tables, peered at him from beneath the tablecloths which covered the tables. O'Fallon felt the headache washing over him and he raised to his full height and sucked in his breath and hammered both fists down on the keyboard, screaming at the top of his lungs, "What will O'Fallon tell this poor boy's widowed mother! What now!" He took up his submachine gun and sprayed it into the piano, the glass shattering, shards of it flying everywhere, the women screaming, his own men stepping back. He wheeled toward the British hostages again. "Bled like a kosher slaughtered steer, he was! And, damn it all, some bloody bastard's gonna pay dear! Dear!" And he jumped from the stage, nearly losing his balance, one of his men reaching out to him, O'Fallon brushing him off.

O'Fallon stopped his headlong rush, swaying on the balls of his feet, his breathing coming faster as the pain filled him. A Brit with red hair and frightened brown eyes. O'Fallon grabbed him up, tearing the adhesive tape from his mouth, plastering it against his forehead then ramming the muzzle of his submachine gun into the man's abdomen. "Fuck you!" O'Fallon triggered a burst, the body twitching, blood vomitting out of the mouth as he shoved the body away and there were more screams. He waved the submachine gun at them, shouting, "Martin! Get me the bloody intercom switched on if it means electrical power for the whole bloody boat! Do it, now!"

He advanced a pace, looked down at his kill and spat on him.

Chapter Twenty-four

There was a loud hum and lights went on everywhere in the corridor, Cross flattening himself against the bulkhead, Comstock hissing, "Good God . . ."

"Hang loose," Cross answered.

The speaker on the opposite bulkhead crackled and a voice—it sounded like the voice of the devil—came over the air. "The rotten bloody bastards who slaughtered Tim McCarthy, the only support of his widowed mother. Listen close now! O'Fallon knows you by name. A Mr. Cross, a Miss Hall, a Mr. Comstock." There was a pause. "Crewman Alvin Leeds."

"Passenger list," Comstock murmured. "But at least they don't have Leeds."

"Listen," came the voice again. There was a woman's scream, and the speaker crackled with terrible static, a noise so loud Cross tried to shield his ears, a sound like something ripping and tearing. Then the voice, the speaker still crackling static. "That was me killin' a bloody British whore. I have me little British brats, too. I start killin' a woman and a child every five minutes until the three of you appear before me in the Seabreeze Lounge. Four minutes, fifty-five seconds!" There was a loud click, and then an even louder one as the lights went out again and the panic lights tried to glow again.

Cross looked back toward where Jenny Hall and Liedecker were, Jenny standing square in the middle of the corridor, mouth open, tears streaming down her cheeks. She took out her pistol and for a moment, Cross thought she was going to shoot herself with it, but she threw it down, Cross dodging back in case it discharged. And then she was running, back along the way they'd come. Cross snapped, "Comstock!" and he pushed the

AKM into the Britisher's hands. "Cover the hold!" Cross was running after her, not daring to shout, Jenny disappearing around a bend in the corridor, the stairwell not far beyond. Cross reached the bend, skidding, half tripping, launching himself into a dead run, arms out at his sides, mouth wide and gulping air.

She was at the entrance to the stairwell now, Cross right behind her.

She disappeared inside. Cross hit the entrance as the door started to slam, punched it back, the door swinging wide, banging against the bulkhead, Jenny taking the stairs two at a time running. Cross threw his body toward her, his left hand catching at her right ankle, closing over it, pulling her down as he hurtled up and forward, his right arm closing around her waist, bulldog-ging her, both of their bodies, intertwined, rolling back down the stairs, Cross taking the impact as they crashed against the deck at the stairs' base.

"Let me—" Cross's hand went over her mouth. She tried biting him, her hands free, scratching at his exposed flesh, clawing at him. His legs scissored around her, trying to pin her, the nails just missing his eye and gouging along his cheek. His right hand flicked outward, slapping her, her head snapping back. She started to scream again and he did the only thing he could. His left hooked upward, catching her at the tip of the chin and decking her. His hands caught at her before she fell back. And Cross held her face in his hands, still straddling her, looking down at her. "I can't let you go." He drew her to him and just held her for a long second. The lights came on again. The speaker in the stairwell over their heads clicked on again. Abe Cross knew what he would hear.

And he knew he'd kill this man O'Fallon for it, not a man at all but a devil incarnate. . . .

Vols advanced on knees and elbows toward the open doors, deciding that with the speaker blaring now was the best time, despite the light. He crawled between the open doors and onto the catwalk, peering down, the shotgun and the AKM left behind with the West German, Liedecker.

A half dozen men, laying out ropes of plastic explosives, the ropes uncoiling from open packing crates.

These madmen had planned this well.

He closed his eyes, trying to clear his head, trying to ignore the horrible voice of this homicidal maniac. It was one thing to kill for your country, to kill men who would just as easily kill you if they had to, but no more willingly. This man—this O'Fallon. Vols opened his eyes. Six men. Each armed with an assault rifle or submachine gun. Could they be taken? Where else were there explosives?

And then he heard the plaintive voice of a young child, saying, crying, "I'm scared! Mommie! Mommie! Mo—" There was the burst of static which Vols knew was gunfire. There were screams, then the shriek of a woman's terror and another burst of static.

And then the voice of O'Fallon. "Five minutes or two more. I got enough to keep this goin' longer than you can keep listenin', I do!"

Vols only realized he'd been biting his lower lip when he tasted the blood.

Chapter Twenty-five

"Ready, Lewis?"

"Ready, Mr. Hughes."

"Whenever you wish then." Hughes gave a final tug at the shooting muffs and raised the Beretta 92F, inserting the magazine up the butt and working the slide release. The slide followed forward and the hammer followed down, the safety on, just as it should be. His right thumb moved the safety up and he snapped the pistol into a two-hand hold and fired, pulling the first shot through double action, emptying all fifteen rounds as fast as he could. Like the other magazines before it, this one functioned flawlessly, the slide locking open over it when the last shot was fired. Hughes bent over to peer through the spotting scope as he moved the DeSantis night-simulation glasses up to his forehead, squinting his eyes against the sudden brightness. He had shot out the chest of the silhouette at twenty-five yards except for one hole which was in the thorax. He theorized this was the first round, the one fired with the stiffer double-action pull.

He looked to his left toward the next position. Lewis Babcock was removing his glasses and inspecting the performance of his pistol as well. It was taking some time, but there would be time enough to reach the objective. The aircraft which would carry them would not be ready for another—Hughes checked the Rolex on his left wrist—thirty-five minutes. That meant another fifteen minutes he could allow for range time.

Time forbade making a test jump, or trying to run through even the most basic aspects of the mission; but, there would be no possibility of success if they could not rely on their weapons.

Babcock was taking up one of the H&K submachine guns, getting ready to try his first magazine. Hughes began the same, stripping away his shooting muffs because they would not be needed.

The Azores were almost due east and the aircraft which would carry them would only dogleg to avoid the islands themselves and any watchful British eyes. Latest information from Argus indicated the SAS were mounting a full-scale attack force that would soon be ready to go, thanks to the cooperation of Portugal. Word also was that O'Fallon and his band of gangsters had begun killing hostages.

As soon as one magazine was emptied, Hughes would load the next, the purpose of the exercise not to test marksmanship. However that might be lacking, now was not the time to correct it. Rather, they were function-testing each weapon they would use and each magazine, only with the first and last magazine from each taking the extra time to test the weapon's accuracy.

Hughes kept firing.

Cross was not the sort of man to sit idly by while O'Fallon executed hostages, which meant one of two things: Cross was either in action somehow, or dead.

Hughes kept firing.

As his hands worked, his mind worked, but to the same end, the success of the mission. Sound and light grenades, ear and eye protection in the event one of the grenades had to be detonated in an area where they would have to remain. Gas cannisters to be utilized if possible, the kind that would knock out everyone who breathed it quickly. But only the innocent would wake up again, because it was predetermined that none of the terrorists would leave the *Empress* except in body bags. Gas masks in sufficient quantity to make available to Cross, this Leeds fellow, the female CIA-er and themselves. And also one more. Just in case it was worthwhile to keep this KGB man Vols conscious.

He kept shooting.

The aircraft to make the pickup, the impact-proof, bullet-resistant flotation pouch for the ampule once it was recovered and the Rube Goldberg device for suspending the pouch so the pickup aircraft could hook it up and snatch it away.

Hughes rammed the last magazine up the H&K's magazine well and worked the bolt, letting it slam forward. It was the last of the weapons testing. He opened fire on what remained of the silhouette target twenty-five yards downrange, firing from the shoulder in three-round bursts, using the Aimpoint sighting system for target aquisition. The H&K was all but soundless in any real sense. The submachine gun empty in his hands, he looked to Babcock beside him. Babcock was just raising his weapon after clearing the magazine. Babcock made a thumbs-up signal. Each of the MP5 SD A3s had functioned flawlessly. They could be serviced aboard the specially modified E-4 Boeing 747, the aircraft stripped and fitted with engine modifications about which Argus had been terribly vague. Hughes had conjectured that the engine modifications had to be quite interesting indeed since in the next breath he had said that they would be over the target in approximately four and one half hours.

"If half the men I've trained or worked with could shoot as well as you two . . ." Argus said from behind them. But he didn't finish it.

"Anyone with reasonably normal vision and gross and fine motor skills can shoot well if they practice at it. Trouble is, there's usually something better to do." He turned around and looked at Argus. "These are good. Can we get these packed in those shock-proof padded cases?"

"I've arranged for it to be done. All the maintenance gear you'll need is ready to go aboard. Parachutes, bouyancy vests, all the chemical weapons you've asked for. Twice as much ammunition as you requested. Got your knives. Everything."

"How do we get away after this thing is over, assuming we're able?" Babcock asked suddenly. "Once we hit, the SAS is going to know about it pretty fast and may get in before we can get out."

"As soon as you two get aboard," Argus told them, taking a small black-surfaced box from his left outside uniform jacket pocket, "one of you will activate one of these. It emits a one-time only radio signal. Trash it afterwards. And please do because this is classified and we can't have you getting caught with it if anything goes wrong."

"Perish the thought," Hughes smiled.

"Yes." Argus nodded. "One of our satellites will pick this up, matter-of-factly log the coordinates even though we know them. It's programmed for it. The signal will be transmitted to a submarine we already have moving into the area. It'll stay out of the hot area until this signal comes, then move in at flank speed. If the British detect it by then they'll have so little time to do anything, it won't matter. By the time the operation is concluded, the submarine should be within visual range of the *Empress*. Get

yourselves into the water on her portside and fire a flare. We'll
come right in to get you.''

"Unless the SAS see us first," Babcock remarked.

"Unless the SAS see you first. We don't want that to happen,
but they are friendly forces so don't try shooting your way out of
anything with them.''

"How about Russian submarines?" Hughes asked.

"Satellites tell us there are two in the immediate vicinity. But I
doubt they'll risk surfacing.''

"What if they do?" Babcock inquired.

"I have no instructions to cover it," Argus told them, looking
at each of them in turn.

"What sort of instructions will the captain of the U.S. submarine have?" Babcock asked very deliberately.

"I had no control over that. He was told to withdraw and leave
you in the water. There was nothing I could do. I'm sorry.''

"Oh, well, that makes it all right, then," Babcock said,
hammering his fist into one of the partitions which separated the
range positions, the spotting scope mounted to it vibrating.

"Things don't really change at all, do they, General." Hughes
said it as a statement, not a question, then looked at his watch; it
was time to go. . . .

Another woman and child were murdered as they listened,
helpless, and soon there would be another. Jenny Hall's action
had left Cross no other choice. He could not trust her alone, nor
could he drag her along kicking and screaming once she woke
up. He had checked; she was regaining consciousness. And he
had taken the strap from her purse and tied her hands with it,
leaving Liedecker to stay with her while he and Comstock took
care of other matters.

They crouched at the top of the catwalk now. Comstock
whispered, "She will hate you for this. And hate me for helping
you.''

"I couldn't have made her understand.''

"I have a feeling you and I may have a falling out, Cross.''

Cross looked at Comstock, puzzled for a moment. "Why?"

"You'll want to kill this man O'Fallon. And so do I. But until
then, allies, hmm?''

"Until then. Ready?''

"Ready. Yes.''

Cross stood up, the AKM in both fists, Comstock beside him,

the Browning High Power in his belt, one 12-gauge in his hands and a second one leaned against the catwalk.

"Now!" Cross shouted, and they both opened fire into the six men below them, the roar of the Soviet assault rifle and the belching of the shotgun blending into a deafening cacaphony, the sound reverberating again and again off the steel walls of the cargo hold all around them and above and below, return fire starting to come up at them, bullets ricocheting off steel plate, Cross feeling something tear at his left thigh, Comstock staggering back, throwing down his shotgun, picking up a second and firing one-handed, the Browning High Power in his left fist.

Cross emptied the AKM and rammed the fresh magazine into place, continued firing until the last of the six were down. Had the men been near the plastic explosives with detonators set, there could have been—but there had been no other choice. And they had waited until the men had been about to leave the hold to do their bloody work.

Cross looked at Comstock. The Englishman's white shirtsleeve was stained red with blood. "Just plenty of blood, but nothing serious I think. Have a look at it, will you, when you get the chance?" And Comstock staggered, almost fell, Cross letting the AKM drop on its sling to his right side, bending down with the man. Cross's left thigh burned.

He inspected the wound to Comstock's arm. "You were right. It doesn't look serious. Betchya it hurts like hell."

"You're right there, old man." And Comstock's eyes flickered to the right for an instant. "Not unscathed either, are we?"

"Just a scratch. Probably a ricochet. Fragment in it feels like. Yours went clean through. I'm making a pressure bandage here," and Cross began cutting away Comstock's right sleeve.

"Don't suppose you'd rather mutilate *your* shirt. Heaven forbid." Comstock grinned.

Cross placed the bandage. "Just keep your elbow crooked until the bleeding slows up. Try to keep it elevated."

"Your thigh, old man."

"One of us has to get down there and hold that position. All the racket we made, they'll be on us quick. Take your time on the stairs. Come down on your butt if you feel light-headed, all right?"

"Yes."

"Right." Cross was up, the half-spent AKM in his right fist, Jenny's stainless Colt Officers ACP in his left. He started down the stairwell off the catwalk. Get the weapons gathered up from the dead, then get to defusing the plastique if it could be done. And the unpleasant but necessary part. If any of the six weren't dead, see that they became that way.

He kept moving. . . .

"Liedecker! Bring her," Vols ordered.

"Yes, Herr Comstock," the recreation officer shouted back.

Vols turned his back and, using one of the shotguns like a cane to support himself, he started back along the corridor toward the catwalk. The lights came on and the speaker crackled and Vols sagged against the bulkhead, a wave of nausea gripping him. "Five minutes have passed. Faith and doesn't it bother ya that innocent women and babies are dyin' now?"

There was a child's voice, crying. Then the first blast of gunfire came. Vols pushed himself upright and quickened his pace. . . .

Babcock followed Hughes's lead, as soon as the craft was airborne getting into a cross-legged sitting position on the fuse-age floor. "All right, lad. Submachine guns first. Complete field strip, light lubrication only, then reassembly. Save loading magazines until the last. There'll be time." Hughes started dismounting one of the three Heckler & Kochs.

Babcock looked at his Rolex. As General Argus had put them aboard, he'd told them, "The Air Force people tell me that some specialized equipment on one of their planes has been picking up traffic between the British vessel off the *Empress*'s portside and the Azores. It was voice; some sort of code; didn't make any sense. Except for one thing. They kept repeating the word 'lighthouse.'" We think it's an attack order." And Babcock wondered if, by the time they got there, there would be anyone left to save. . . .

Only one of the six hadn't been dead already. With the knife he'd borrowed from Jenny earlier, he corrected that, as quickly as he could and as mercifully, the man unconscious anyway. Three UZI submachine guns, fine weapons but the cyclic rate too fast for some applications; two more AKMs and two spare magazines for each of them; two revolvers and three semiautomatic pistols; an assortment of cheap knives. He looked up the stairwell, Jenny Hall being taken down toward them by Liedecker, her hands still evidently bound behind her to keep her from getting away to turn herself in. Coming along just ahead of them, looking a little wobbly, Comstock.

Cross gave the Englishman credit. SIS men were tough if this man were in any way typical. Only two of the pistols were decent, one of them a Browning High Power like Comstock already had, the other a SIG-Sauer P-226 9mm. The revolver was an old, blue worn Model 10 M&P Heavy Barrel Smith. Cross unloaded the cylinder and checked the timing. Satisfactory, the action wear-smoothed feeling. He reloaded it. "Liedecker! Get down here and check the bodies for spare magazines or ammo, pocketknives, anything we might be able to use for anything."

Cross stood up. He licked his lips nervously. He had experience with explosives, but nobody except an idiot liked dismantling something already set to go off. And these things were. He wished Darwin Hughes were here, because Hughes was the best explosives man Cross had ever seen. Cross set to work, using the Gerber with its spearpoint blade as his probe, starting on the first confluence of plastique ropes.

The announcements had stopped coming and Cross prayed that the killing of hostages had stopped as well. Comstock joined him. "I'm not half bad at this stuff. May I?"

"Please. Those guys looked like a bunch of schlubs."

"Schlubs?"

"No talent dumb asses."

"Ahh." Comstock nodded as Cross looked at him for an instant.

Then Cross put his attention back to the explosives. "But I don't think they were. You have any experience with hidden detonators?"

"A bit. Let's have a look."

"See if you get the same idea I do," Cross said. He lit a cigarette. Smoking wouldn't cause the stuff to blow.

"Yes," Comstock nodded, probing with the knife, "this one for sure. Fake detonator here, as you supposed, but beneath it buried in the plastique—oh, well. So much for this."

There was some movement coming from decks above them now, but Cross didn't think that O'Fallon had enough manpower to launch a major attack, at least not so rapidly. "Liedecker. You any good with a rifle?"

"Try me."

"Good. I'll do that. Burrow in someplace and shoot the first thing that moves above us, right?"

"All right!"

O'Fallon's men would know about the charges and be doubly reluctant to shoot down at them; the terrorists, after all, weren't trained combat marksmen, just a bunch of homicidally delinquent sociopaths. Cross didn't feel safe, but the danger wasn't so immediate, either.

Cross looked at Comstock. "Any brilliant ideas?"

"And I was just about to ask you. One thing, while we think, let's get that bullet fragment out of your leg."

"I was afraid you'd remember."

They found some shelter beneath a reasonably solid steel overhang that supported a wide conveyor belt used to move cargo, Comstock taking out a Zippo lighter much like Cross's own, heating the primary blade of the Swiss Army Knife copy they'd taken off the dead man near the ship's armory. As Comstock fanned the blade on the air to cool it, he said under his breath, "Those are radio detonators, you know."

Cross nodded, saying nothing.

"And," Comstock continued, "I'd wager if our friend has that degree of sophistication, he's likely planted similar devices aboard the yacht they used to intercept us. Which means we can't get out of here with this thing Alvin Leeds is carrying, and we can't stay here either. Stickier than I'd supposed, actually. As soon as you have some marvelously innovative idea beyond the obvious one of getting O'Fallon and neutralizing his detonators, let me know, would you?"

Cross started to say that he didn't have any marvelously innovative ideas, but then Comstock started probing for the fragment in his leg and it was all he could do to keep from screaming or biting off his tongue.

Then Jenny Hall started to speak, her voice lifeless sounding. Her jaw was bruising where he'd knocked her out, and there was a reddish mark where he'd slapped her. It had all gone wrong between them, he knew. "I know you did what was practical. Abe, I know you did. But I'm going to have to live with those deaths for the rest of my life. If I'd turned myself in, maybe they would have stopped."

He wanted to tell her they would only have killed her. But there wasn't any use to doing it. . . .

* * *

Babcock looked up from what he was doing. Hughes was inspecting the parachutes. All the weapons had been serviced, all the magazines loaded, the edges of the knives touched up. Babcock smiled momentarily at that. Hughes had brought one of the Cold Steel Magnum Tantos to give to Cross. Babcock shook his head. The drone of the aircraft was not so terribly loud, just incessant. Babcock looked back to the deck plans he studied. There were acres of deck space, hundreds of people O'Fallon was using as a shield. And what would a man like Alvin Leeds have done with the ampule? At first, he would have hidden it someplace accessible only to crewmen like himself. That much seemed obvious. Restrict the access and you restrict the number of people who might stumble onto it. But if Leeds had kept himself free, had he left the ampule in its original hiding place? Was it on his person? What were his plans? Was he just going to wait for the hostage crisis to be resolved? Did Leeds know that the contents of the ampule were capable of producing death on an almost unprecedented scale?

Babcock closed the file containing the plans to the *Empress*. He opened the file with the photographs. Alvin Leeds, as General Argus had put it, was indeed black, like he—Babcock—was. But his skin looked darker in the photographs, front view and right and left profiles. A high forehead, thinner lips than normal and a crooked sort of smile. What was Leeds's real name? He looked then at the photos of the girl singer, Jennifer Hall. Very pretty with strong features and a look in her eyes that was at once defiant, yet gentle. The next photos were not posed, but blown up candids, very grainy. They showed a tall, good-looking man with sandy hair and, as best Babcock could tell from the photos, a look of amusement in his eyes. This was the KGB man, Vols or Volshinsky or whatever.

Babcock turned to the last group of photos. Dark hair that looked as though it had been combed with the fingers and needed a washing. Deepset dark eyes, the face and the look it held almost Rasputin-like in the image it projected. Seamus Colin O'Fallon. Babcock closed the photo file; O'Fallon's face gave him the chills.

Chapter Twenty-six

The sandy-haired man he had seen prowling about below decks had to be a Russian agent, he had told himself. Otherwise, why would the man have been looking for the ampule? There had been a poker game going with some of the other men from the boiler crew and, once the game had broken up, he had retrieved the ampule from its hiding place, determined to keep it on his person to better guard it.

And then some of the men from the crew had produced guns, shot the Chief when he'd gone after them with a wrench. And he had used the opportunity to slip away, the big military Beretta and the spare magazines for it still hidden among the maze of pipes, and the six rounds in the inherited PPK Alyard had given him not enough to do anything with against four handguns and one of those miniaturized submachine guns.

Then he had decided to hide the ampule again, first retrieving the Beretta then working his way as far aft along the shafts as possible, where the heat from the steam was almost intense enough to make him pass out. But there was a circuit-breaker box with a few inches of free space at its base. He couldn't fit the watertight bag into the gap, nor even the little maroon foam-padded box, but the ampule itself fit there as perfectly as if the space had been made for it and, by pulling down some of the wires, he was able to camouflage its appearance completely.

Planning ahead, he stored the empty maroon case and the watertight, cushioned bag back among the piping, just in case. He would, after all, need something in which to safely transport the ampule once he retrieved it.

And then the business was survival, to hide out and wait it out until the hijacking thing was resolved, if it would be resolved at all, or find some other means of getting the ampule to safety if it came to that.

He had heard each episode of the grisly execution drama unfold over the PA system. And he knew then how it would be resolved. The British, whose ship-of-the-line this was, would have no choice but to send in their crack Special Air Service people, perhaps the best unit-sized counter-terrorist force in the world. But then he had seen them planting the charges of plastic explosives in the main hold, left the area immediately, seen the evidence of more plastique planted elsewhere. He'd had elementary demolitions training. Not that he qualified as any expert, but he knew enough to recognize a setup that would be enormously difficult if not impossible to safely defuse.

Thomas Griffeth had always prided himself on making advantage out of adversity. If the *Empress Britannia* went down, then ''Alvin Leeds'' would go down with it, and the Russians would think the United States had lost the ampule, enhancing the strategic advantage possession of the ampule represented. The Russian program to duplicate the processes by which the contents of the ampule had been developed would not need to be so accelerated when they were convinced that the Americans didn't have it.

''Alvin Leeds'' would die, taking his precious cargo with him. But Thomas Griffeth, his military pistol and spare magazines hidden on his body, would find the means to escape, confirm the chances, return to the electrical box where he had stored the ampule, then get away.

He had climbed down into one of the lifeboats from the deck above; despite the cool temperatures, the air beneath the heavy tarp was stiflingly warm. Sentries moved about on the deck above and below, but when it was safe to do so, he would peer out. After looking at it several times, he decided. The yacht. There was no one aboard her in open view, likely no one aboard her at all. And under cover of darkness, he could slip her moorings and get her round behind the *Empress*'s radar image and make good his escape with the ampule. The British vessel off the port bow would be none the wiser until it was too late, nor would the sentries aboard the *Empress*. There was always the chance a stray shot would get him, but here the only certainty was death. He would wait until just before dawn, slip below and retrieve the ampule, then make for the yacht. . . .

*　　*　　*

"Mr. Hughes?"

"Yes, Lewis?" Hughes was into his black BDUs and securing equipment, Babcock doing the same.

"What if we can't locate the ampule? I mean, what if we can't find Leeds or something's happened to him?"

"Well, what alternatives suggest themselves?"

"The SAS will go over the ship with a fine-tooth comb. They'd find it. And we don't want that to happen, especially since no one's telling them how dangerous it is. And there's always the possibility that if this O'Fallon has the *Empress* wired, we can't neutralize the explosives. I mean, you're the expert. There are some charges that can't be defused, right?"

"Indeed there are. So, then what will we do, Lewis?"

"Get everybody off the *Empress* and scuttle her, right."

"Yes," Hughes agreed. "Yes. That's just what we'd do, Lewis. Help me with this parachute harness—needs tightening over here."

Babcock started working the strap.

Chapter Twenty-seven

There was no sign of any of the crew, and as they moved through the bowels of the *Empress*, all they found were more signs of explosives planted with radio detonators, the detonators so constructed that even a genius with explosives, like Darwin Hughes, would likely have been unable to defuse them safely. The explosives were planted, as best Cross could tell (and Comstock concurred with his judgement), to blow out a fore-to-aft gash on either side of the *Empress* below her waterline. Coupled with the massive explosives package in the hold, which would blow off much of the forward section of the vessel and gut the base of her hull with a hole big enough to drive a truck through, she would sink in minutes. There wouldn't be time to lower her lifeboats; or, if they were lowered already when she blew, there wouldn't be time enough to get far enough away to avoid the lifeboats being sucked down after her.

It was a perfect setup for mass murder, Cross realized, and the only way to prevent the deaths of all passengers and hands was to prevent O'Fallon and his gang of hijackers from using the detonators.

Because Liedecker was with them, with his superior firsthand knowledge of the *Empress*'s layout below decks, it proved a relatively simple matter to lose the party of hijackers who had followed after them once they evacuated the hold. Armed with an adequate number of automatic weapons, they had the equipment to go after O'Fallon and his men, but a plan was still lacking.

And the enormity of the *Empress* below decks convinced Cross of two things: First, they would not find Alvin Leeds unless sheerly by accident; second, finding whatever it was exactly that had been taken from the Russians, if Leeds had hidden it, equated on level of difficulty with a blind man searching for a needle in a haystack while wearing metal mittens.

They sat in a circle on the floor in the mouth of a massive ventilation pipe, secure from observation above or below and with clear fields of fire fore and aft, their voices low as they spoke to avoid them being carried. "We tell this O'Fallon monster that we're armed and that if he and his men don't leave the *Empress*, they're in for it," Jenny Hall said with all the authority of Moses reading the riot act to the People of Israel. Unfortunately, she lacked the same wisdom, Cross realized.

"We can't do that. A: Once he stops laughing he'll remember he's supposed to be killing hostages; B: He already knows we're reasonably well armed and I doubt he's preparing to depart; C: In for what? Once we lose what little element of surprise we've got, then what? We're still outnumbered. He still has hostages. If you're gonna play in the mud, you gotta expect to get your dress a little dirty, kid."

"I'm not wearing a dress. But there has to be some kind of solution besides just killing and more killing."

"You think I like it? You're nuts. You're still beautiful. I still love you. But, you're a friggin' nutball."

"Eat it," she sneered.

"Really," Comstock interjected. "I think this is getting us nowhere. We can't find Leeds. Can't find this precious thing he's taking away from our Russian chums. We can't just sit about waiting for O'Fallon to kill more hostages or blow up the bloody ship."

Cross looked at Liedecker. The man shrugged his shoulders. "I have a responsibility to the passengers and the crew as a ship's officer. It seems clear to me that, overall, fewer lives will be endangered if we take some positive action. I know nothing about explosives, terrorists or anything else. But my parents survived the Nazi era, and one time my mother told me that all of them, those who weren't Nazis, distrusted the Nazis, distrusted war as a means of achieving greatness—that all of them kept waiting for something to happen, for someone else to stop what was going on. But no one ever did until the war ended, and by then, so much had changed forever. I think we must do something; or else, this madman will blow up the *Empress* and every one of the passengers and the crew will die for certain."

Cross looked at Jenny Hall. "What's Leeds got?"

"What?"

"What'd he steal from the Russians, Jenny?"

"Some kind of lab sample. That's all I know," she said almost indifferently.

"That's, ah, not entirely true, is it Miss Hall?"

Cross looked sharply at Comstock.

"Unless I miss my guess, you know exactly what it is, or they wouldn't have sent you along to serve as nanny for it, would they?"

Her pretty eyes hardened.

"What the hell is it, then?" Cross asked, not knowing who to ask. Did Comstock know? Or was he baiting her with a bluff that seemed to be working?

"Why would anybody have told you?" Jenny whispered.

"The question is, why won't you tell us?" Comstock smiled.

Cross closed his eyes, shook his head to clear it. "What's the deal, here, huh?"

"Now perhaps Miss Hall really doesn't know, and the United States government just trusted a foreign secret service with more information than one of their own officers. Is that it?" Comstock asked her.

"It's a sample of biological warfare agent," she said so softly Cross could barely hear her.

"Biological warfare what?"

Comstock cleared his throat. "It's some sort of viral agent. Very deadly. Causes flu-like symptoms for about twenty-four hours, is what we got. Then after that, the virus mutates as the patient of course gets worse and worse. It attacks the cerebral cortex and kills, death in thirty-six hours after infection and incubation. They told us, too, there's no vaccine against it. Our undercover people got some word on it, by the by, while involved in something else and we've done our best to monitor the development. Might have tried stealing it ourselves if you Yanks hadn't beaten us to it." He smiled. "The idea, I presume, behind CIA going after it was that our Russian chums wouldn't dare use it if both sides had it. And, if my days down at university haven't gone all foggy on me, it seems it might be capable of being airborne. Aren't most influenza strains?"

Cross stared at Jenny Hall. "I'm a bloodthirsty killer because I want to fight terrorists rather than surrender to them? And you're Miss Pureheart because you're smuggling biowarfare materials aboard a passenger vessel?"

"What if—and this is just a theory, of course . . ." Comstock began. "But, what if the *Empress Britannia* does blow up? Couldn't the heat of the explosion drive this virus up into the atmosphere and the prevailing winds take it across Europe or something? And don't viruses and nasty things like that thrive in warmth?"

"*Mein Gott*," Liedecker murmured.

"Epidemic. A manmade plague?" Cross asked, rhetorically really.

"We didn't develop the thing. The Russians did!" Jenny insisted.

"Ironic, isn't it, that the champion of Western democracy would unleash it then, what?"

She looked at Comstock as if she wanted to kill him.

Cross asked a question then that had started gnawing at him and worked its way up until he couldn't do anything but ask it. "This Alvin Leeds—does he know what he's got?"

Jenny closed her eyes and the life was gone from her face. "No. He doesn't know anything about it except that if he opens it, breaks it or otherwise releases it the stuff could be dangerous."

Comstock laughed. "And they say we British are the masters of understatement!"

Chapter Twenty-eight

"Let's go over it once more," Darwin Hughes said slowly. Babcock looked at his Rolex. Five minutes until they were to move to the door, seven minutes before the door would be opened, nine minutes before they would leap out into the pre-dawn blackness over the target. "There's a small transponder inside the equipment package. The transponder will activate automatically when the chute opens. If the chute doesn't open, I don't think the package would survive the impact sufficiently that anything would be useable. The transponder's signal will only carry for about five hundred yards; so, it is imperative, Lewis, that you spot the third chute as it opens. Once the package hits the water, the flotation device will activate, but there's only enough flotation to keep it just slightly above the surface. So, you won't be able to spot it visually. And with the seas getting choppier down there, that goes double. I'm going to the yacht as soon as I ditch my parachute, then getting aboard her."

"The chute for the equipment package is rigged to the altimeter?"

"Right."

Babcock nodded. "You go to the yacht and take out anyone aboard her, then I join you with the equipment package and we gear up, then go up onto the *Empress*."

"From what I recall of her, that time I was aboard her, the deck plans haven't changed at all when compared to the diagrams. That's an advantage, having at least a vague physical familiarity with the terrain we'll be working. What then?"

"We're on board and we remove any sentries in the immediate vicinity as quickly as possible. Then we recon to ascertain where the bulk of the hostages are being held."

Hughes nodded, glancing at his watch. "Then we ascertain as best as possible where the control for the demolitions is headquartered. We take out the demolitions control—"

"And we take action to free the hostages, physically freeing the ship's officers first so they can supervise the evacuation."

Hughes smiled, the lines in his cheeks furrowing deeply, his eyebrows cocking upward. "With all those people in lifeboats, once we have the job done, no Russian submarine's going to dare surface. They wouldn't have the room."

"And we find Cross and the girl and this Russian guy and then we get Leeds to take us to the ampule."

"Sounds so easy, doesn't it?" Hughes smiled again. And he looked at his watch. "Time, lad." Hughes offered his hand. Babcock took it.

Hughes started into his helmet, Lewis Babcock doing the same, Hughes starting to check Babcock's equipment. "Good!"

Babcock turned and did an equipment check on Hughes. Both men bent to the cargo package, checking that it was secure, that the chute was rigged properly to it. They hefted the cargo package—it wasn't light—and brought it to the door.

The crewman who had bobbed in and out several times throughout the journey stood beside the fuselage door. Hughes secured his helmet chin strap, then pulled his oxygen mask up. Babcock did the same. "Let's go on oxygen then one last radio check." The headset radios were an emergency item only, radio silence to be maintained unless one of the two of them were in imminent danger.

"Testing one, two, three—Lewis?"

"I have you, Mr. Hughes. Am I coming through?"

"Reading you loud and clear, Lewis. Headsets off."

Lewis Babcock shut down, checking the readings on his oxygen mask. The pilot's voice came over the intercom. "We are depressurizing on my mark. Go to oxygen." Babcock secured his mask, turning on the oxygen supply. The pilot's voice again. "All personnel are on oxygen. Commence countdown to depressurization. Ten . . . nine . . . eight . . . seven . . ." Babcock checked each strap, each gauge, checked the position of the Gerber BMF lashed to his right thigh, checked the safety strap and the thong, secured it into the synthetic sheath. ". . . four . . . three . . . two . . . one . . . MARK!" A klaxon sounded and Babcock reminded himself to breathe, a hissing sound growing progressively louder, his ears feeling strangely hollow, his sinuses starting to run. He sniffed back. The pilot's voice again. "Cabin is depressurized to atmosphere. I say again. Cabin is depressurized to atmosphere." The door was starting to open. There was a loud rushing sound of the slipstream passing around the fuselage.

Lewis Babcock looked to the jump signal. The red light changed in that instant to amber.

Babcock reached to the gear package, Hughes already starting to move it. The man beside the door, secured into the fuselage with webbing safety straps, reached down, grabbed at the package and consulted a stopwatch. He nodded, Babcock and Hughes throwing their weight behind it as the man at the door drew it outward, the package suddenly gone.

Babcock looked up.

Amber light still. He stepped into the door. Green light. Thumbs up from Hughes. A tap on the shoulder from the man at the door. Babcock jumped, tumbling, the wind rush around him deafening for an instant. His arms and legs—he slowly spread them, getting his attitude correct, sailing forward, arms outspread like the wings of a bird. He saw the package, tumbling what looked like a mile beneath him. But it was only his perception.

His eyes came to the altimeter. He watched the needle spinning crazily downward, shifted his eyes from it for a moment. The package! He couldn't—he spotted it, barely visible against the night as it descended below the horizon, now lost entirely. He checked his altimeter. He swallowed hard. His pulse was racing. It always did when he jumped because the thought of hurtling down into the night, on one level of consciousness, terrified him. And he tried to keep that level submerged in the technical details of the jump.

He checked his altimeter constantly now, watching the needle, watching the digital readout, ready to pull the ripcord. The numbers were dropping more rapidly.

"Shit!" Babcock growled into his mask.

He pulled the cord, the snap, his shoulders hauled up, his body wrenched.

He thought he saw a splashdown beneath him, but couldn't be sure. . . .

Darwin Hughes had waited longer, controlling his rate of descent with body movement, aiming himself toward the white blotch beside the white mass, the yacht moored beside the *Em-*

press. Above and to his right, he saw Lewis Babcock's chute open.

Hughes glanced at his altimeter. He was getting too old for this sort of thing, he realized almost absently. He could feel his pulse racing maddeningly. Men his age had heart attacks and strokes, were at greater risk. Few men his age did what he did. What would happen if— He pushed the thought from his mind, the altimeter reading right, his angle right. He pulled the cord, his body whiplashing, the sea yawning up below him, the yacht suddenly gone. He turned his head, had it and worked his chute toward it. If someone with keen eyes spotted him from the deck of the *Empress* and were a good enough shot— But he told himself they would be looking for dozens of men, the SAS coming, not one man or two and a third chute for cargo.

The water was slamming up faster now and he at once braced and relaxed as he readied to hit.

He glided into it, but still the impact to his body took his breath away and he gagged for an instant beneath his mask, his body chilled beyond endurance for a split second. And his hands found the quick release for the chute and he punched it, the chute billowing around him, then gone, the weights added to the pack bringing it down. He turned away from it, his face feeling the pressure of his goggle gasket from the water. He broke surface and ripped away his oxygen mask and sucked air, a whitecap crashing over him.

Hughes tugged at the helmet chin strap, pulling the helmet from his head and trashing it into the water. It, too, was weighted to go down. He began orienting himself as he worked at the straps binding the breathing unit to him. He had them, shrugged out of it. Two hundred yards to the stern of the yacht. He started to swim, keeping his mouth closed, his nose and eyes just above the surface, whitecaps breaking over him.

Hughes looked back once.

There was no sign of Lewis Babcock.

Hughes told himself that Babcock had made it, then pushed the thought from his mind that somehow Babcock hadn't. He kept swimming.

Fifty yards down. One hundred and fifty to go, the yacht's definition growing. He could see a yellow light burning in what had to be the wheelhouse.

One hundred yards gone, one hundred remaining now. He treaded water for an instant, reaching down to his thigh for the reassurance of the Gerber knife. It was there. He started forward again, varying his stroke to conserve energy.

Fifty yards more.

He tucked down beneath the surface, gulping air as he did, swimming more easily now beneath the choppy topside, a dull grey blur ahead of him, the hull of the yacht. He surfaced, gulped air, and tucked down again, swimming easily now because the end was in sight and because he would need strength and breath control more above the surface than below.

His left hand reached out along the surface of the hull and he followed it up, breaking the surface, taking air. His right hand moved to his waist to release the weight belt, then down along his thigh, his skintight gloved fingers undoing the knot then opening the safety strap on the Gerber's sheath. He withdrew the knife, putting it between his teeth pirate fashion as he moved along the hull, the yacht between him and the towering hull of the *Empress*. He found the anchor chain and reached up, biting down harder on the knife, pulling himself along its links hand over hand. He got one foot purchased against a drain hole, pushing himself up, eyes just at the level of the deck.

He saw no one, pulled himself up and slid under the rail, flattening himself against the decking.

Hughes took the knife from his teeth and resheathed it, then pushed up on right knee and left elbow, his right hand jerking down the zipper front of his black wetsuit, then moving beneath it. He felt the plastic bag, drew it out, tore the plastic open and closed his fist over the gunbutt.

To his knees, then to a full crouch, he started forward, the plastic bag balled tight in his left fist, his right thumb sweeping up the silenced Walther PP .22's safety.

The wheelhouse was just ahead, a darker shape against the yellow light. He dropped flat, the Walther ready. Nothing. He moved along on knees and elbows now until he was beside the superstructure, then drew himself up again into a crouch.

The wheelhouse windows—he ducked down.

Past the windows.

Darwin Hughes rose to his full height. He approached the wheelhouse door. It was closed against the night cold. He could see the door handle faintly. He moved his left fist down against it and the door swung open inward. Hughes stepped into the doorway, the door creaking on its hinges, the man at the chart table spilling his coffee as he turned around, the man's right hand holding a large-caliber revolver. Hughes stabbed the PP toward him and fired once, then again, shooting out the left eye with the first shot, the second shot going into the open mouth.

The body flopped back, the right fist tightening on the gun, then the revolver falling, clattering against the table and the body knocking it over, slipping from the chair to lie in a heap against the overturned table.

If there was anyone else aboard the vessel, they'd heard the noise of the table falling. He wheeled toward the companionway steps, racing toward them, a trash basket beside them. He flipped the crumpled plastic bag into it, taking the steps down two at a time, no allowance for caution.

A man was sitting up in a berth near the base of the steps and Hughes shot him once between the eyes. As the head flopped back, Hughes ripped the pillow from beneath it, smothering the pillow over the mouth in case an instant's life were still in the man.

He left the pillow where he'd put it and quickly now explored below decks. Only the two men. No one else. But ten fifty-gallon drums in the compartment amidships, the smell overpowering. And, they didn't smell like diesel.

He had no time to open them, but suspected that here was the much-threatened-with jellied gasoline, the napalm not yet transferred to the *Empress* perhaps, or perhaps too its proximity to charges set aboard the *Empress* deemed enough. Hughes kept moving forward, nothing in the galley except garbage someone had been too lazy to pick up and the smell of onions. He cautiously opened the forward stateroom door, the silenced Walther tight in his fist. He closed his eyes for an instant. Plastic explosives were roped about the cabin like tinsel on a Christmas tree.

Hughes's eyes followed the ropes, all of them coming together at the head of the master bed, right where the hull tapered to form the bow. And just below the waterline. He approached the bed. At the confluence of the ropes of plastique there was an obvious detonator. Too obvious. He touched at the plastique into which it was imbedded, feeling a stiffness below it that could only mean one thing. A concealed detonator. There was no time. And, if there had been, there was no guarantee it was defuseable. Hughes closed the cabin door after him.

Hurriedly, Hughes walked back the way he had come, took the companionway steps three at a time, passed through the wheelhouse, cautiously stepped out onto the deck. Keeping to the heaviest shadows, he made a complete round of the yacht's topside. No one else, a sentry barely visible from the prow standing looking over the railing of the *Empress*.

"Damn!" Hughes hissed under his breath. It was an impossible shot with a handgun, at least for him. He drew back deeper into the shadows, then more quickly made his way aft.

There was no sophisticated signal between them. He simply leaned over the stern rail and hissed into the darkness, "Lewis!"

"Here, Mr. Hughes."

"Company on the portside rail of the *Empress*. Mum's the word," Hughes hissed back as he worked the hammer-drop safety and put the Walther away. "By the anchor, Lewis. Keep low."

He caught the line Babcock flipped up, caught it on the first try, then began to pull.

There was a clanging sound and Hughes ducked, drawing the Walther from beneath his wetsuit again. It was the cargo package hitting the hull. Hughes licked his lips, worked the safety on again and put the Walther onto the deck beside his feet, then kept pulling. In a moment, Babcock was pulling beside him.

"Two here, two gone. Safe as church except for the five hundred gallons of napalm. Keep pulling, Lewis!"

"Napalm?"

"That and the plastic explosives with the hidden detonator. Keep pulling!" They had it up, only the weight of a man or so, but awkward, especially to do in silence. "Into the wheelhouse, lad." They carried it between them, through the door, dropping to their knees as they lowered it. Hughes had his knife out, slashing away the lashings over the watertight case. They pried open the lid, each man reaching for one of the Aimpoint-fitted MP5 SD A3s. "Stand guard while I gear up. Won't be a moment. Watch the man on the deck of the *Empress*. Stay aft. Go on!" And Babcock was through the door.

He took the battle vest with the magazine pouches for the subgun and the extension magazines for the Beretta. He zipped it closed. Hughes took his own pistol belt—they had marked each with tape—and cinched it around his waist, checking the magazine and Swiss Army Knife and mini-Maglite pouches by feel. He took the sheath from his leg and pulled away the lashings, opened the Bianchi fastener and closed it over his belt, then resheathed the knife. The hood from his wetsuit. He stripped it away with a snapping sound, then opened the small utility pouch on the battle vest, pulling out first the other hood then the earplugs. They would not prohibit sound, but only serve to break it up. Hughes put the plugs into his ears, then pulled the mask/hood over his head and down along his throat, adjusting it to line up the eye holes, for an instant feeling as though it were going to smother him. He ignored the feeling. He stripped away his diving boots and pulled on boot socks, then stuffed his feet into his combat boots and speed-laced them.

To his feet, the H&K submachine gun in his right fist. And then he bent over the open waterproof container and took out one other object. It was a stock Cold Steel Magnum Tanto. He'd promised himself he'd deliver it to a friend. He slipped it into the loops at the front of his battle vest—he'd sewn them in on board the aircraft—and secured them. He caught up his gas mask bag and slung it, then his musette bag with the stun grenades and the smoke and gas grenades.

Hughes stepped out of the wheelhouse. "Lewis—you take Cross's things. Then we take out our friend on the rail of the *Empress*."

Babcock nodded, disappearing into the wheelhouse.

Slowly, silently as he could, Hughes drew back the bolt of the H&K, then eased it forward, stripping the top round from the magazine and chambering it. His thumb played with the safety.

In just over a minute as he ticked it off mentally, Babcock was out of the wheelhouse, the second pistol belt strapped across his chest, the pistol beneath his left arm, the second submachine gun slung across his back.

Hughes looked at him. Babcock nodded. Hughes wondered if he looked as unearthly with the hood pulled over his face as Babcock did? He suspected that he did.

Quickly, silently, they moved forward along the starboard side, keeping in low crouches, hugging against the superstructure as they neared the bow rail.

The man Hughes had seen before lounged there still, a cigarette glowing in his fingers.

Hughes already had the H&K's stock retracted and he shouldered the weapon now, set to semiauto. The light was poor, but he trained often with poor light intentionally. He held over a little because of the extreme angle and fired, aiming for the head.

There was the tiniest plop, the body rocking, collapsing over the rail. "We live right—if he'd fallen to the deck here or into

the water, only a deaf man couldn't have heard it. Come on!''
And they started for the gangplank lowered from the *Empress* to
the level of the yacht's deck. . . .

Thomas Griffeth pushed up the edge of the tarp which covered
the lifeboat. He saw no one. The military pistol in his fist, he
pushed the tarp up further and swung one leg over, the lifeboat
swaying in its berth. Then he swung his other leg out and
dropped. He was instantly chilled, sweating under the tarp which
prevented any sort of air circulation, and now the cold predawn
air making him shiver. He started aft toward the companionway
steps. First get the cases for it, then the ampule itself, then back
topside and down to the yacht.

Griffeth started moving. A voice came out of the shadows.
''Faith now, blackie. You wouldn't be this Leeds feller we
been lookin' after findin', would ya now?''

Griffeth had already turned toward the voice, saw no one. And
then he felt the thing, colder than the sweat which bathed him
or the night air which cocooned him, so cold as it penetrated into
the very heart of his being. He fumbled for the safety, but the
strength was all gone from his hand.

''Looks like we won't be needin' to look for you no more,
blackie.''

Griffeth felt an emptiness and he suddenly realized he was
dying. . . .

Abe Cross moved quickly down the corridor toward the casino's main entrance, nervous-sounding chatter coming through the
open doors, the nervous chatter of people consumed with fear.
He'd heard it before. He looked across the corridor to the opposite side, Comstock moving as he did, flat against the bulkhead,
an Uzi submachine gun in each fist, a pistol stuffed in his belt.

They stopped just before the doors.

He looked back down the corridor.

She stood there, waiting. Cross nodded to her. She started
walking, on the balls of her feet as if she were wearing high
heels, hips swaying an imaginary skirt, head high, hair tossed
back. He'd asked her, ''Will you? It's the only diversion we've
got. We need something.''

Naked except for her bra and panties, Jenny Hall walked past
him straight through the open doorway, Comstock's expression
half arousal and half amusement.

There were shouts. There was a whistle. A catcall. A scream, he assumed from one of the women passengers.

Cross nodded to Comstock.

They stepped through the doorway.

Jenny Hall, standing in the middle of a crap table, tore off her bra and threw it into the knot of terrorist gunmen around her. Cross shouted, ''Hostages down!'' And the first fingers of each hand touched the triggers of the Uzi submachine guns. A heavier roar came from his right. It would be Liedecker with one of the AKMs. Terrorists, shock registering in their faces, fear in their eyes, were wheeling toward them. A flash of pink bare flesh as Jenny dove off the table to cover. Cross tracked his subguns toward the crap table now. She knew the chances. He kept firing, the one in his right fist out, chunks of furniture and ceiling fixtures flying around the room, pieces of wall and ceiling tile disintegrating, the dust spraying everywhere. His second Uzi was gone and he let them drop at his side and drew the Colt Officers ACP that was cocked and locked in his waistband. He extended his right hand, fired, acquired a new target, fired, his left hand grasping the liberated Smith & Wesson M&P .38, thumb-cocking it, firing, acquiring another target, firing. He shot one of the terrorists in the mouth with the .45, another twice in the throat with the .38, another one gutshot with the .45. Liedecker fired on the terrorist too, the already dying man's body flopping back as the round from the AKM hit. Cross looked right. Comstock, a Browning High Power in each hand, fired point-blank into the chest of a man charging at him with just bare hands, then wheeled, firing into the head of a terrorist crawling across the floor toward his assault rifle.

Cross looked toward the center of the casino floor. There were whimpering sounds, and children cried, and there were murmurs of ''Oh, my God,'' and Jenny Hall stood there, nothing on but her panties, her arms folded across her to cover her bare breasts. He saw her bra and told Liedecker, ''Get that for her, huh?'' And he started around the room, checking bodies. Comstock was doing the same, a grim set to his features like nothing Cross had ever seen before. Cross had decided: Any who weren't dead would get that way. With the arms and ammunition from these men, he had the rounds to waste. And there would not be enough medical personnel or lifeboat room for the terrorists anyway. They had stepped out of the human community when they had become terrorists.

One of the terrorists moved, reached up, clawed at his trouser leg. Cross turned toward him and moved the muzzle of the revolver on line with the man's forehead. "Die." Cross pulled the trigger. Sometimes, he thought, a person really did get what he earned. . . .

They had crossed up onto the *Empress*, dragged the body of the man he had shot off the rail, putting it inside the darkened doorway of the snack shop.

There was gunfire aft, Hughes signaling Babcock. "The casino. Either they're executing hostages or someone's doing some rescuing of his own. We go to the Seabreeze Lounge—hurry!" There were steps leading up to the decks above, Hughes running toward them, dodging left as he heard the racking of a submachine-gun bolt, but tripping on something as he moved deeper into the shadows. "Company!" Hughes dropped to one knee, punching the H&K toward the steps as soon as he saw a target, firing, the ones from the steps returning fire, chunks of the bulkhead beside Hughes blasting away, Hughes drawing back.

He looked down in the darkness to find what he'd tripped over. It was the body of a man.

Hughes stabbed the H&K round the edge of his cover and fired a short burst.

They had rehearsed the responses to specific situations with predetermined, numbered routines. "Alpha!" Hughes shouted. "Number Three!" Hughes called again, reaching to his musette bag, taking one of the sound and light grenades from it, pulling the pin. As he hurtled it, he closed his eyes, turning his face away, the palms of his hands cupping over his ears, his shoulders hunching.

Despite the plugs in his ears and his hands shielding them, he could hear the high-pitched whine, almost deafeningly loud. It was deafening to unprotected ears, the flash of light from the grenade blindingly bright, the effect wearing off in a few hours totally. But these people would never be alive long enough for that. There was sporadic submachine-gunfire audible as Hughes started forward in a dead run, Babcock right beside him, both men spraying their weapons into the writhing bodies of the three terrorists. "Toss their weapons over the side. Something I have to do." Hughes ran back, to where he had tripped over the body. From the pouch at his belt, he took the mini-Maglite, twisting the flashlight's head and shining it over up along the body and toward the face. There was a huge, open wound in the abdomen, as though a long knife had gutted the man, the man's hands clasped over it in death. And the face.

Hughes dropped to his knees and detail-searched the body.

"Damn!" He rose to his feet, twisting off the flashlight, running to rejoin Lewis Babcock. Babcock was already halfway up the steps, Hughes picking his way over the bodies to join him. "That was our friend Alvin Leeds. Dead. No ampule. Nothing. Which means unless somebody else has it, the blasted thing's hidden aboard the *Empress.*"

"We scuttle her?"

"We scuttle her." Hughes nodded.

He reached the head of the steps just behind Babcock. It took only a second to orient himself, then he rasped, "Follow me and be ready with the gas but don't use it unless I say so. We can't load hundreds of unconscious passengers into lifeboats." He broke into a run for the Seabreeze Lounge. . . .

Nineteen of the men and two of the women from among the passengers who had been held captive in the casino had some type of military experience. Cross ordered Liedecker to parcel out the captured weapons and the shotguns taken earlier as best he could. He stepped up onto the crap table. "This is gonna be short, so listen. There are passengers and crew—the ones with British passports, it appears—and the ship's officers held in the Seabreeze Lounge. We're going after them now. This vessel is mined with high explosives and there doesn't seem to be any way to defuse them." There were screams, cries. Cross shouted over them. "Listen. There are plenty of lifeboats. You can't go to your cabins for your life vests so you're just going to have to be a little more careful. Mr. Liedecker, as a ship's officer, is in complete command. Anyone who doesn't cooperate or panics he has authority to shoot. Now, under Mr. Liedecker, move quietly and safely toward the lifeboats. He will direct you. Mr. Liedecker!"

"Here." And Liedecker stepped up onto a roulette table. "Everyone was given a lifeboat assignment when they came aboard. We will have to alter that procedure. Families whose last names beginning with the letters A through M will assemble on the portside of the casino—to my left," and he began gesturing to his left.

Cross tapped Comstock on the shoulder. "Still game?"

"As a matter of fact, I am old boy."

"Count me in," Jenny Hall told them, coming to stand beside them, fully dressed now. "I took another Uzi and rounded up a half dozen more spare magazines."

Cross smiled at her. "All right." They started out of the casino. . . .

Seamus O'Fallon screamed his orders from the stage. "All the children in the bathrooms. Get 'em, lads!"

Paddy Kehoe, still wiping off his knife, tapped two of the others on the shoulder, young Martin one of them, then sprinted off toward the restrooms where the British children—more than a dozen and a half of them—were incarcerated.

"All of ya—your damned SAS won't save ya!" And he looked to the half dozen men he had left. "Jack. You've got the responsibility, lad. Bunch the hostages around ya and take 'em topside. Demand that they withdraw. Hurry!"

There were screams, the voices of people begging not to be separated from their children. As O'Fallon stepped from the stage, a woman in a stained dress ran to him and fell to her knees at his feet. "Please, my children!"

O'Fallon kicked her away. "Paddy!"

"Comin', Seamus!" They were dragging some of the children, pushing the rest, O'Fallon fighting his way through the crowd toward them as Jack and the other lads assembled the adult hostages around them.

O'Fallon reached Paddy, Biff, and young Martin and the children. "All right, now, lads, stick with me." And he bent down to a little girl and swept her up in his arms.

"Let me go!"

"Shut your bloody little mouth, girl," O'Fallon hissed, crushing her close to him. "Each of ya grab a child into your arms. Can't shoot when you're holdin' a kid. Come on!" The radio detonator was in his pocket. All he needed was to flip the cover and pull the antenna and push the switch into the on position. But if he led the SAS a merry chase through the bowels of the *Empress*, he'd take more of them with him.

"Come on, lads!" The headache was intensifying. . . .

Darwin Hughes skidded on his boot heels, throwing himself against the flat of the bulkhead, then edging forward along its length. There was an easeled poster advertising a singer named Jennifer Hall and a pianist named Abe Cross.

He peered around the corner, and from between the open glass doors with etched birds and palm trees on them, he saw a group of dissheveled men and women, clothes rumpled and stained, hair uncombed, faces dirty, fear in their eyes, some of the women crying, all of them bunched together, all of them with their hands bound, some of them with adhesive tape patches over their mouthes.

"We've got trouble," Hughes told Lewis Babcock.

Hughes called out. "The game is up! O'Fallon's men! The game is up! Lay down your weapons and release the hostages!"

"Fuck off, SAS-er. Or they all get it here and now!"

Hughes was warm beneath the mask. Suddenly warmer. He licked his lips. "Look. We aren't the SAS. We only care about the hostages being freed. Then do what you want. All right?"

He was lying, but it didn't matter now.

There was a burst of submachine-gun fire and a scream, Hughes stepping partway from cover so he could see, react if he could. Two of the hostages were on the floor, bleeding. The rest, screaming, crying, were bunched around the terrorists so tightly Hughes couldn't even see how many of them there were.

Hughes ducked back rather than provoke another outburst of killing. Babcock whispered beside him, "Mr. Hughes. The stun grenades?"

"No, no, we can't. They'd still have time to fire out their weapons into the people around them. It'd be a bloodbath. The same for the gas. Even with the glass enclosure to the seaward side, there's too much ventillation. Never work in time. Damn!" Hughes hammered his fist against the bulkhead. His mind raced as he ran the options. There were none.

Hughes called out again to the terrorists. "What do you want?"

"A bloody boat."

"You have the yacht already," Hughes called back, stalling.

There was a laugh. "You can have that boat, copper."

"Look. Fine, we'll get you a boat. Just release the hostages and you're all free to go. O'Fallon's got this boat wired to blow," Hughes said, gambling, "and the yacht, too. What's the sense of everybody dying? If you had a point to prove to the Brits, you've proved it. Save your lives, damnit!"

"Bleedin' British lies, copper! We're comin' out—don't try nothin' or they all dies!" Hughes swapped magazines in his submachine gun.

Hughes looked at Babcock. Lewis Babcock was doing the

same. "If you have a brilliant stratagem in mind, Lewis, this is no time to hold back."

Babcock shook his head.

Hughes peered round the corner. They were coming—but behind them. He blinked his eyes. Through his teeth, Hughes hissed, "Be ready, lad. Only guns."

Two men were just inside the double doorway, one of them was Abe Cross and the other face—Hughes couldn't be sure—he thought was the Russian, Vols or Volshinsky or whatever his proper name was.

Cross was armed, but nothing was in his hands except a knife. The Russian was holding a knife, too. "My God," Hughes hissed to Babcock. "No guns. Be ready with your knife, lad."

Cross and the Russian were slowly moving forward, each of them in a low crouch. Hughes felt his body tense. The nearest of the hostages was less than three yards from him now.

"We're comin' through, we are," the terrorist who'd spoken before snarled.

"Well. Then come ahead," Hughes told him, letting his submachine gun fall to his side on its sling, starting to move his hands outward and away from his torso.

Cross jumped. Hughes reached to his fighting knife. The Russian charged forward like a benighted football player trying to break up a huddle instead of a play. Hughes snapped, "Now, lad!" to Babcock, then hurtled himself toward the knot of hostages and the terrorists within it, Cross visible for an instant at the edge of Hughes's peripheral vision, a head snapping back, a throat slit. Hughes shoved aside a woman, ramming the blade of his knife into the throat of one of the terrorists. A submachine gun discharged. There was screaming. Hughes saw Babcock, left fist flashing out, catching one of the terrorists in the mouth, the right hand driving his knife forward and into the terrorist's chest.

Hughes felt something cold, then suddenly hot across his back and he stumbled forward as he heard the burst of submachine gun fire. He hit the deck and rolled, his knife slashing across the right kneecap and left thigh of the terrorist. As the man recoiled from the knife, the Russian was suddenly there, driving his smallish blade home like a rapier, into the right side of the terrorist's neck.

Hughes was up, Cross locked in combat with the last of the men as best Hughes could tell. Babcock stepped forward, swinging the butt of his submachine gun as if it were a baseball bat, the terrorist's head snapping left, Cross stepping in, driving his knife into the man's throat to the hilt. The body fell.

Hughes swung his submachine gun on line, covering a quadrant of the lounge foyer at a time.

Abe Cross spoke. "Three more, plus O'Fallon himself. Jenny followed after them. They were going below. Had about eighteen kids with them ranging in ages from early teens to preschoolers. It was either go after them or help you, and you sounded like you needed it."

"We did, lad. Your Russian friend's a good fighter."

"Russ—" Cross wheeled toward Vols, but Vols had his submachine gun up and aimed at Cross and Babcock. Hughes leveled his weapon at Vols.

"Everybody down!" Babcock ordered, the hostages still screaming, crying, terrified, huddled around them.

"I have no desire to hurt anyone, sir," Vols said, a smile on his face but his eyes not smiling at all. "All I want is the opportunity to recover the property stolen from my nation by your nation. Ask Mr. Cross. I've assisted him throughout. I only came for the rightful property of my country."

Hughes lowered his submachine gun. "Well, I'm sorry, Major Vols, but there's a bit of a problem with that. I found a body on the deck out there, down on the boat deck. It was Alvin Leeds. I bet you know who he is."

Vols's right eye twitched.

Hughes said, "I searched him quite thoroughly. We were briefed concerning the viral agent. He didn't have it. There was nothing on him to indicate where he'd hidden it. Is the *Empress* wired?"

"Radio-controlled detonators," Vols said. "Cross and I—we inspected them. They are booby-trapped. Can't be defused, I doubt even by an expert."

"And you know what will happen to the viral agent if it becomes heated and gets into the upper air currents, don't you?"

"You are telling me the truth, then? Finding the ampule is hopeless?"

Hughes nodded. "Finding the ampule is hopeless. We've got to scuttle the ship before O'Fallon can blow it. It's the only way to neutralize the contents of the ampule."

Vols looked at Cross. "I trust you, Cross. Is he telling me the truth?"

"Yes. He's telling you the truth."

Vols nodded. He looked at Babcock, then at Hughes. "I would think a truce might be in order, then, sir. We have to free those children."

"Good man," Hughes said softly.

He heard Cross saying, "Russian, gee whiz." And as Hughes looked, Vols lowered his submachine gun and Cross clapped him on the shoulder.

"This is ridiculous," Lewis Babcock remarked. "Let me look at your back," and he came over to Hughes. "Looks like a graze. The vest deflected it."

Hughes looked to the hostages huddled around them. "All right. Give me your attention, please. The crisis is over for you, but we have to get all of you off the *Empress* . . ."

"My children!" a woman screamed from beside him. Hughes dropped to a crouch before her, gently helped her to her feet. "That devil's got my—"

"We'll get them back for you, 'ma'am. We specialize in fighting devils."

And the hostages all began to stand now, Babcock and Cross and the Russian, Vols, aiding them to their feet. There wasn't much time left.

Cross said, his voice low, "All the ship's officers. They're dead on the floor in there, in the lounge, hands cuffed behind them, bags over their heads, strangled or throats slit. She's right about the devil part."

Chapter Twenty-nine

Darwin Hughes, Lewis Babcock, Vols and Abe Cross moved into the companionway, a lipstick slash arrow pointing the way as Jenny Hall followed after O'Fallon and his men and the hostage British children.

They paused at the head of the companionway steps, Cross buckling on the gunbelt Hughes and Babcock had brought for him, drawing the Magnum Tanto and its sheath from his trouser belt where he'd placed it and stuffing it between the front of his pistol belt and his abdomen. He took back the H&K from Vols, whom he'd given it to as he put on the belt.

Hughes started down the companionway steps, virtually no light here at all; but, to have used their flashlights would have alerted anyone ahead of them. All they were able to risk was one of the mini-lights, the beam shielded within a fist and moved up and down the bulkhead surface to look for more arrows, more signs Jenny had passed this way following after O'Fallon.

The course they followed was taking them inexorably deeper into the bowels of the *Empress Britannia*, and suddenly Cross knew exactly where O'Fallon was headed.

Vols whispered in his ear, "I know where O'Fallon's going—the madman!"

"To the cargo hold," Cross whispered back. He stopped Hughes and Babcock. "Vols and I both agree. There's only one place he's going. He may want to die, but he won't want to drown like the rat he is. He's taking the kids to the main cargo hold where he's got most of the explosives."

"Is there a faster way to get there? To beat him there, maybe?" Lewis Babcock asked.

"There might be," Vols volunteered. "I just had a flash of an idea. O'Fallon took his men and the children below decks immediately to get out of sight. He thought the SAS was coming and his game was up. But wouldn't it be more direct to cross along the boat deck, and then rope it down into the cargo hold or something?''

''Vols is right,'' Cross said slowly. ''If we go back topside and cut over, then the two of you follow them, we'd at least have them between us.''

''Quickly, then,'' Hughes began. ''You've both seen the explosives. What are the chances a gunfight would set things off? Any chance of using stun grenades or gas?''

Cross closed his eyes, picturing the hold. He opened his eyes. ''We fired down into the hold and took out six of their guys. But we waited until they were leaving through an access door and as far away from the explosives as they could get and still be in sight. That'd be the only way. Stun grenades could be effective, but O'Fallon's men—''

''Would shoot the children,'' Babcock supplied.

Cross said, ''Yeah. Same with gas unless it were instantaneous in effect.''

''Too strong an updraft, I'd think,'' Vols interjected.

''He might be right,'' Cross agreed. ''There are four of them, counting O'Fallon. There are four of us and Jenny. If we could box 'em in, we could go after them like we did the guys topside by the lounge.''

''Let's not forget that O'Fallon will have his detonator with him, could use it instantly in any likelihood,'' Hughes murmured. ''But it's the best plan we've got. Abe, you and Major Vols try to cut them off. We'll stay after the girl and meet you there.''

''We'll need some kind of signal for when we're all in position and ready to hit,'' Babcock said, sounding as if he were thinking aloud.

''I've got a flare pistol,'' Hughes said. ''We'll have to assume both of you are into position ahead of us. When we're in position, I'll fire the flare and then we go for it, instantly. Because we won't have any time.''

''Better brief Jenny where to take the kids.''

''Good idea, lad. Tell me something—you and Jennifer Hall—anything I could say to her that would instantly take care of the introductions?''

''Tell her I'm sorry I clipped her in the jaw.''

Cross heard Hughes chuckle softly. "All right. Good luck." Hughes started past him, Babcock after him. Cross started back up the companionway steps, Vols right behind him.

They reached the boat deck level, the sun already beginning to rise over the water, the sounds of shouted orders and boats' winches and children crying filling the air, the lifeboats lowering, better than a half dozen of them visible in the water below.

Cross ran, his left thigh burning from the dugout bullet fragment, Vols sprinting along beside him, the Russian's left arm stiff at his side, but a pistol clutched in the left fist, and an Uzi in his right.

People stared at them as they ran, shrieked in terror from the sight of armed men running, Cross shoving past the lines for the lifeboats, no time to explain.

He saw Liedecker ahead, increased his pace. "Liedecker! Liedecker!"

"Cross!"

Cross shouldered past more of the fleeing passengers, getting to Liedecker, grabbing the man by the shoulders. "All the hostages are accounted for as best we can tell. Except about eighteen children. All the ship's officers were murdered . . ."

"*Gott in Himmell* . . ." And Liedecker made the sign of the cross.

"Look. We've gotta have a lifeboat standing by if one'll hold 'em."

Liedecker's eyes seemed glazed. He was stunned. Cross shook the man. "Liedecker!"

"Yes, all right. A lifeboat for eighteen children. I will personally see that it is standing by. You and Herr Comstock—you go to rescue them?"

"To try, yes." And Cross edged through the crowd, picking up his pace, shouting back to Liedecker as he ran, shouldering ahead, "Remember! Eighteen kids, then shove off! Don't wait for us! Remember!" But he knew his words would be lost by now in the frantically shouted orders, the men and women and children searching for loved ones, clamboring aboard the lifeboats.

They reached the spot above the cargo hold as best Cross could tell, swinging over the deck rail to peer toward the hull, confirming the opening there well above the water line, the opening sealed.

"Over here, Cross! I say, here!" Cross looked around, spotted Vols by steps leading below, Vols shouting again, "This way!"

Vols vanished into the well for the steps, Cross shoving his way after him, reaching the steps, starting down in a run. He could see Vols for an instant as the steps diagonaled back and downward off the landing below. Cross started taking the steps two at a time, jumping the last three to the landing, taking the next flight down, flipping the rail to the landing from four steps up, right behind Vols now, Vols tripping, catching himself, jumping to the landing below.

There was a door, watertight and massive, a warning sign proclaiming entry restricted. "The hold," Vols panted.

Cross nodded, throwing his weight to the wheel that operated the locking mechanism, the armatures moving in a zigzagging pattern as they pulled the bolts from their receptacles. Cross stepped back, Vols swung open the door.

It was all or nothing. They both knew that.

Beyond the door was a catwalk and as Cross and Vols stepped through the door simultaneously, the cargo hold yawned open below them, the light from the battery-operated lanterns by which the terrorists had set their explosives yellowed now and nearly dead.

O'Fallon wasn't there yet.

Cross took to the catwalk steps, both fists on the rails, skidding down to the next landing, Vols running, flipping the railing to the landing, just behind him. Cross kept running, his eyes scanning the door opening into the bottom of the hold, seeing no one. He kept running.

He flipped the rail and came down in a crouch on the deck of the hold, his left leg screaming at him that he was an idiot, Vols still coming, Cross sweeping the hold with the muzzle of his H&K, settling it on the door. Still no one.

Vols rasped from behind him. "Here, behind these crates. There's a way up on top of them if we need it."

Cross only nodded, walking backwards slowly, the submachine gun still aimed toward the door. He dodged behind the packing crates, Vols there, his knife already out. "So," Vols whispered, barely audible, "you're one of these commando chappies? You Americans are versatile, indeed. Pianist. Commando. Do you do rope tricks?" And Vols smiled.

"And you're one of these slimeball KGB guys, huh?" Cross grinned.

"Oh, the slimiest, yes. Are you? One of them?"

"I was. What's a decent guy like you doin' with an outfit like the KGB?"

"Almost sounded like that old line about 'What's a nice girl like you doing,' etc., for a moment. What am I doing with the KGB? Right now, I'm not so sure. Usually, just my patriotic bit for Mother Russia and all that. Whatever you do, if we get out of this flap alive, don't go back and tell your CIA that I helped you. The crowd at Derzhinsky Square won't be too happy with me at any event by then."

"I'd never tell anybody that I had a KGB Major as a friend— don't worry," Cross hissed, eyeing the door.

"You mean that? I mean, the friend part?"

"Yeah. Wanna make somethin' of it?"

"Actually, I feel the same way. And don't worry. I'd never admit to having a money-grubbing corrupt capitalist exploiter of the working classes for a friend either."

Vols shifted his knife to his left hand, extending his right hand. "Let's hope we never meet professionally, hmm?"

Cross took it. "Amen."

And then he heard a child crying and he looked back to the doorway. Nothing in sight, but he heard the child again. He set the safety on the H&K and shifted it back, his right fist closing on the haft of the Magnum Tanto, his left unsheathing the smaller Tanto he'd borrowed from Jenny Hall.

The larger blade he held against his right forearm, edge outward, the smaller blade he held like a dagger.

He felt Vols tap him on the shoulder, gesturing toward the top of the crates. Cross nodded. Vols sheathed his knife, started to climb.

Cross looked around his position. Ropes of plastic explosives were entwined everywhere. If something went wrong, he'd never have the chance to know it.

There were the cries of many children now, the hesitantly defiant voice of a young girl, the blunt sounding threat of a boy whose voice hadn't quite changed. And the children were herded and pushed inside the hold like animals, some of the smaller ones thrown to the steel deck plates.

And he saw O'Fallon. It had to be O'Fallon. Eyes like death, the face of a prophet or a madman, perhaps both. There was an Uzi submachine gun slung casually off his right shoulder, a revolver in his right fist.

Slouch hat, brown corduroy sportcoat, lighter corduroy slacks, a cigarette hung from his mouth, the mouth downturned at the corners.

"Keep the the little bastards quiet, Martin! Paddy—that bitch with the loud mouth—" and he gestured toward a girl of about thirteen, dissheveled looking but pretty, the flashing blue eyes and dark curls and upturned nose only marred by the braces visible as she opened her mouth to scream or curse O'Fallon. "That one—miss prissy, there. Cut her damn tongue out if she lets out a peep, Paddy."

"Right, Seamus," and Paddy—a leer on his face that said he liked to do other things with young girls—drew his right hand from his coat pocket and there was a loud click. A switchblade, the blade itself of enormous seeming proportions. He leaned toward the girl and she screamed.

"Cut that foul tongue out of her head!" O'Fallon shrieked, both his hands going to his head, rubbing at his temples. "Cut it out of her head, Paddy!"

He wasn't just a devil. He was also stark, raving mad, Cross realized.

Paddy started for the girl. She screamed again and O'Fallon stomped his feet and shrieked unintelligibly.

Cross looked upward, not for inspiration but for some sign of Hughes and Babcock. No flare. Nothing.

"Hold it!"

Cross looked toward the doorway. It was Jenny Hall, her shiny .45 automatic in both tiny fists, the muzzle aimed for O'Fallon's head.

Cross started to move. There wasn't time. The third flunkie to O'Fallon stepped from the shadows beside the doorway and the pistol in his right fist belched a tongue of flame as the hold reverberated with the sound waves of the gunshot. Paddy grabbed the dark-haired girl by the hair in the same instant and brought the knife down toward her mouth as she screamed, the scream lost in the gunshot. A small child shrieked with fear. Cross's right hand snapped outward as his body lunged, the blade of the Magnum Tanto swinging outward in a ninety-degree arc, intercepting Paddy's switchblade. "Try me, asshole," Cross snarled.

"Now!" It was Hughes's voice. Cross didn't know from where, and there was no time to look, Paddy throwing the girl against Cross, then diving toward him with the knife. Cross stumbled, turned to push the girl behind him, felt the knife as it skated over his ribcage. Cross shoved the girl away and wheeled, hacking outward with the larger Tanto, drawing off Paddy's blade. He saw a blur of movement as Vols dove from the top of the stacked packing crates onto the back of one of the other terrorists. Cross's left hand snaked forward, the mini-Tanto striking for the throat, missing as Paddy dodged, wheeled, his knife streaking toward Cross's face. Cross snapped his head back, nearly losing his balance, the tip of Paddy's blade missing Cross's face by inches. Cross's left leg snapped out as he wheeled right and ducked. The toe of his left foot hammered against the side of Paddy's right knee. Paddy stumbled back.

Cross finished the turn, both blades ready in his hands, spinning in his fingers.

He saw Hughes and Babcock coming down the catwalk steps, Hughes flipping over the rail from the last landing, throwing himself toward the man who'd shot Jenny, Babcock running straight for O'Fallon.

And then the devil voice he'd heard, hated over the loudspeaker during the hostage executions, came in a high-pitched shout. "Freeze! Or the detonator gets its pretty button pushed, now!"

Cross held his blades, his eyes passing from Paddy—who stood stock still—to Babcock—stopped dead in his tracks less than six feet from O'Fallon—to O'Fallon himself. O'Fallon's right hand was raised high over his head, a small box in his outstretched fingers, thumb poised over a red button.

"Ya bloody peelers! We'll be together in Hell!"

Cross started to move, a blur of motion at his left, Vols diving for O'Fallon. Hughes—Cross saw the gun rising in Hughes's hand. Babcock was hurtling himself toward O'Fallon.

And then a carrot-haired boy, not much more than an older teenager—the one O'Fallon had called Martin—jumped up as if he were going for a slam dunk in basketball, his hands closing over O'Fallon's right hand, O'Fallon hurtled back against the bulkhead. O'Fallon's left hand moved. There was the blast of a gunshot and the carrot-haired boy was blown back. Babcock's head impacted O'Fallon in the crotch, the revolver discharging a second time. Vols threw his body upward, hands groping for O'Fallon's hand that held the detonator. Hughes fired, O'Fallon's right cheek blown away. Cross was suddenly there, not knowing how he'd gotten there, but simply being there, his right hand arcing downward, the long-bladed Tanto's blade biting through flesh, catching an instant, then passing through, O'Fallon letting out a hideous shriek as his thumb was severed.

Cross saw it, the thumb flying outward, the detonator, its antenna extended, tumbling from the thumbless hand. He threw himself after it, his body twisting as he impacted the deck plates, the Tanto falling from his fingers, his hands reaching.

His hands closed over the detonator, his own right thumb almost depressing it.

He saw a blur of motion coming for him. It was Paddy, still with his knife. Lewis Babcock twisted round and in his right hand was his pistol. The Beretta fired twice, then twice again, Paddy's body spinning, falling, Cross edging back to avoid the knife as Paddy fell.

"We did it," Hughes said quietly. And he turned for the doorway. Children were screaming. "God forgive me this," and the Beretta in Hughes's hand fired once. Cross twisted over onto his stomach and looked toward the doorway. The last of the terrorists slumped against the bulkhead, turned around, eyes wide open in death, then slipped to the deck as if he were just sitting.

Darwin Hughes turned to the children, dropped to his knees, holstering his gun. He tore off the mask which covered his face. "Children. I'm sorry you saw this. But there was no other way." Some of the children began approaching him, the grey hair, the smile Cross knew was there, like an exceedingly fit, melifluous voiced grandfather cum hero. He outstretched his arms, drawing some of the children to him, holding them. "There are bad men in the world. You all know that. And sometimes, to stop bad men, we have to be bad ourselves. But none of you—none of you walk away from this taking human life cheaply. You have your lives. Respect life whether it's yours or someone else's."

Cross watched, listened, picked himself up off the floor. It was like listening to Batman or The Lone Ranger, but he didn't feel like laughing. He started to disarm the detonator but realized his hands were trembling too badly.

He looked around behind him, remembering Jenny. Vols had her propped against him, and she was breathing. "I wonder if a KGB Major and a CIA case officer could ever make a go of it, Cross?"

Cross just stood there, then Lewis Babcock, taking the mask from his face, reached out for the detonator. "Give me that."

Cross gave it to him.

Chapter Thirty

Abe Cross looked out over the twenty-three steps that led down from the front porch. He lit a cigarette. Hughes and Babcock were inside, Hughes being beaten at chess.

O'Fallon had raped the *Empress*. Cross himself and Hughes and Babcock had done no better by her, opening her wide to the sea, the last intimate portion of her violated. And after not very much time at all, the *Empress* had bowed beneath the waves and the ocean itself had seemed to spasm with her coming.

Over twenty-two thousand feet deep according to the charts. Until diving technology took a quantum leap forward, a detailed enough exploration of the *Empress Britannia* to recover the ampule from the bottom of the Atlantic would be impossible. And, by that time, the Russians would have reinvented their virus or developed something worse and the United States would have its own version of the virus or its own version of something worse.

Or just maybe, nobody would want to bother with something like that by then. But Abe Cross doubted that part. Which, he supposed, was the reason he had told Darwin Hughes and Lewis Babcock that he'd come in it with them again.

It was a clear night and cool.

Jenny Hall's voice had been that way on the telephone from West Germany. She would be released in a few days. But no, she didn't want him to go to all the trouble of flying over. She didn't know when she'd be back. This time, she wanted to see a little of Europe, not just the nightclubs and lounges, and not just after most sane people were asleep. But when she came back—she would keep up her singing, not the other thing—she would make it a point to call him. She really would.

Good-bye.

The telephone rang. Abe Cross felt as if his heart had jumped into his throat. He heard Babcock's voice answering it. Then, "Abe, it's for you."

He snapped the cigarette into the night and tore open the screen door, crossing the room in three wide strides, almost ripping the phone from Babcock's hand. "Thanks, Lew." He spoke into the receiver. "Hello. Hey, listen, we can—"

"Cross?"

He knew the voice. He swallowed hard. "Vols?"

"Don't ask how I got your telephone number, old man. I've always had good connections." There was silence, the kind between bad jokes from a stand-up comic. "Anyway, thought you'd like to know. I got back to Moscow and what do you suppose?"

"I don't know. They were pissed?"

"No—they gave me a medal! Can you believe that? Anyway, I was going to show Anna—remember the girl I mentioned to you while we were all floating around at sea waiting for your submarine to get us? And by the by, thanks awfully for doing your part about keeping me free."

"You'll never be free there, doing what you do."

"Oddly enough, I arrived at the same conclusion. I told the people on Derzhinsky Square that your chaps had gotten the ampule after betraying me and leaving me for dead. Sorry over that, but it was necessary. Rather thought it might give your johnnies the chance to neutralize the military potential of the bloody virus after all, our chaps having less of an incentive and all to use it with you having it."

"What did you mean about arriving at the same conclusion, man?" Cross asked.

"Checked our files, actually. Found out some of our people had been indirectly working O'Fallon for years. Spread chaos in the West; that sort of thing. It didn't sit well, Cross. Anna and I are in West Berlin now. I'm on a coin telephone from the lobby of your Embassy. Never guess."

"You're not—"

"We're defecting, yes. But we're still patriotic Russians and all that. Not going to tell anything damning to the Mother country. Just enough to qualify for new identities and passports after all the interminable questions."

Cross lit a cigarette. "They'll get you eventually, Comstock—Vols, I mean."

"Eventually's a long time off. Look here, I don't think we'll likely speak again. But, well, maybe we'll meet again in that place O'Fallon suggested. Good-bye, old man."

"Vols—"

The line went dead.

"What did he want? Everything all right?" Babcock asked.

Cross looked at Lewis Babcock, then at Darwin Hughes. The board between them showed that Hughes was about to be checkmated.

"What did he want?" Hughes asked.

"Aw, nothing much. Tell ya later. But he did suggest a place where we could get together sometime. But, well, I didn't have the heart to tell him."

"Tell him what?" Babcock asked.

"They don't let guys like him in down there." Cross stubbed out his cigarette.